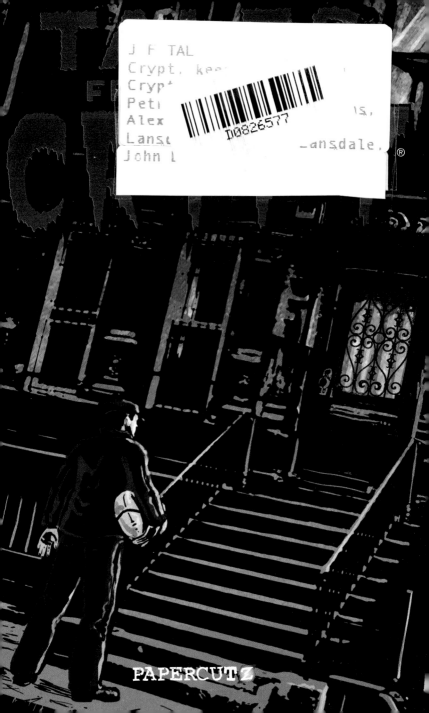

PAPERCUTZ

TALES FROM THE CRYPT®

Graphic Novels Available from Papercutz

ALL-NEW STORIES! FULL-COLOR GRAPHIC NOVEL!
TERROR
NO. 1
TALES FROM THE CRYPT
FEATURING...
THE CRYPT-KEEPER
THE OLD WITCH
THE VAULT-KEEPER

ALL-NEW STORIES! FULL-COLOR GRAPHIC NOVEL!
TERROR
NO. 2
TALES FROM THE CRYPT
FEATURING...
THE CRYPT-KEEPER
THE OLD WITCH
THE VAULT-KEEPER

TERROR
NO. 3
TALES FROM THE CRYPT
FEATURING...
THE CRYPT-KEEPER
THE OLD WITCH
THE VAULT-KEEPER
PAPERCUTZ

ALL-NEW STORIES! FULL-COLOR GRAPHIC NOVEL!
TERROR
NO. 4
TALES FROM THE CRYPT
FEATURING...
THE CRYPT-KEEPER
THE OLD WITCH
THE VAULT-KEEPER
PAPERCUTZ

ALL-NEW STORIES! FULL-COLOR GRAPHIC NOVEL!
TERROR
NO. 5
TALES FROM THE CRYPT
FEATURING...
THE CRYPT-KEEPER
THE OLD WITCH
THE VAULT-KEEPER
PAPERCUTZ

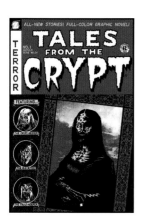

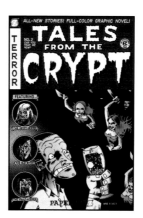

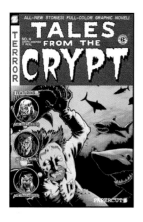

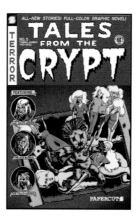

Graphic Novel #1
"Ghouls Gone Wild!"

Graphic Novel #2
"Can You Fear Me Now

Graphic Novel #3
"Zombielicious"

Graphic Novel #4
"Crypt-Keeping It Real

Coming October 2008:
Graphic Novel #5
"Yabba Dabba Voodoo"

$7.95 each in paperback, $12.95 each in hardcover. Please add $4.00 for postage and handling for the first book, add $1.00 for each additional book. Send to: Papercutz, 40 Exchange Place, Suite 1308, New York, NY 1000 • www.papercutz.com

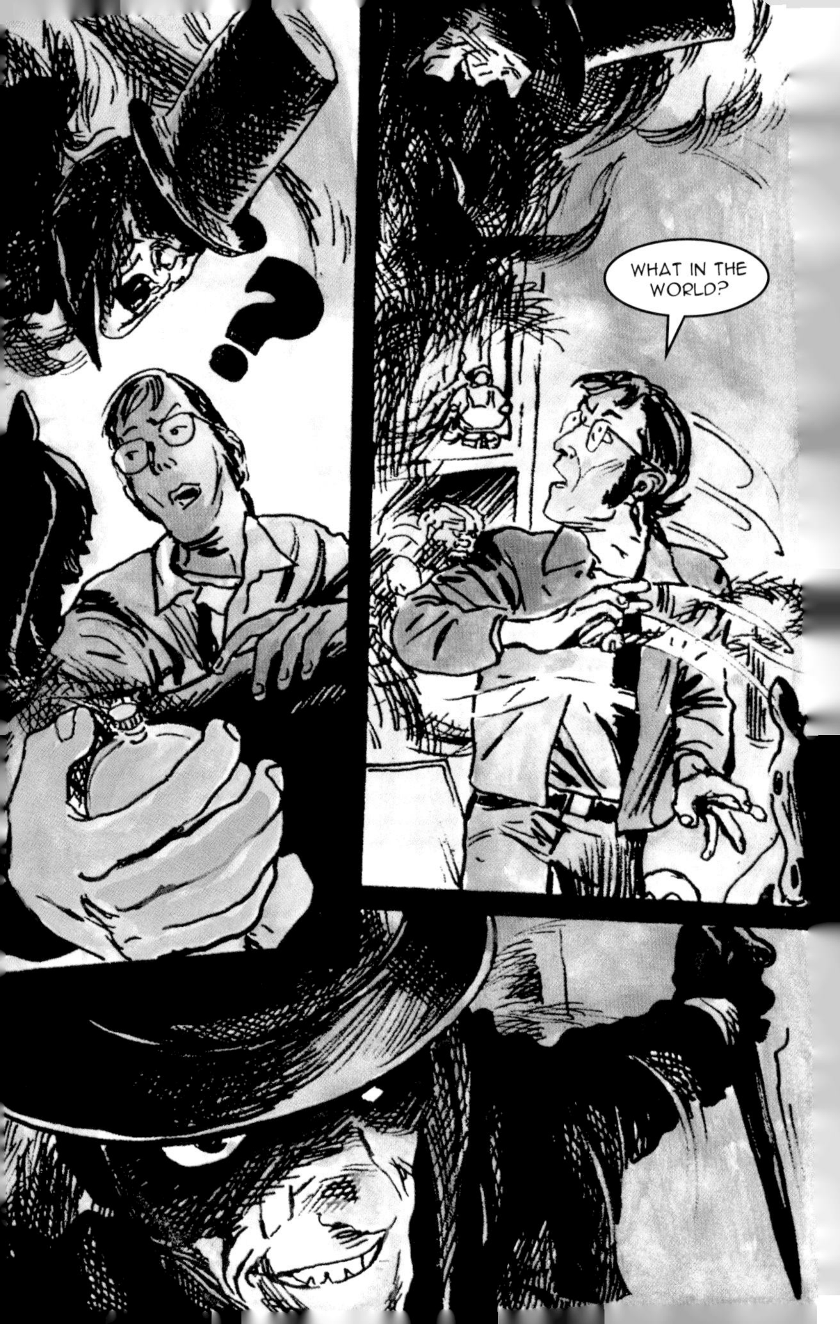
?
WHAT IN THE WORLD?

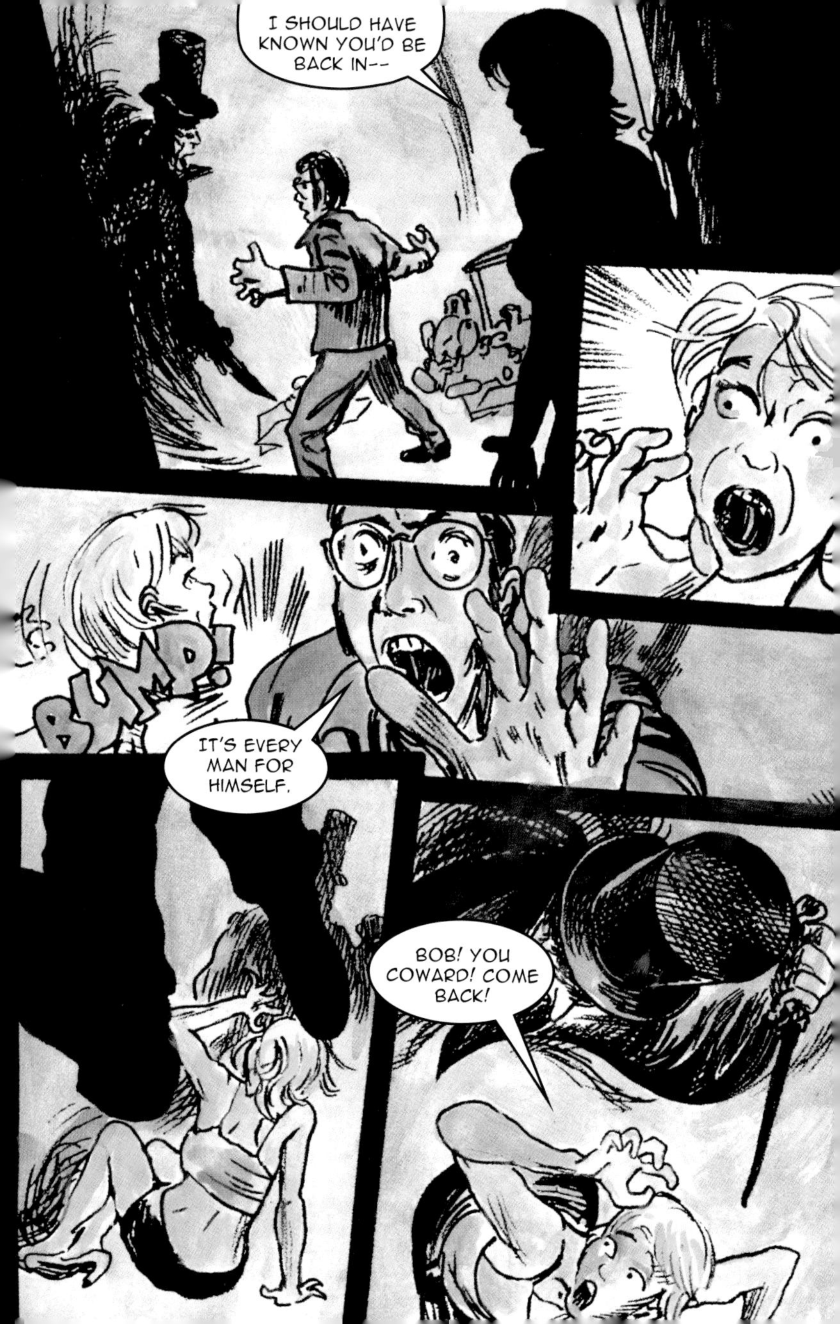
I SHOULD HAVE KNOWN YOU'D BE BACK IN--
BUMP!
IT'S EVERY MAN FOR HIMSELF.
BOB! YOU COWARD! COME BACK!

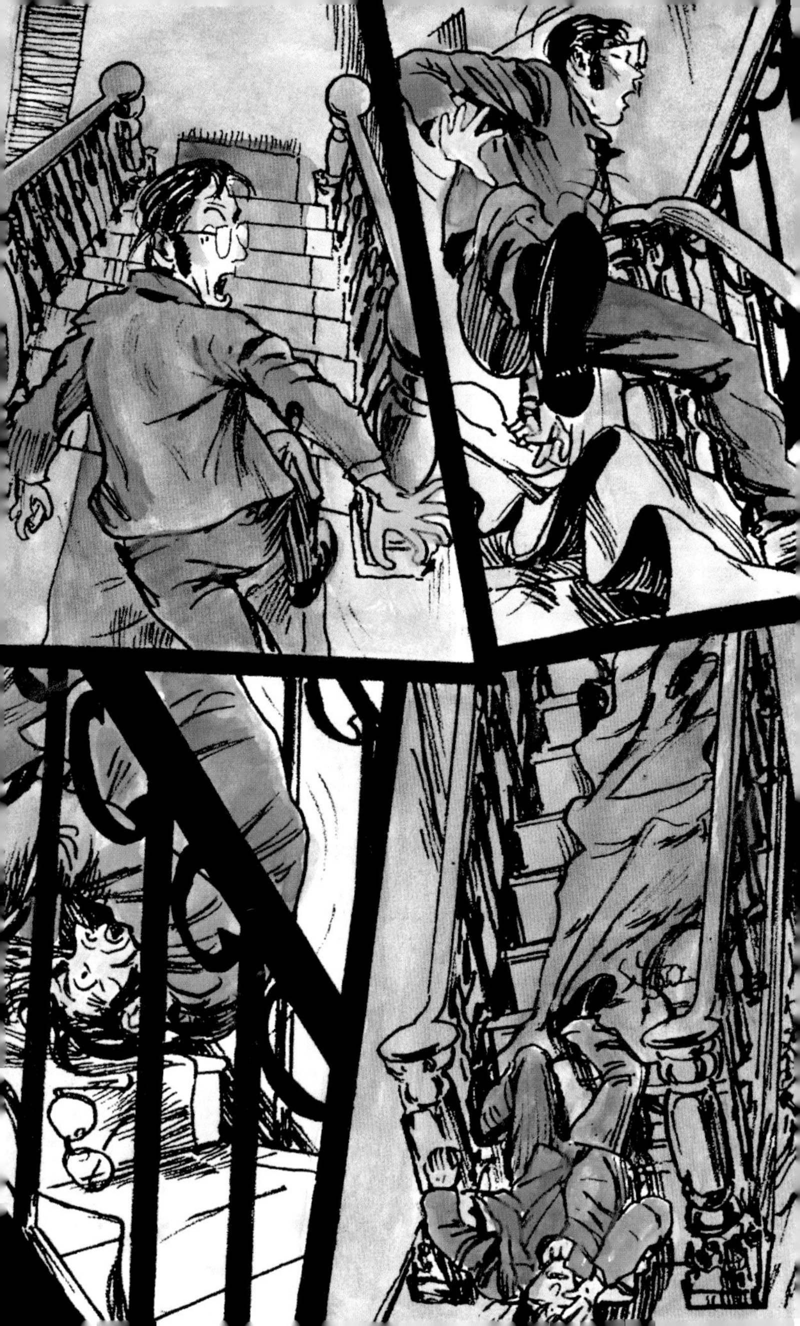

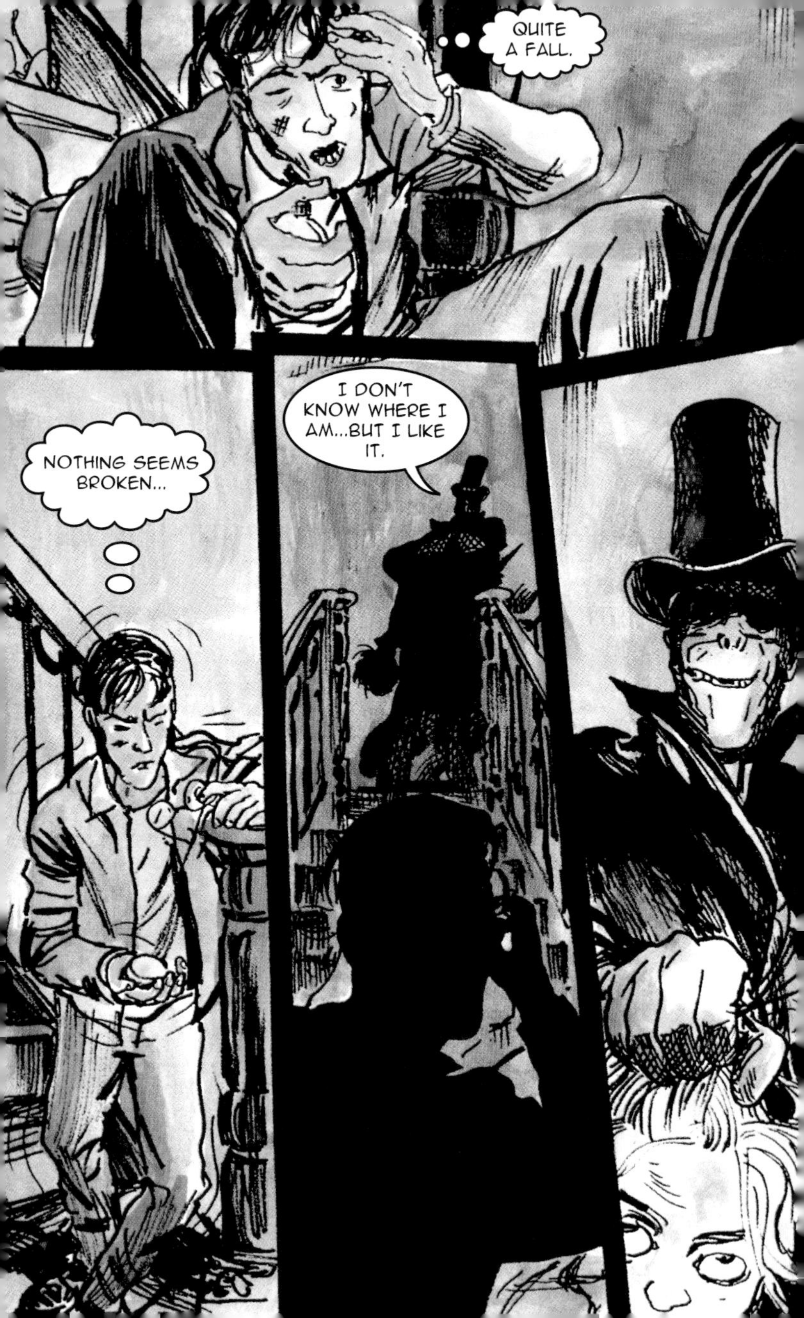
QUITE A FALL.
NOTHING SEEMS BROKEN...
I DON'T KNOW WHERE I AM...BUT I LIKE IT.

TALES FROM THE CRYPT ®

NO. 4 – Crypt-Keeping It Real!

STEFAN PETRUCHA
ALEX SIMMONS
SCOTT LOBDELL
JOE R. LANSDALE
JOHN L. LANSDALE
ARIE KAPLAN
JIM SALICRUP
Writers

TIM SMITH 3
FACUNDO VELILLA
ALEJANDRO CABRAL
JEZIEL SANCHEZ
MARTINEZ
CHRIS NOETH
MR. EXES
JAMES ROMBERGER
RICK PARKER
Artists

MR. EXES
Cover Artist

Based on the classic EC Comics series.

PAPERCUTZ™
New York

"YOU TOOMB"
STEFAN PETRUCHA — Writer
TIM SMITH 3 — Artist
BRYAN SENKA — Letterer
MAGIC EYE STUDIO — Color

"THE CREDITOR"
ALEX SIMMONS — Writer
MORT TODD — Artist, Letterer

"DUMPED"
SCOTT LOBDELL — Writer
FACUNDO VELILLA & ALEJANDRO CABRAL — Artists
JOHN McCARTHY — Letterer

"ROSES BEDIGHT"
STEFAN PETRUCHA — Writer
JEZIEL SANCHEZ MARTINEZ — Artist
SEAN TAYLOR — Letterer
MAGIC EYE STUDIO — Color

"MOONLIGHT SONATA"
JOE R. LANSDALE & JOHN L. LANSDALE — Writers
CHRIS NOETH — Artist
BRYAN SENKA — Letterer

"JUMPING THE SHARK"
ARIE KAPLAN — Writer
MR. EXES — Artist
MARK LERER — Letterer

"A RIPPING GOOD TIME"
JOE R. LANSDALE and JOHN L. LANSDALE — writers
JAMES ROMBERGER — Artist
MARK LERER — Letterer
MARGUERITE VAN COOK — Colorist

GHOULUNATIC SEQUENCES
JIM SALICRUP — Writer
RICK PARKER — Artist, Title Letterer, Colorist
JOHN McCARTHY – Letterer

PREVIEW OF "IGNOBLE ROT"
FRED VAN LENTE – Writer
MORT TODD – Artist, Letterer

JOHN McCARTHY
Production

JIM SALICRUP
Editor–in–Chief

ISBN 10: 1-59707-104-8 paperback edition
ISBN 13: 978-1-59707-104-8 paperback edition
ISBN 10: 1-59707-105-6 hardcover edition
ISBN 13: 978-1-59707-105-5 hardcover edition

10 9 8 7 6 5 4 3 2 1

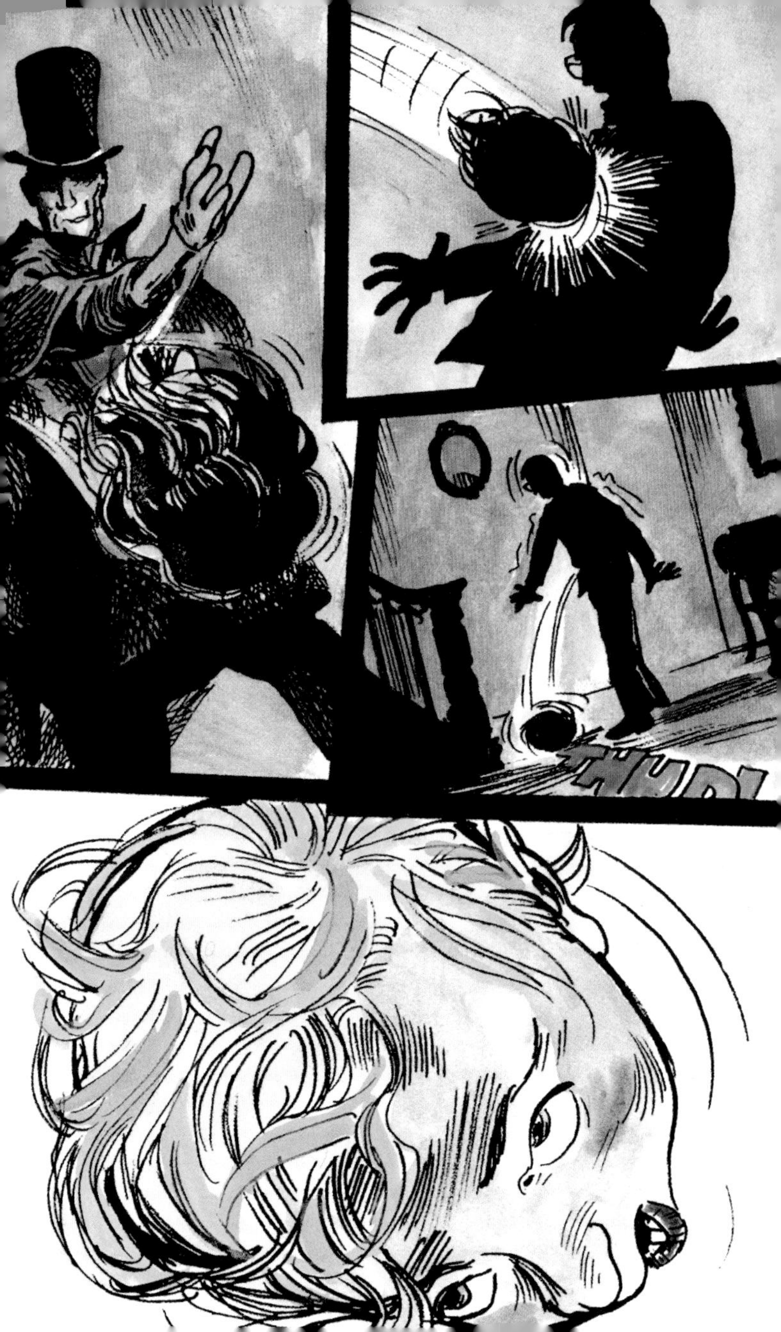
THUD!

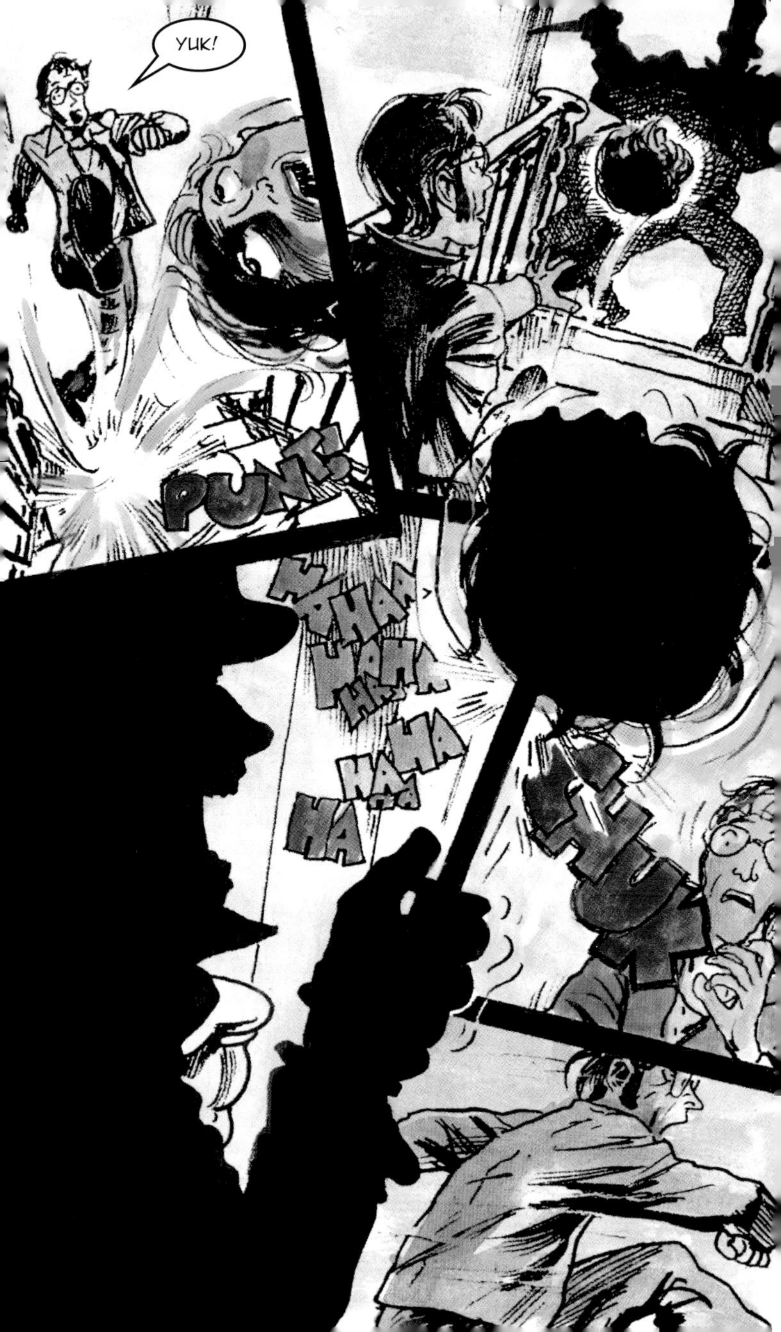
YUK!
PUNT!
HAHA
HAHA
HAHA
HA

THE CRYPT OF TERROR

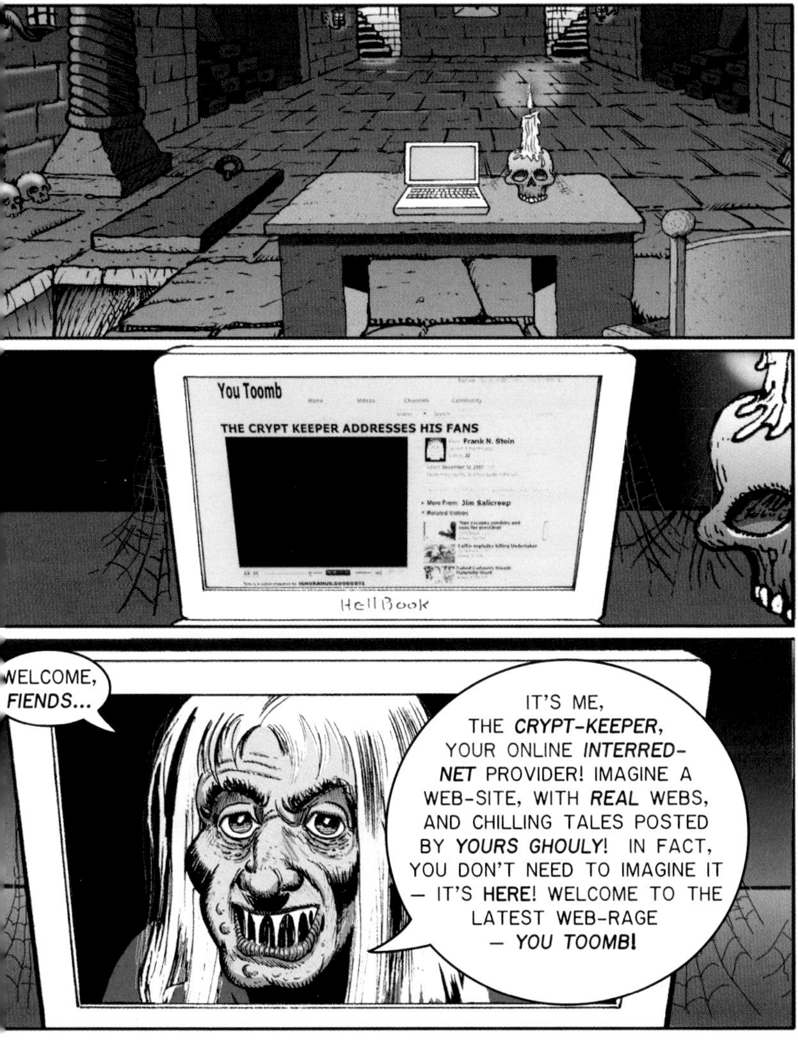
You Toomb
THE CRYPT KEEPER ADDRESSES HIS FANS
Frank N. Stein
More From: Jim Salicreep
Related Videos
HellBook
WELCOME, FIENDS...
IT'S ME, THE *CRYPT-KEEPER*, YOUR ONLINE *INTERRED-NET* PROVIDER! IMAGINE A WEB-SITE, WITH *REAL* WEBS, AND CHILLING TALES POSTED BY *YOURS GHOULY*! IN FACT, YOU DON'T NEED TO IMAGINE IT — IT'S **HERE**! WELCOME TO THE LATEST WEB-RAGE — ***YOU TOOMB!***

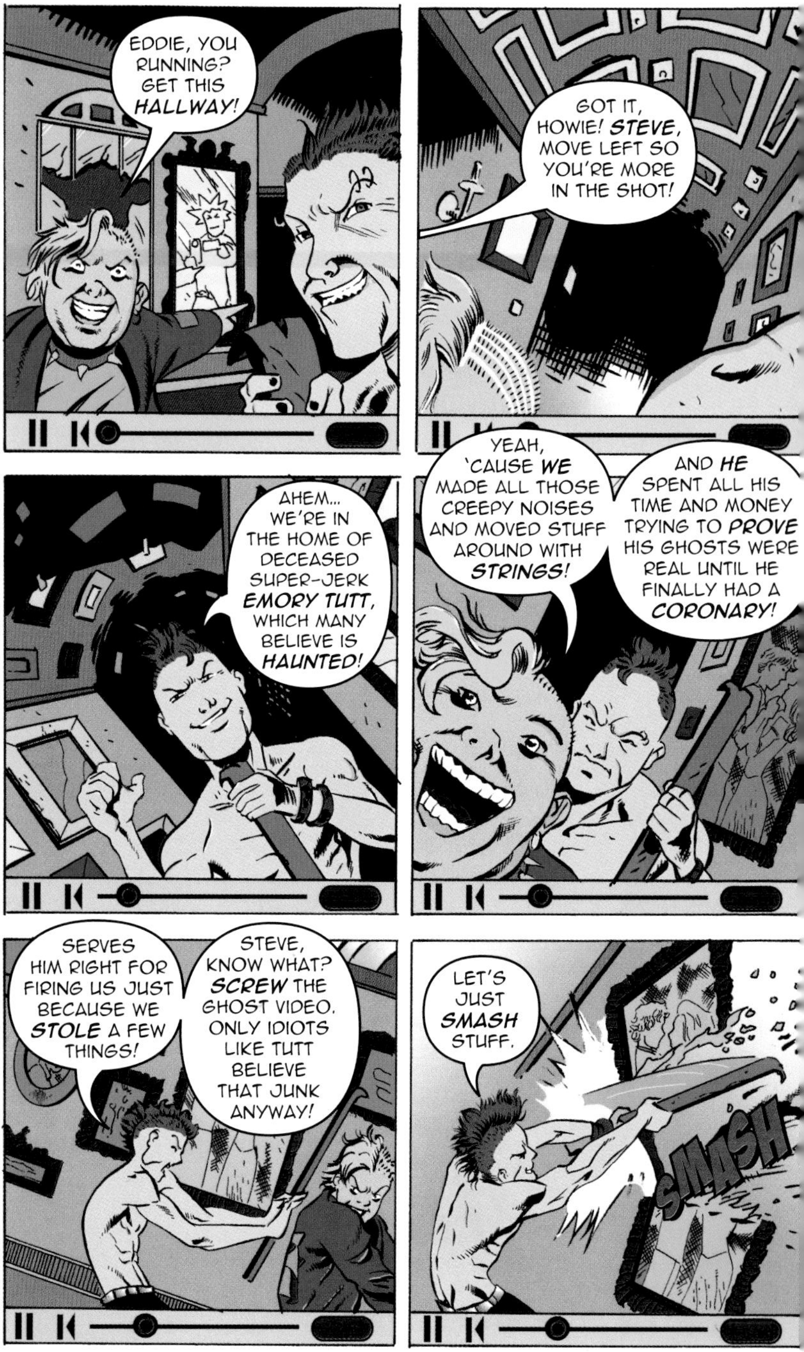
EDDIE, YOU RUNNING? GET THIS HALLWAY!
GOT IT, HOWIE! STEVE, MOVE LEFT SO YOU'RE MORE IN THE SHOT!
AHEM... WE'RE IN THE HOME OF DECEASED SUPER-JERK EMORY TUTT, WHICH MANY BELIEVE IS HAUNTED!
YEAH, 'CAUSE WE MADE ALL THOSE CREEPY NOISES AND MOVED STUFF AROUND WITH STRINGS!
AND HE SPENT ALL HIS TIME AND MONEY TRYING TO PROVE HIS GHOSTS WERE REAL UNTIL HE FINALLY HAD A CORONARY!
SERVES HIM RIGHT FOR FIRING US JUST BECAUSE WE STOLE A FEW THINGS!
STEVE, KNOW WHAT? SCREW THE GHOST VIDEO. ONLY IDIOTS LIKE TUTT BELIEVE THAT JUNK ANYWAY!
LET'S JUST SMASH STUFF.
SMASH

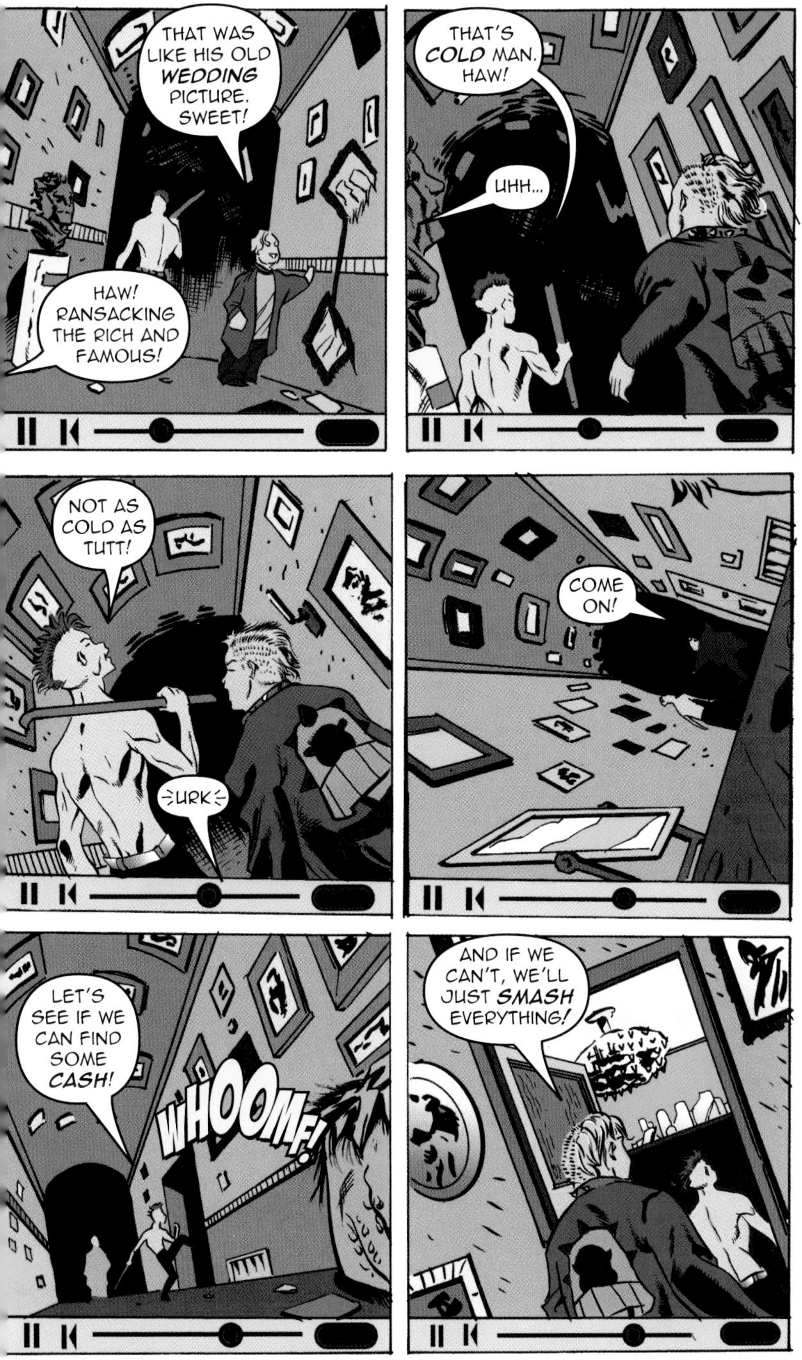
THAT WAS LIKE HIS OLD WEDDING PICTURE. SWEET!
HAW! RANSACKING THE RICH AND FAMOUS!
THAT'S COLD MAN. HAW!
UHH...
NOT AS COLD AS TUTT!
URK
COME ON!
LET'S SEE IF WE CAN FIND SOME CASH!
WHOOMF!
AND IF WE CAN'T, WE'LL JUST SMASH EVERYTHING!

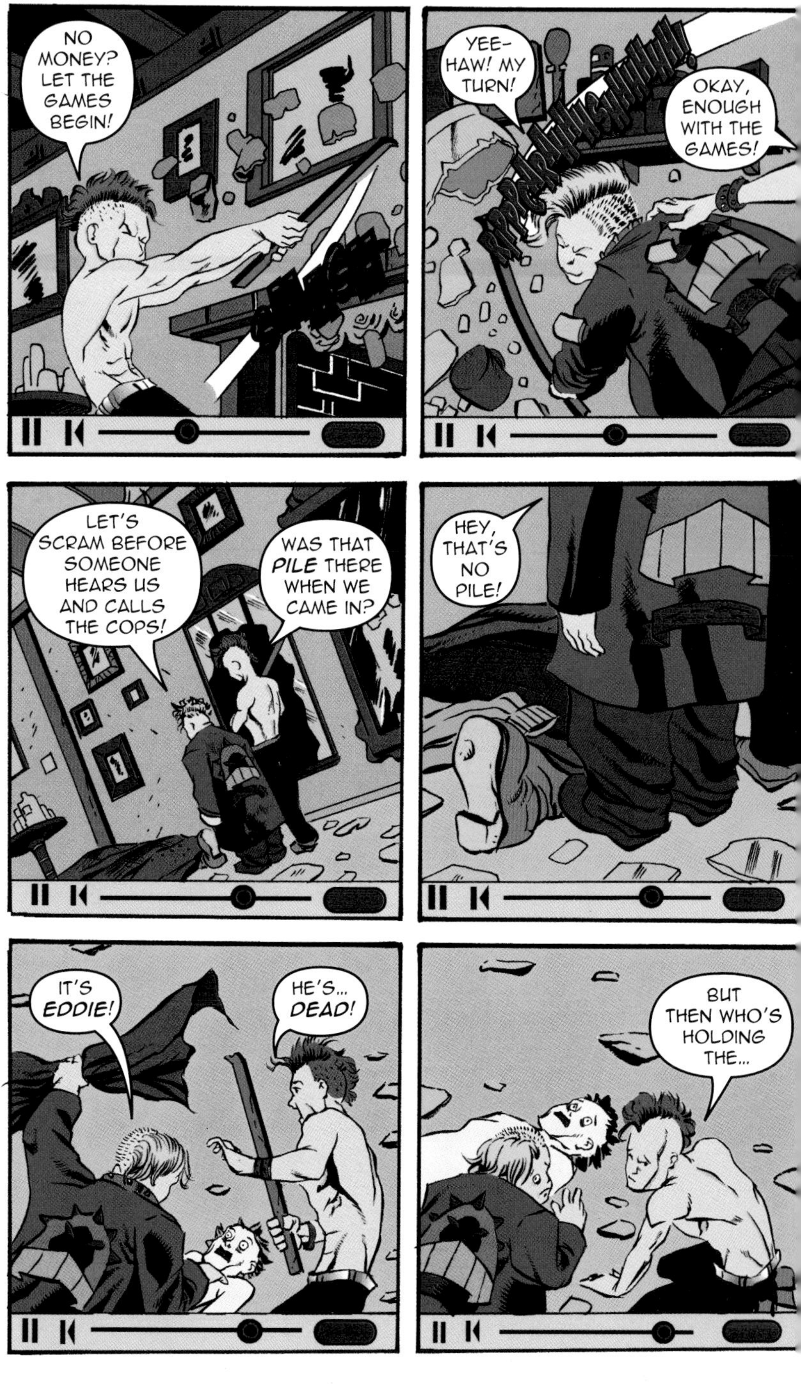
NO MONEY? LET THE GAMES BEGIN!
YEE-HAW! MY TURN!
OKAY, ENOUGH WITH THE GAMES!
LET'S SCRAM BEFORE SOMEONE HEARS US AND CALLS THE COPS!
WAS THAT *PILE* THERE WHEN WE CAME IN?
HEY, THAT'S NO PILE!
IT'S *EDDIE!*
HE'S... *DEAD!*
BUT THEN WHO'S HOLDING THE...

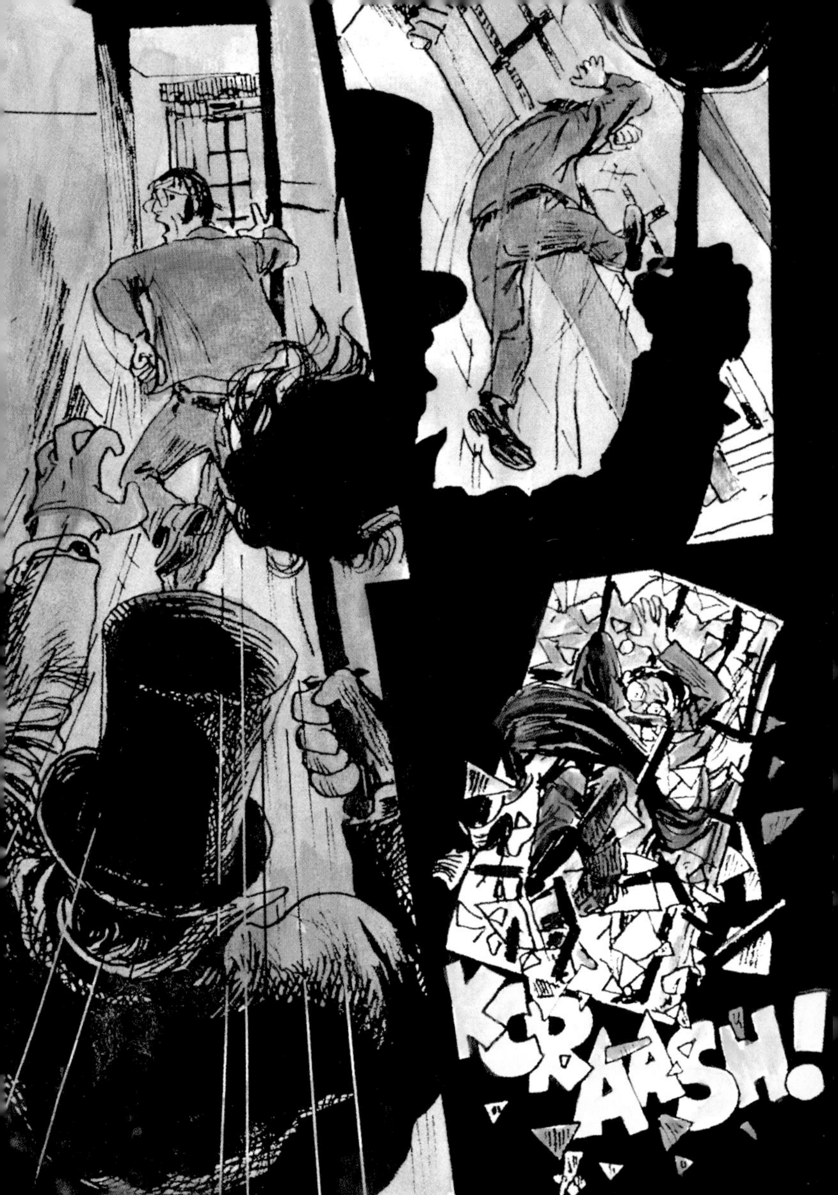
KRRAASH!

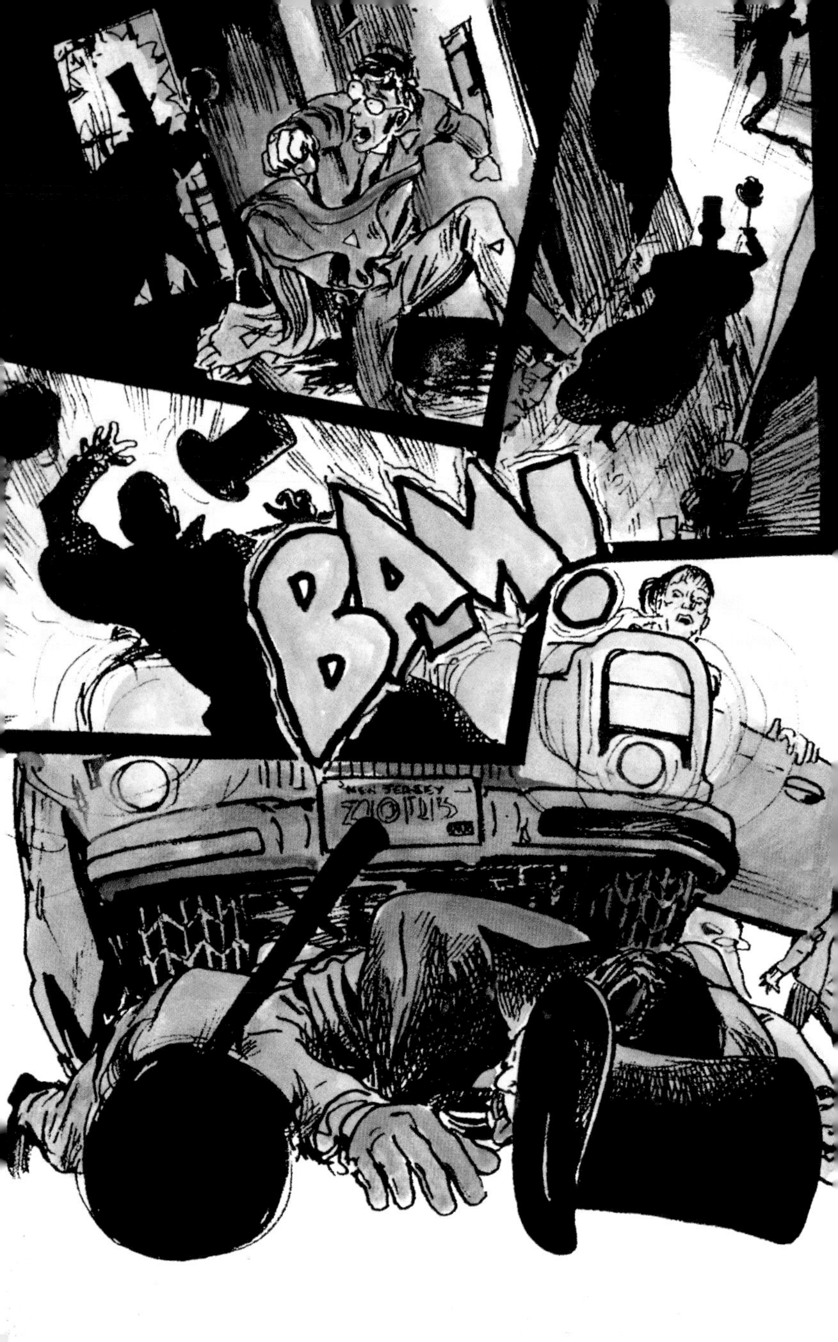
BAM!
NEW JERSEY

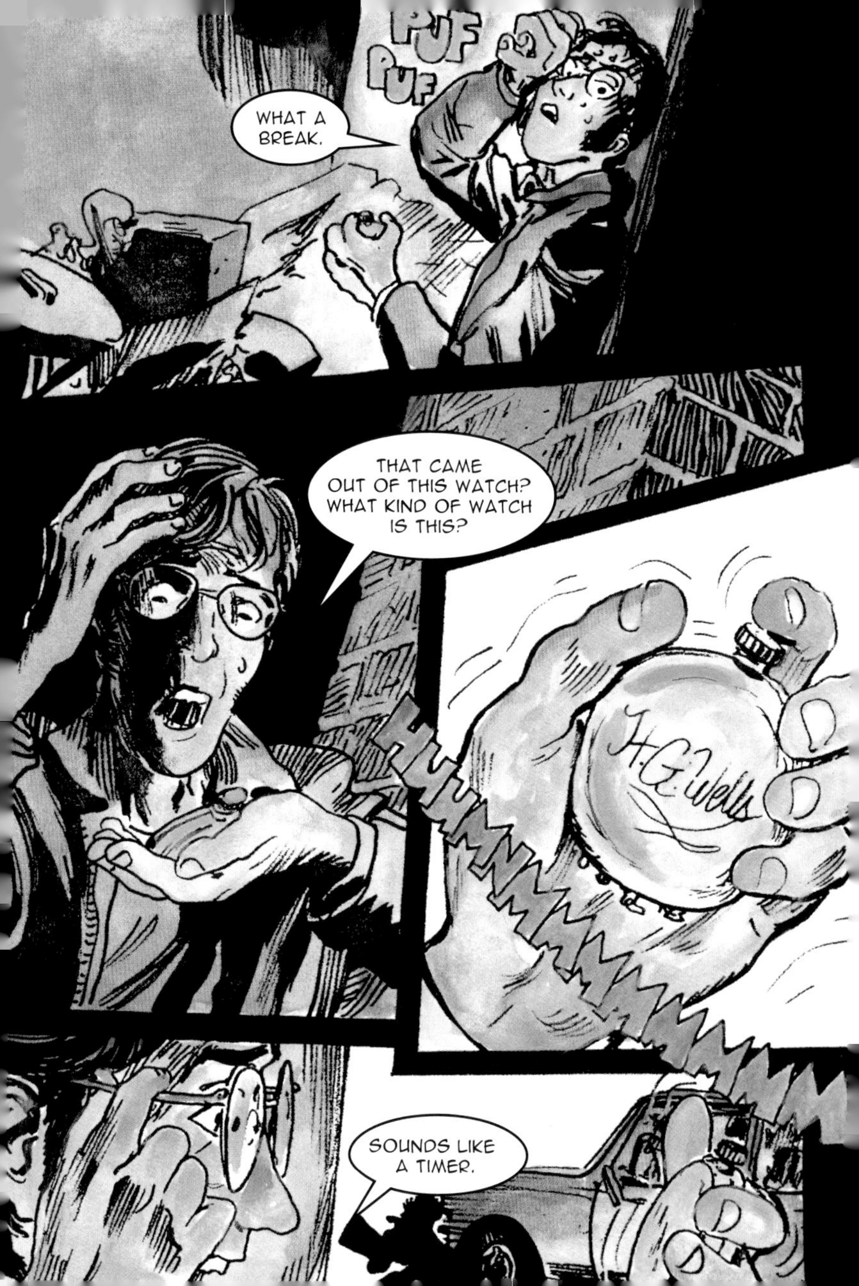
PUF
PUF
WHAT A BREAK.
THAT CAME OUT OF THIS WATCH? WHAT KIND OF WATCH IS THIS?
H.G. Wells
HUMMMMMMMM
SOUNDS LIKE A TIMER.

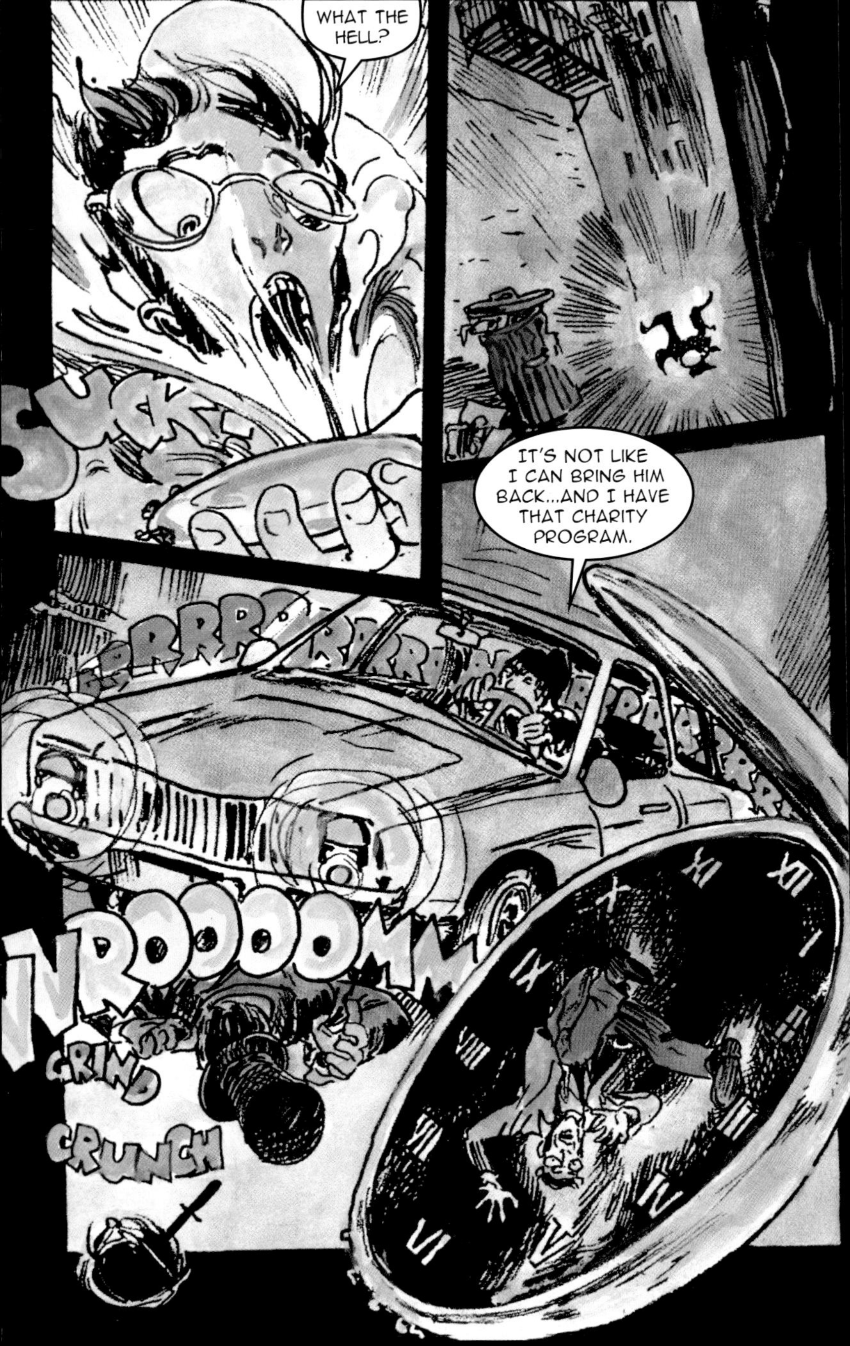
WHAT THE HELL?
SUCK
IT'S NOT LIKE I CAN BRING HIM BACK...AND I HAVE THAT CHARITY PROGRAM.
VROOOOM
GRIND
CRUNCH

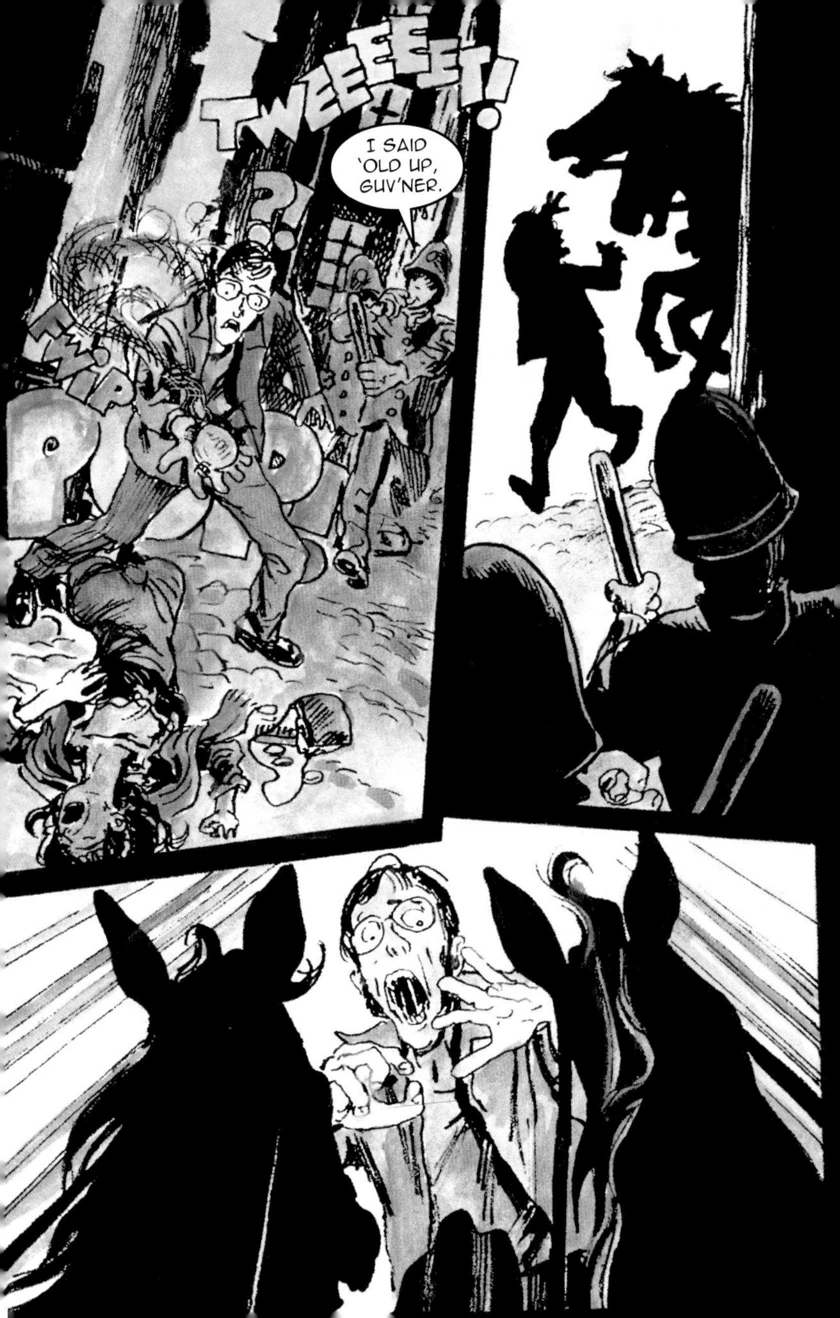
TWEEEEET!
I SAID 'OLD UP, GUV'NER.
WHIP

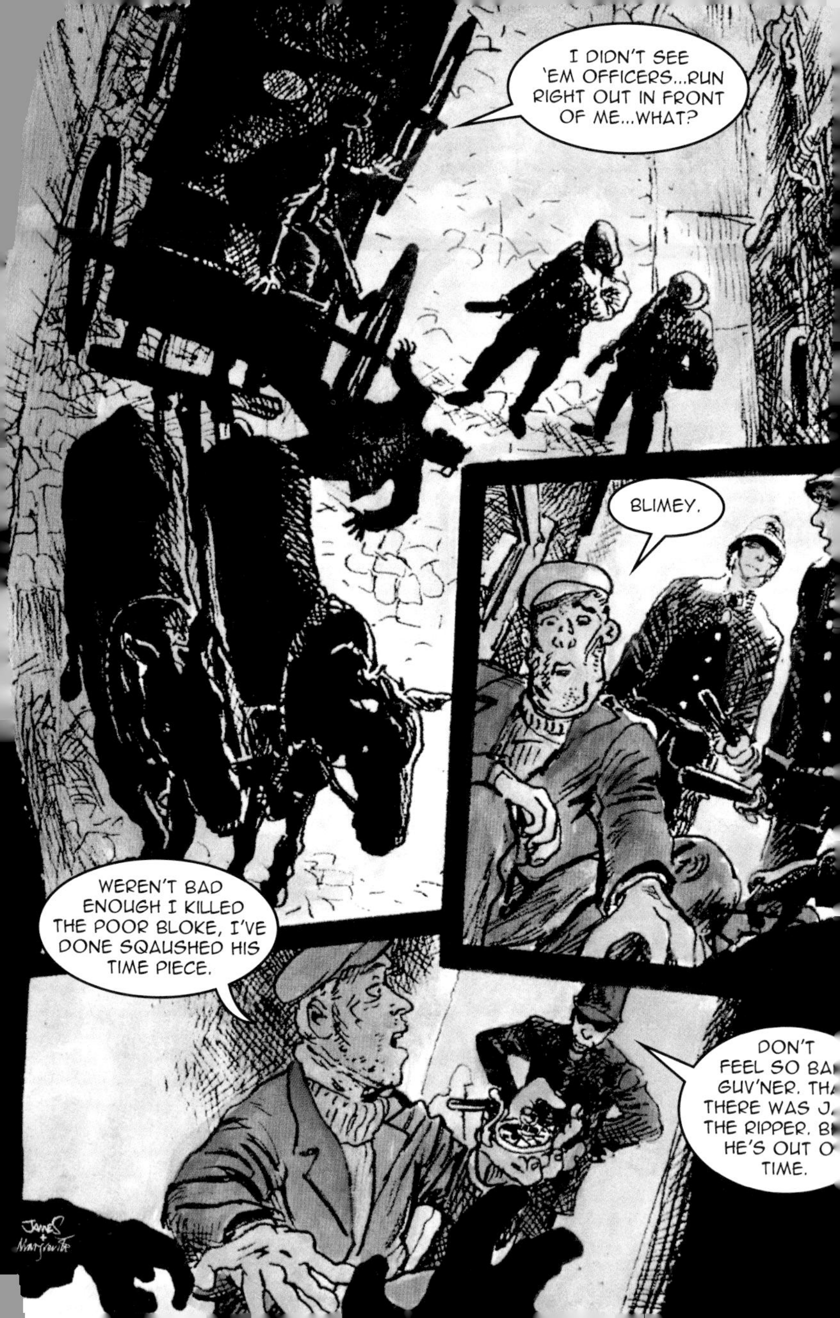
I DIDN'T SEE 'EM OFFICERS...RUN RIGHT OUT IN FRONT OF ME...WHAT?
BLIMEY.
WEREN'T BAD ENOUGH I KILLED THE POOR BLOKE, I'VE DONE SQAUSHED HIS TIME PIECE.
DON'T FEEL SO BA GUV'NER. TH THERE WAS J THE RIPPER. B HE'S OUT O TIME.
JAMES + Naismith

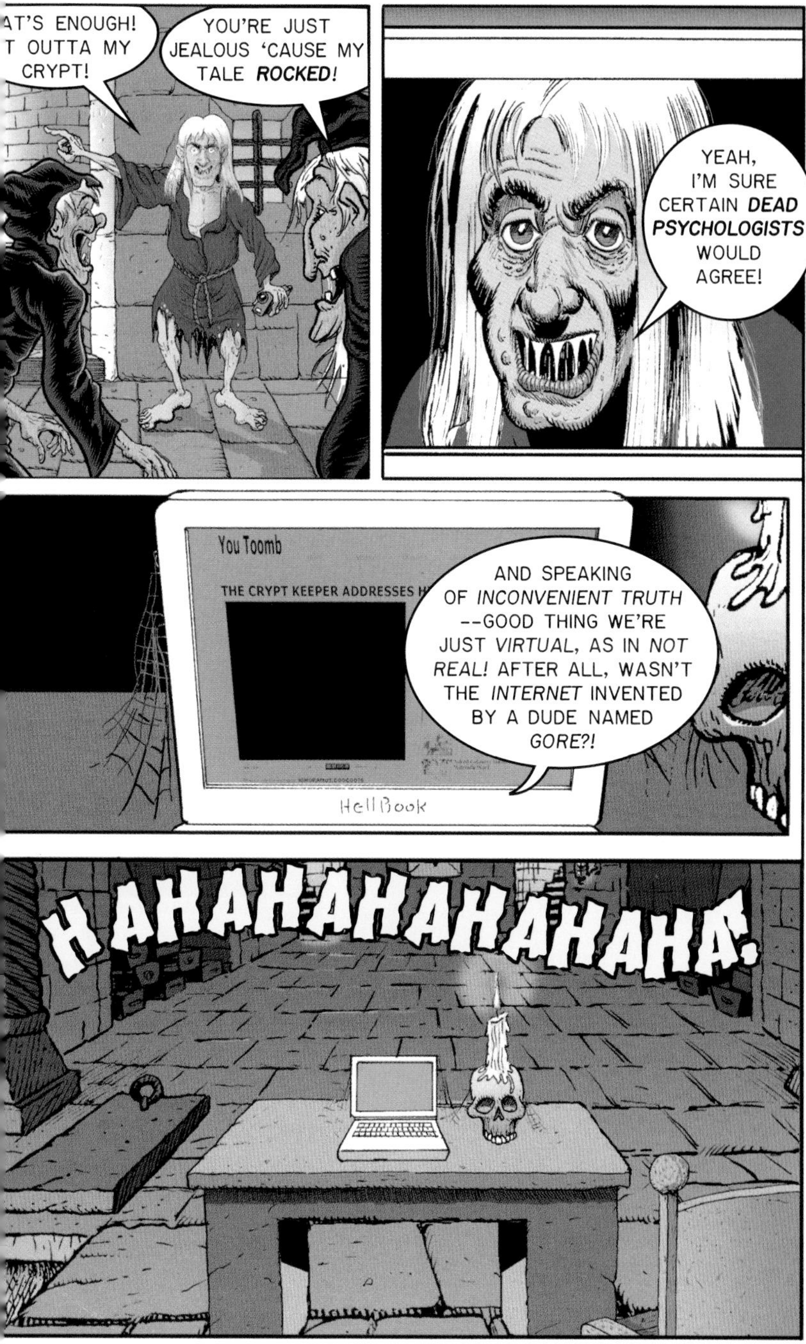
AT'S ENOUGH! T OUTTA MY CRYPT!
YOU'RE JUST JEALOUS 'CAUSE MY TALE ROCKED!
YEAH, I'M SURE CERTAIN DEAD PSYCHOLOGISTS WOULD AGREE!
You Toomb
THE CRYPT KEEPER ADDRESSES H
HellBook
AND SPEAKING OF INCONVENIENT TRUTH --GOOD THING WE'RE JUST VIRTUAL, AS IN NOT REAL! AFTER ALL, WASN'T THE INTERNET INVENTED BY A DUDE NAMED GORE?!
HAHAHAHAHAHAHA!

HERE'S A SNEAK PEAK AT TALES FROM THE CRYPT NO. 5
--“YABBA DABBA VOODOO”

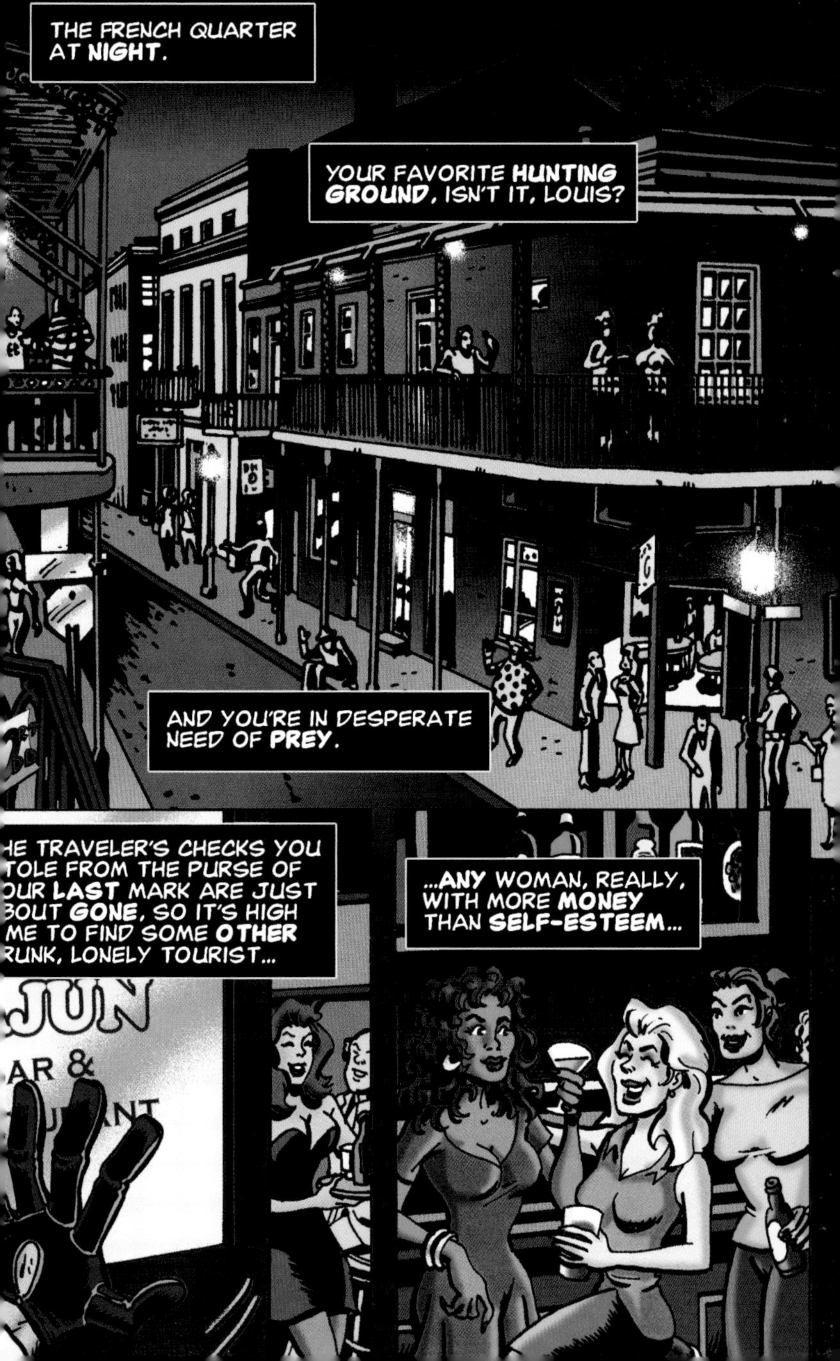
THE FRENCH QUARTER AT NIGHT.
YOUR FAVORITE HUNTING GROUND, ISN'T IT, LOUIS?
AND YOU'RE IN DESPERATE NEED OF PREY.
HE TRAVELER'S CHECKS YOU TOLE FROM THE PURSE OF OUR LAST MARK ARE JUST BOUT GONE, SO IT'S HIGH ME TO FIND SOME OTHER RUNK, LONELY TOURIST...
...ANY WOMAN, REALLY, WITH MORE MONEY THAN SELF-ESTEEM...
JUN
AR &

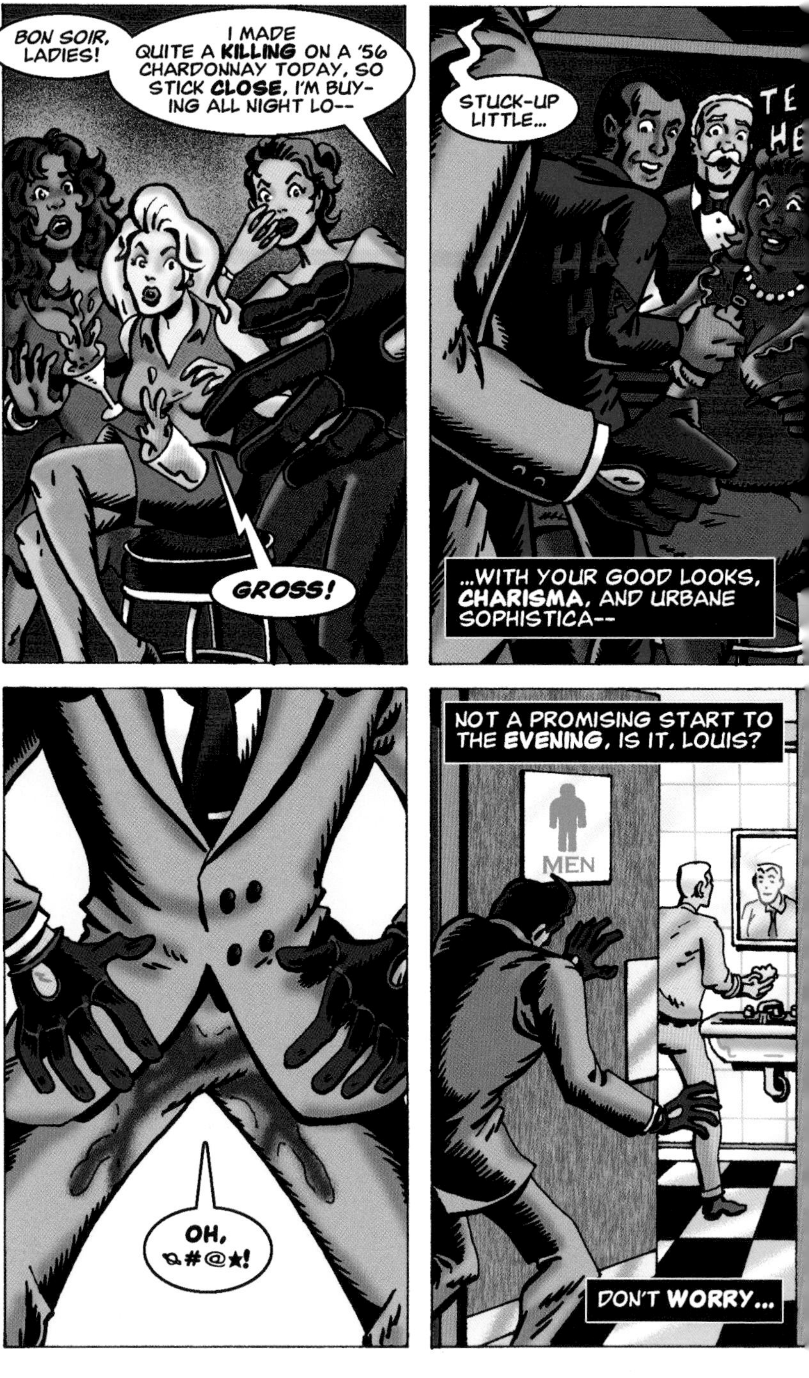

BON SOIR, LADIES!
I MADE QUITE A KILLING ON A '56 CHARDONNAY TODAY, SO STICK CLOSE, I'M BUYING ALL NIGHT LO--
GROSS!
STUCK-UP LITTLE...
...WITH YOUR GOOD LOOKS, CHARISMA, AND URBANE SOPHISTICA--
OH, &#@★!
NOT A PROMISING START TO THE EVENING, IS IT, LOUIS?
MEN
DON'T WORRY...

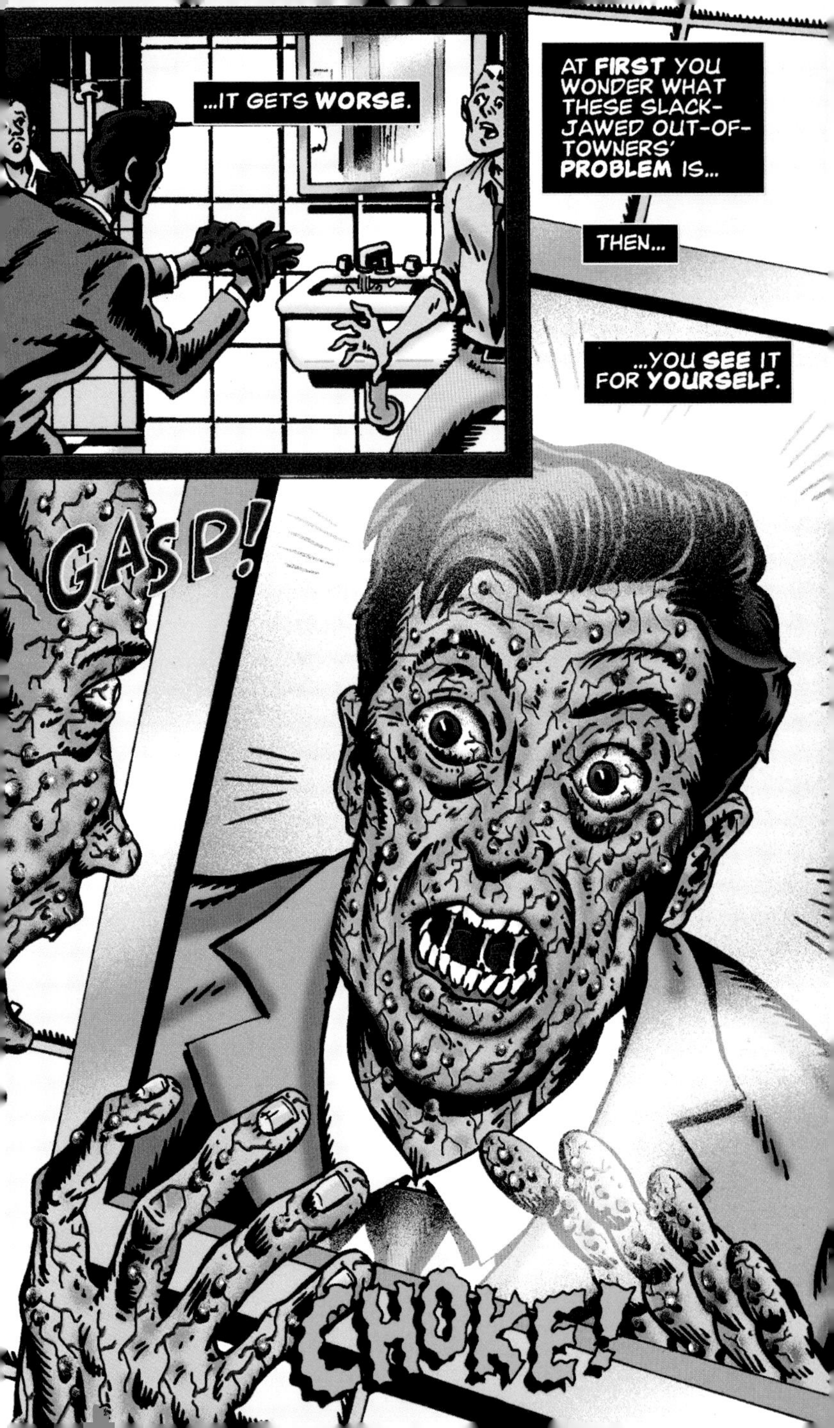

...IT GETS WORSE.
AT FIRST YOU WONDER WHAT THESE SLACK-JAWED OUT-OF-TOWNERS' PROBLEM IS...
THEN...
...YOU SEE IT FOR YOURSELF.
GASP!
CHOKE!

WHAT Y
SEE IS B
ENOUGH
...BUT IT'S WHAT YOU DON'T SEE THAT TERRIFIES YOU
YOU DON'T SEE FOG ON THE MIRROR FROM YOUR BREATH! FOR NO MATTER HOW HARD YOU STRAIN YOUR LUNGS...
...YOU CANNO
BREATH
NOR IS THERE A PULSE BENEATH YOUR WRIST---
---AND THE SKIN IS COLD AND CLAMMY TO THE TOUCH--- LIKE RUBBER LEFT OUTSIDE OVER-NIGHT!
THERE'S ONLY ONE POSSIBLE EXPLANATION, NO MATTER HO IMPOSSIBLE IT SEEMS:
I-I'M...
I'M DEAD!!

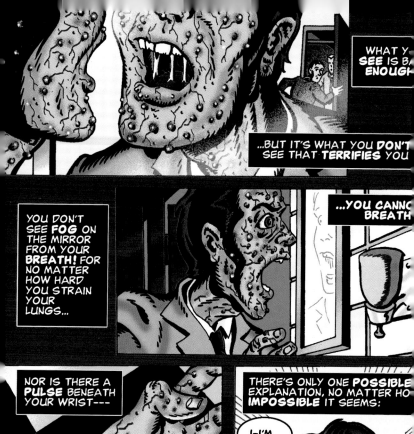

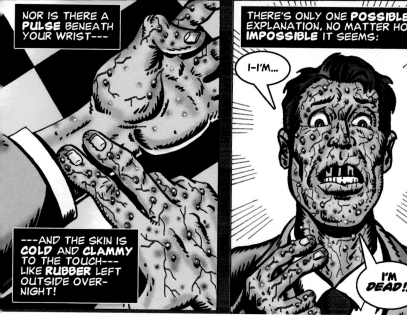

DON'T MISS TALES FROM THE CRYPT NO. 5
"YABBA DABBA VOODOO"

NANCY DREW

IEW GRAPHIC NOVEL EVERY 3 MONTHS!

"The Demon of River Heights"
N 1-59707-000-9 pb.
"Writ In Stone" ISBN 1-59707-002-5 pb.
"The Haunted Dollhouse"
N 1-59707-008-4 pb.
"The Girl Who Wasn't There"
N 1-59707-012-2 pb.
"The Fake Heir" ISBN 1-59707-024-6 pb.
"Mr. Cheeters Is Missing"
N 1-59707-030-0 pb.
"The Charmed Bracelet"
N 1-59707-036-X pb.
"Global Warning" ISBN 1-59707-051-3 pb.
"Ghost in the Machinery"
N 1-59707-058-0 pb.
) "The Disoriented Express"
N 1-59707-066-1 pb.
1 "Monkey Wrench Blues"
N 1-59707-076-9 pb.
v #12 "Dress Reversal"
N 1-59707-086-6 pb.

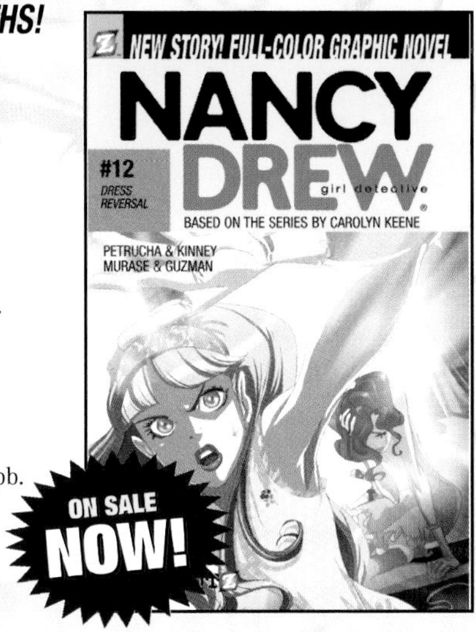
NEW STORY! FULL-COLOR GRAPHIC NOVEL
NANCY DREW
girl detective
#12
DRESS REVERSAL
BASED ON THE SERIES BY CAROLYN KEENE
PETRUCHA & KINNEY
MURASE & GUZMAN
ON SALE NOW!

All: Pocket sized, 96-112pp., full color, $7.95
Also available in hardcover! $12.95 each.

ncy Drew
xed Set #1-4
pages of color comics!
N 1-59707-038-6

ncy Drew
xed Set #5-8
pages of color comics!
.95 ISBN 1-59707-074-4

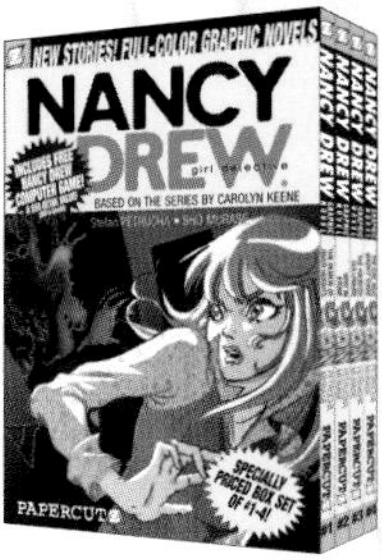
NEW STORIES! FULL-COLOR GRAPHIC NOVELS
NANCY DREW
girl detective
BASED ON THE SERIES BY CAROLYN KEENE
SPECIALLY PRICED BOX SET OF #1-4!
PAPERCUTZ

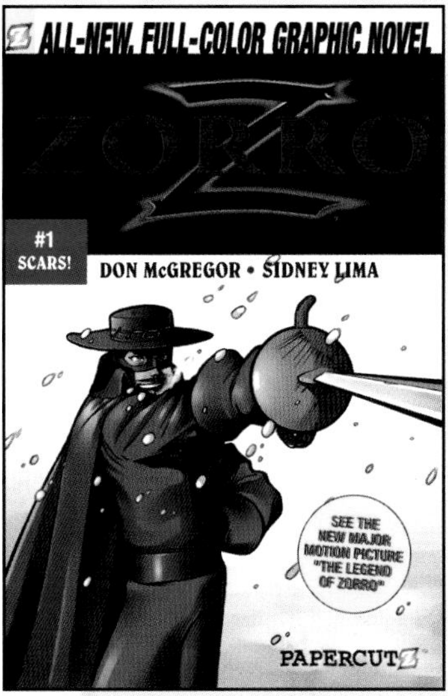
ALL-NEW, FULL-COLOR GRAPHIC NOVEL
ZORRO
#1
SCARS!
DON McGREGOR • SIDNEY LIMA
SEE THE NEW MAJOR MOTION PICTURE "THE LEGEND OF ZORRO"
PAPERCUTZ

ORRO

'Scars!" ISBN 1-59707-016-5
'Drownings!" ISBN 1-59707-018-1
'Vultures!" ISBN 1-59707-020-3

5x7 1/2, 96pp., full color paperback: $7.95
available in hardcover! $12.95 each.

At your store or order at Papercutz, 40 Exchange Place, Ste. 1308,
New York NY 10005, 1-800-886-1223

PAPERCUTZ

WATCH OUT FOR PAPERCUTZ™

If this is your very first Papercutz graphic novel, then allow me, Jim Salicrup, your humble and lovable Editor-in-Chief, to welcome you to the Papercutz Backpages where we check out what's happening in the ever-expanding Papercutz Universe! If you're a long-time Papercutz fan, then welcome back, friend!

Things really have been popping at Papercutz! In the last few editions of the Backpages we've announced new titles such as TALES FROM THE CRYPT, CLASSICS ILLUSTRATED, and CLASSICS ILLUSTRATED DELUXE. Well, guess what? The tradition continues, and we're announcing yet another addition to our line-up of blockbuster titles. So, what is our latest and greatest title? We'll give you just one hint — the stars of the next Papercutz graphic novel series just happen to be the biggest, most exciting line of constructible action figures ever created! That's right -- BIONICLE is here! Check out the power-packed preview pages ahead!

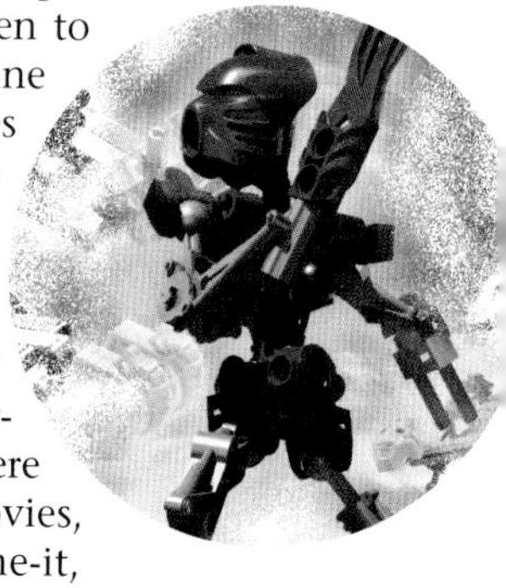

Before I run out of room, let me say that we're always interested in what you think! Are there characters, TV shows, movies, books, videogames, you-name-it, that you'd like to see Papercutz turn into graphic novels? Don't be shy, let's us know! You can contact me at salicrup@papercutz.com or Jim Salicrup, PAPERCUTZ, 40 Exchange Place, Ste. 1308, New York, NY 10005 and let us know how we're doing. After all, we want you to be as excited about Papercutz as we are!

Thanks,

Jim

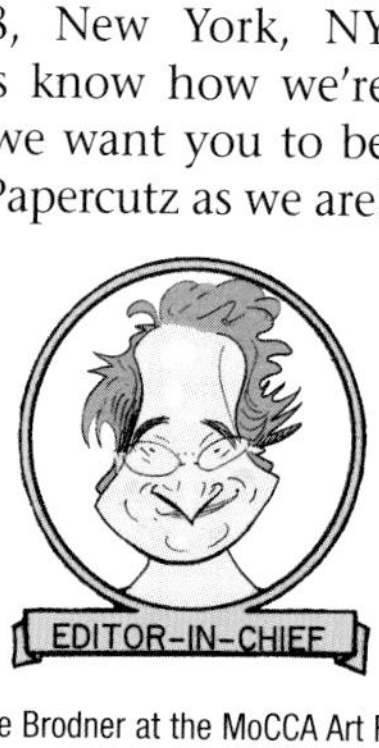
EDITOR-IN-CHIEF

Caricature drawn by Steve Brodner at the MoCCA Art Fest.

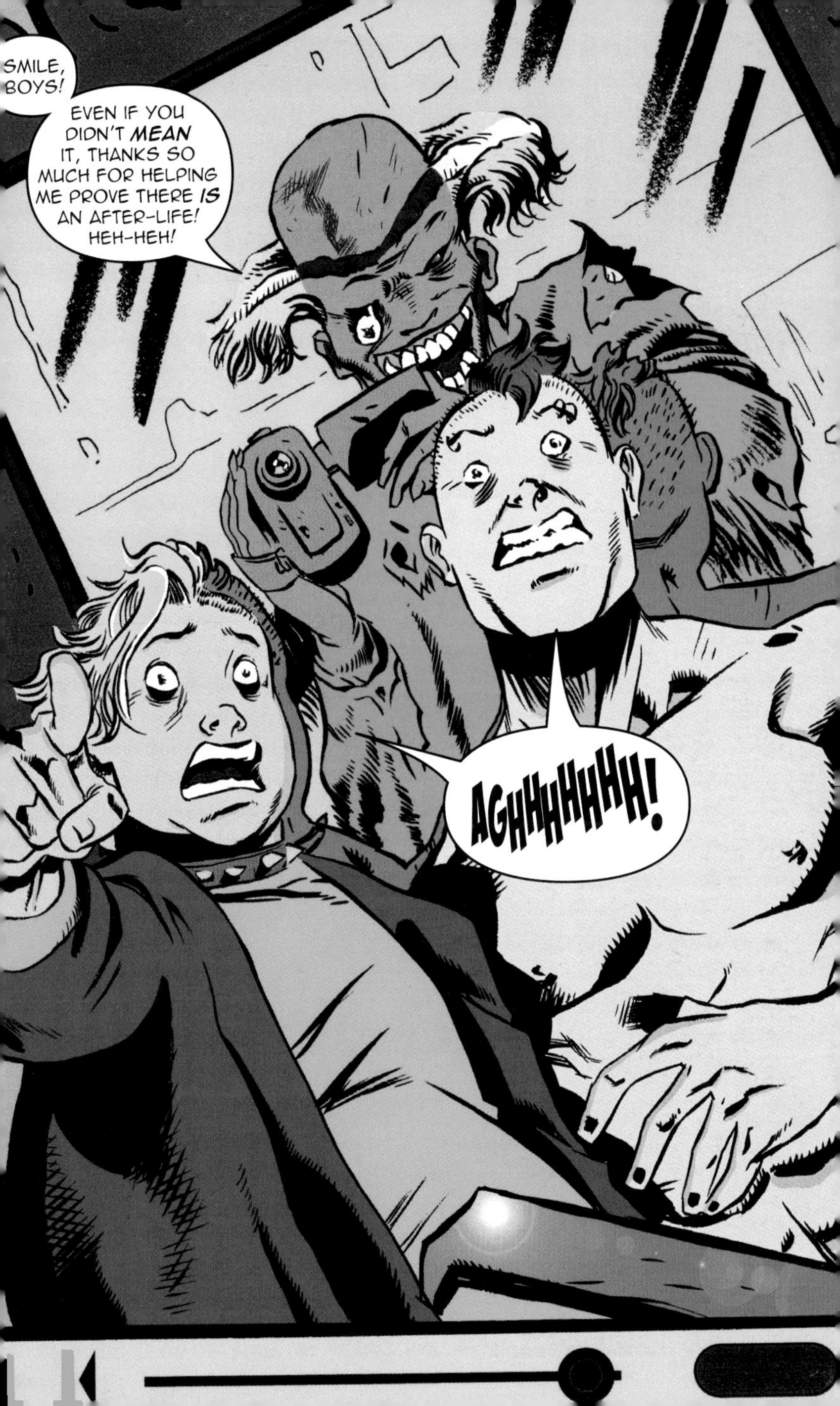

SMILE, BOYS!
EVEN IF YOU DIDN'T **MEAN** IT, THANKS SO MUCH FOR HELPING ME PROVE THERE **IS** AN AFTER-LIFE! HEH-HEH!
AGHHHHHHH!

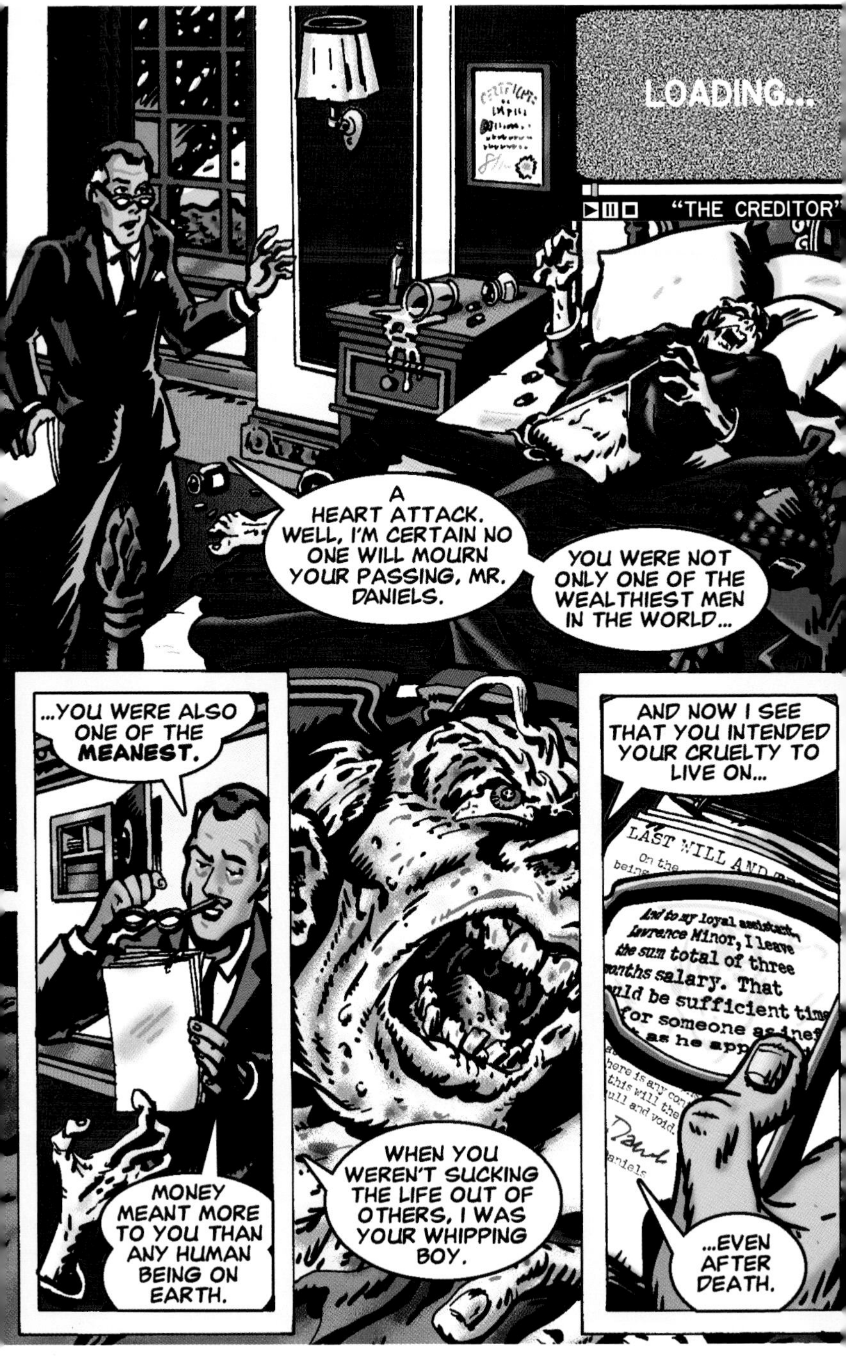
LOADING...
"THE CREDITOR"
A HEART ATTACK. WELL, I'M CERTAIN NO ONE WILL MOURN YOUR PASSING, MR. DANIELS.
YOU WERE NOT ONLY ONE OF THE WEALTHIEST MEN IN THE WORLD...
...YOU WERE ALSO ONE OF THE **MEANEST**.
MONEY MEANT MORE TO YOU THAN ANY HUMAN BEING ON EARTH.
WHEN YOU WEREN'T SUCKING THE LIFE OUT OF OTHERS, I WAS YOUR WHIPPING BOY.
AND NOW I SEE THAT YOU INTENDED YOUR CRUELTY TO LIVE ON...
LAST WILL AND
And to my loyal assistant,
Lawrence Minor, I leave
the sum total of three
salary. That
sufficient time
...EVEN AFTER DEATH.

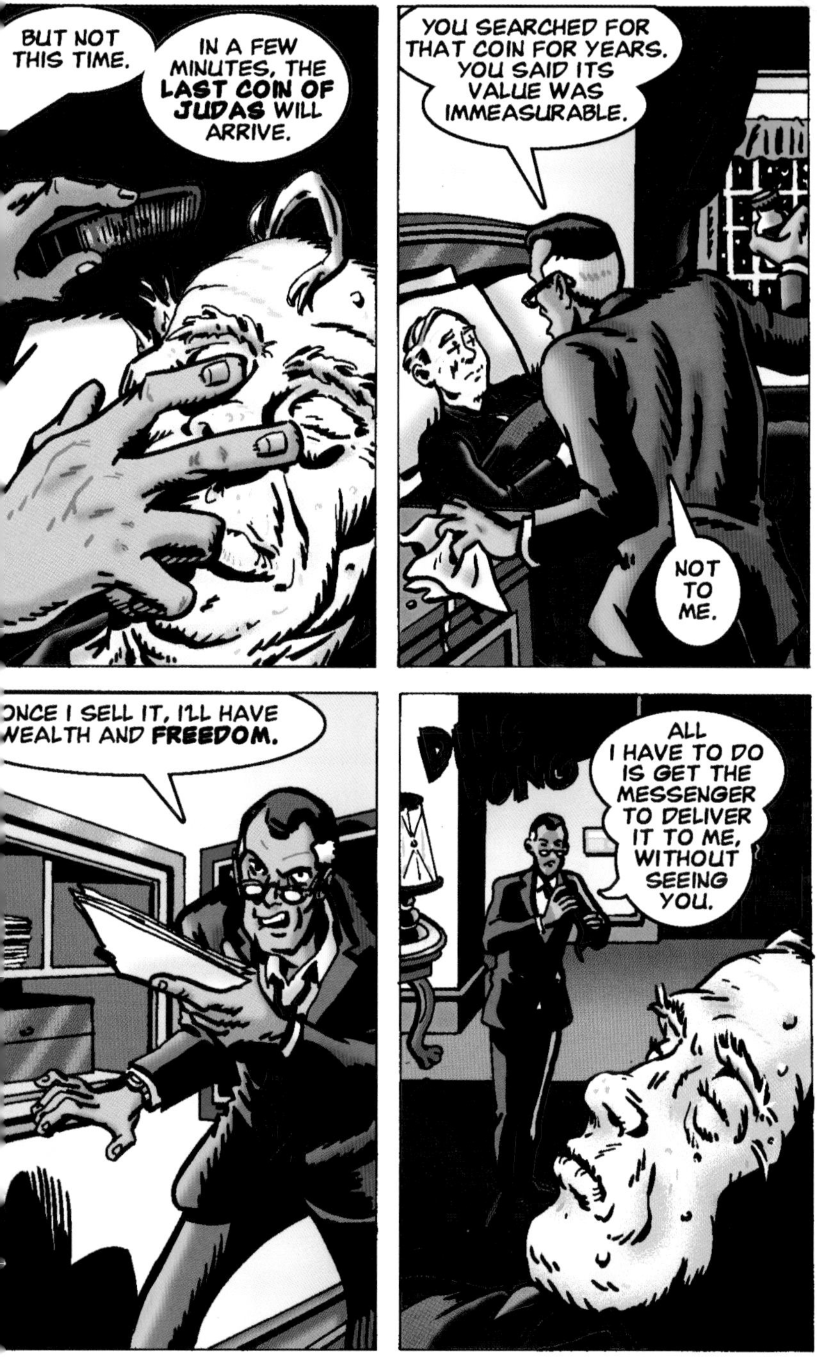
BUT NOT THIS TIME.
IN A FEW MINUTES, THE **LAST COIN OF JUDAS** WILL ARRIVE.
YOU SEARCHED FOR THAT COIN FOR YEARS. YOU SAID ITS VALUE WAS IMMEASURABLE.
NOT TO ME.
ONCE I SELL IT, I'LL HAVE WEALTH AND **FREEDOM.**
ALL I HAVE TO DO IS GET THE MESSENGER TO DELIVER IT TO ME, WITHOUT SEEING YOU.

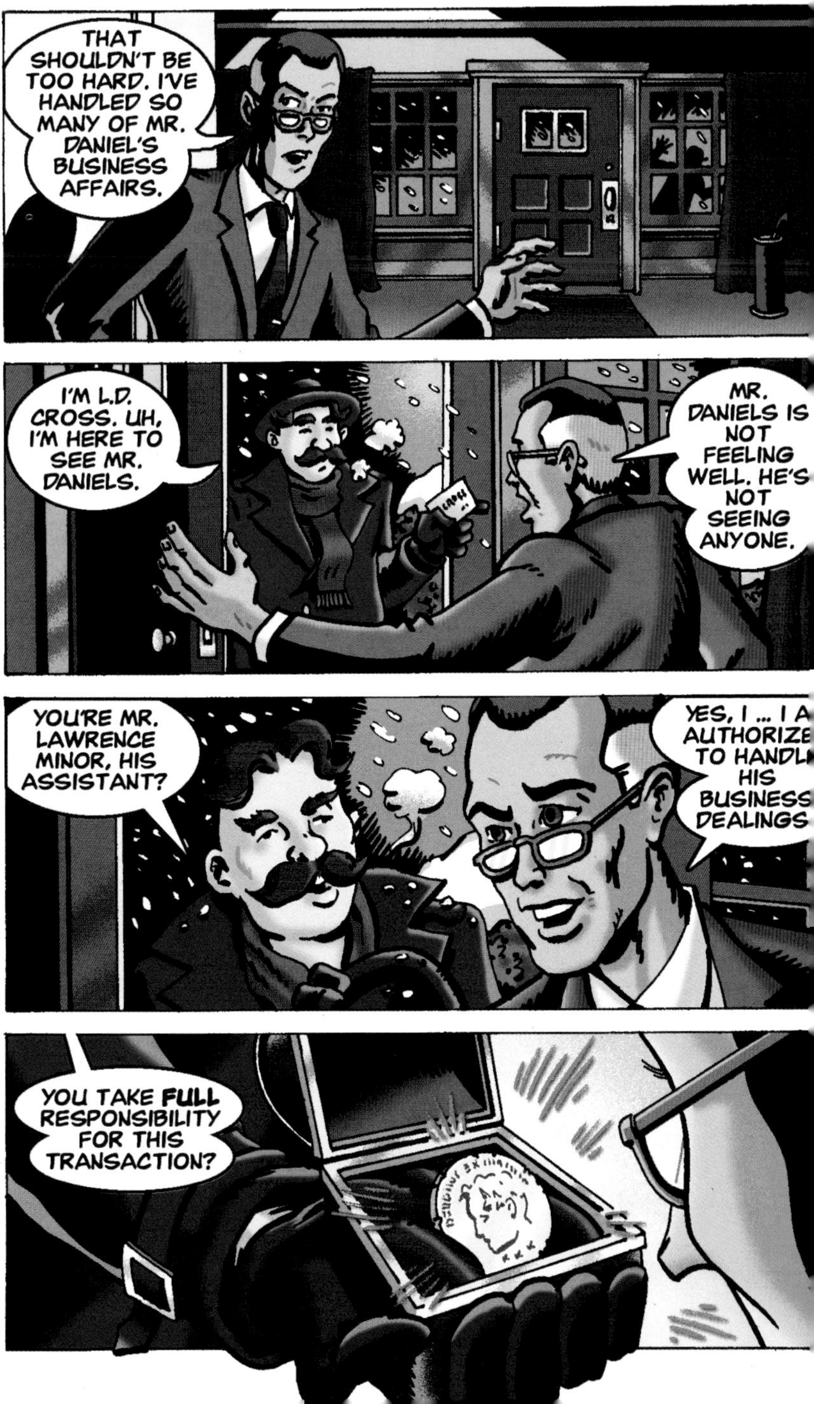
THAT SHOULDN'T BE TOO HARD. I'VE HANDLED SO MANY OF MR. DANIEL'S BUSINESS AFFAIRS.
I'M L.D. CROSS. UH, I'M HERE TO SEE MR. DANIELS.
MR. DANIELS IS NOT FEELING WELL. HE'S NOT SEEING ANYONE.
YOU'RE MR. LAWRENCE MINOR, HIS ASSISTANT?
YES, I ... I A AUTHORIZE TO HANDL HIS BUSINESS DEALINGS
YOU TAKE **FULL** RESPONSIBILITY FOR THIS TRANSACTION?

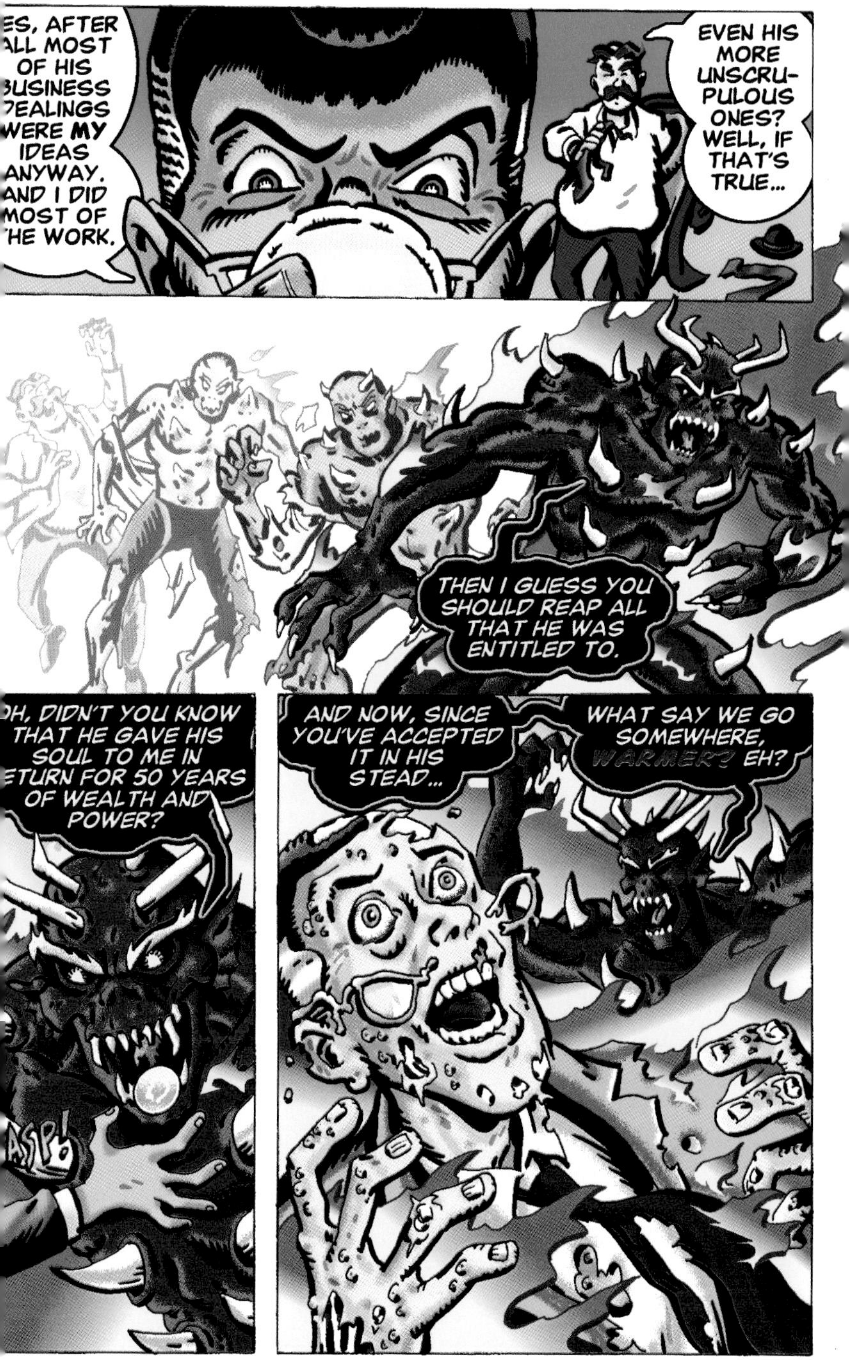
ES, AFTER ALL MOST OF HIS BUSINESS DEALINGS WERE MY IDEAS ANYWAY. AND I DID MOST OF THE WORK.
EVEN HIS MORE UNSCRUPULOUS ONES? WELL, IF THAT'S TRUE...
THEN I GUESS YOU SHOULD REAP ALL THAT HE WAS ENTITLED TO.
OH, DIDN'T YOU KNOW THAT HE GAVE HIS SOUL TO ME IN RETURN FOR 50 YEARS OF WEALTH AND POWER?
ASP!
AND NOW, SINCE YOU'VE ACCEPTED IT IN HIS STEAD...
WHAT SAY WE GO SOMEWHERE, WARMER? EH?

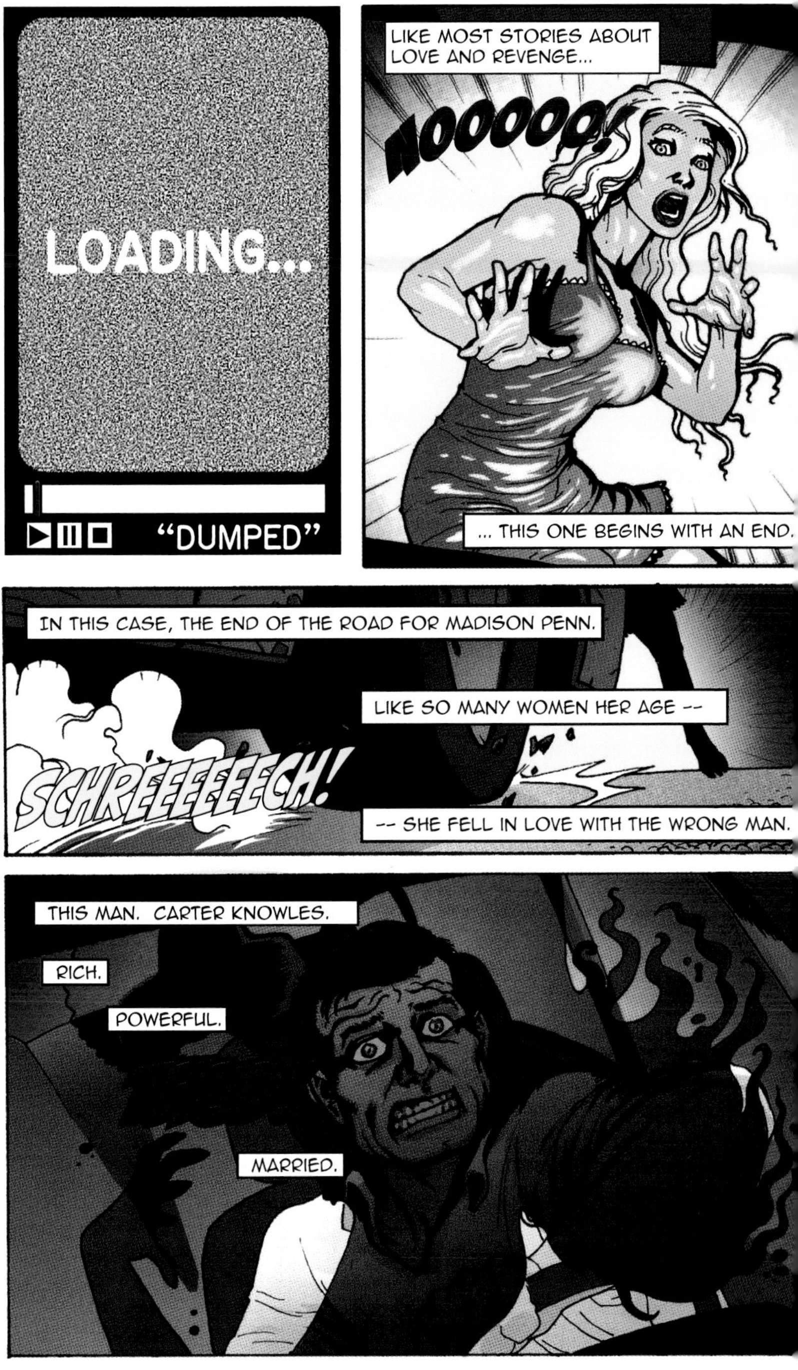
LOADING...
"DUMPED"
LIKE MOST STORIES ABOUT LOVE AND REVENGE...
NOOOOO!
... THIS ONE BEGINS WITH AN END.
IN THIS CASE, THE END OF THE ROAD FOR MADISON PENN.
LIKE SO MANY WOMEN HER AGE --
SCHREEEEEEECH!
-- SHE FELL IN LOVE WITH THE WRONG MAN.
THIS MAN. CARTER KNOWLES.
RICH.
POWERFUL.
MARRIED.

Behold. . .

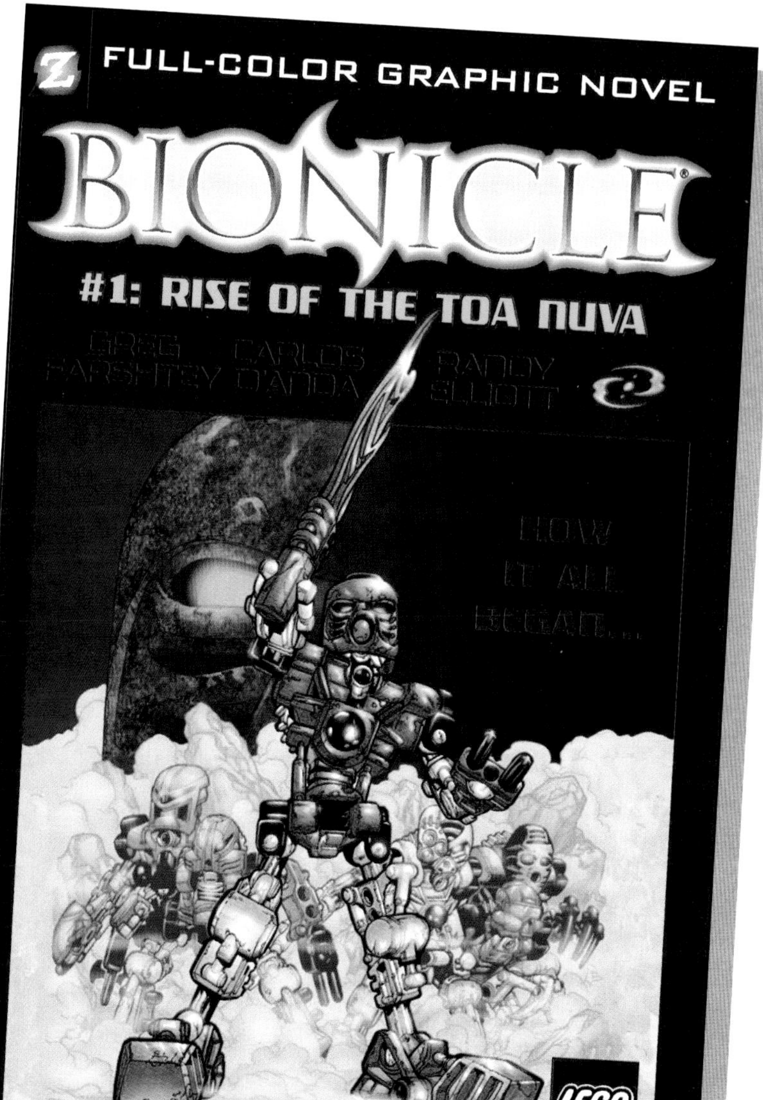

FULL-COLOR GRAPHIC NOVEL
BIONICLE®
#1: RISE OF THE TOA NUVA
GREG FARSHTEY
CARLOS D'ANDA
RANDY ELLIOTT
HOW IT ALL BEGAN...
PAPERCUTZ
LEGO

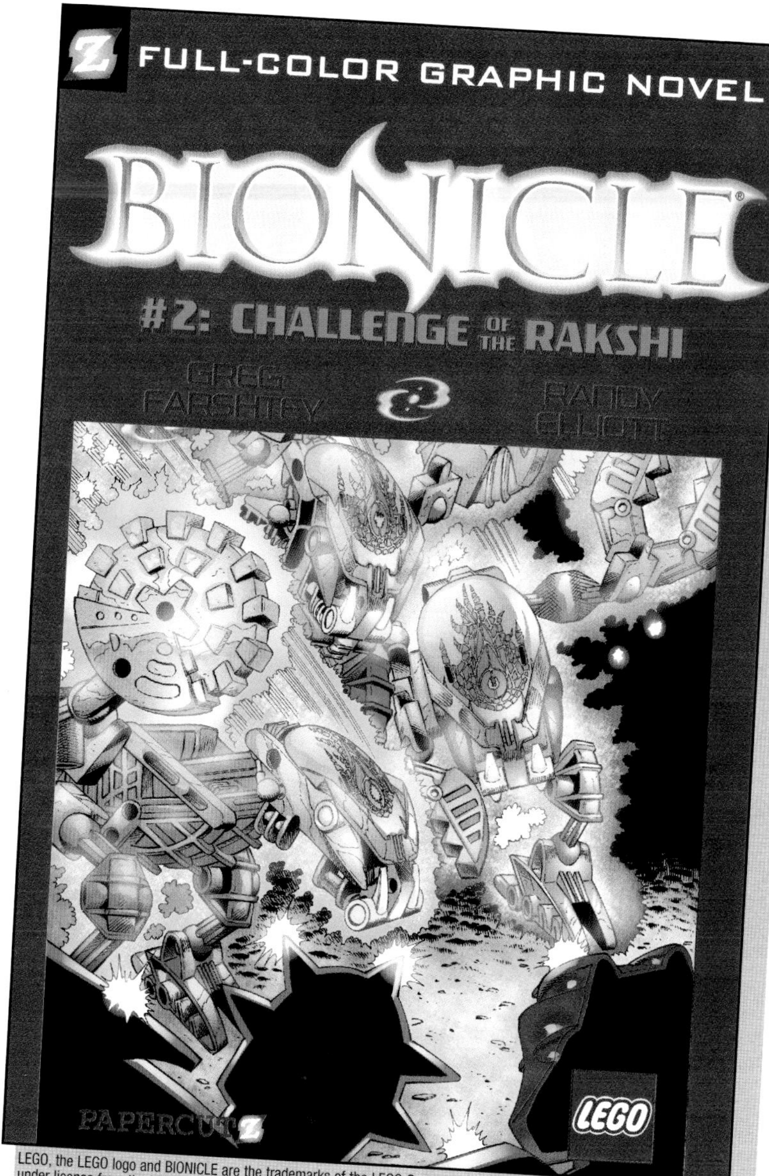

FULL-COLOR GRAPHIC NOVEL
BIONICLE®
#2: CHALLENGE OF THE RAKSHI
GREG FARSHTEY
RANDY ELLIOTT
PAPERCUTZ
LEGO

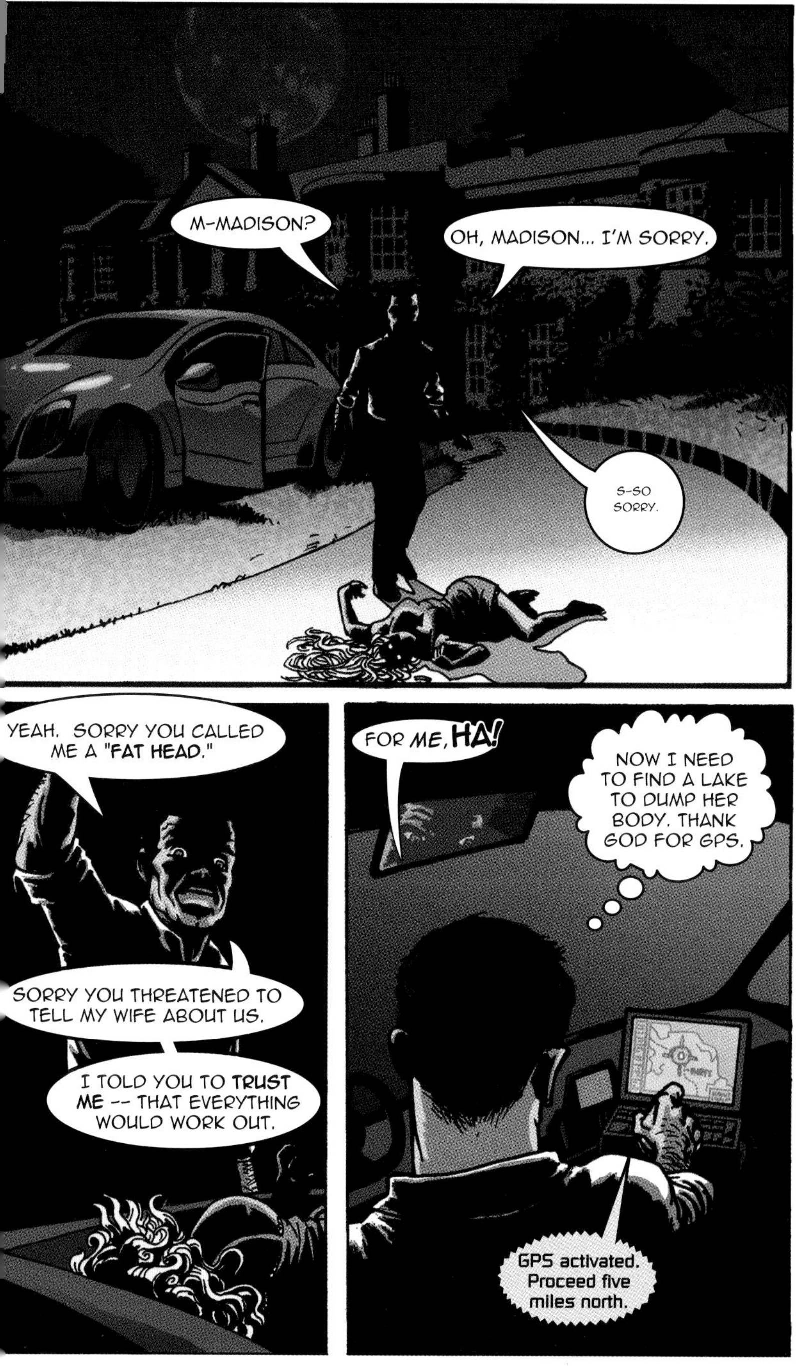
M-MADISON?
OH, MADISON... I'M SORRY.
S-SO SORRY.
YEAH. SORRY YOU CALLED ME A "FAT HEAD."
SORRY YOU THREATENED TO TELL MY WIFE ABOUT US.
I TOLD YOU TO TRUST ME -- THAT EVERYTHING WOULD WORK OUT.
FOR ME, HA!
NOW I NEED TO FIND A LAKE TO DUMP HER BODY. THANK GOD FOR GPS.
GPS activated. Proceed five miles north.

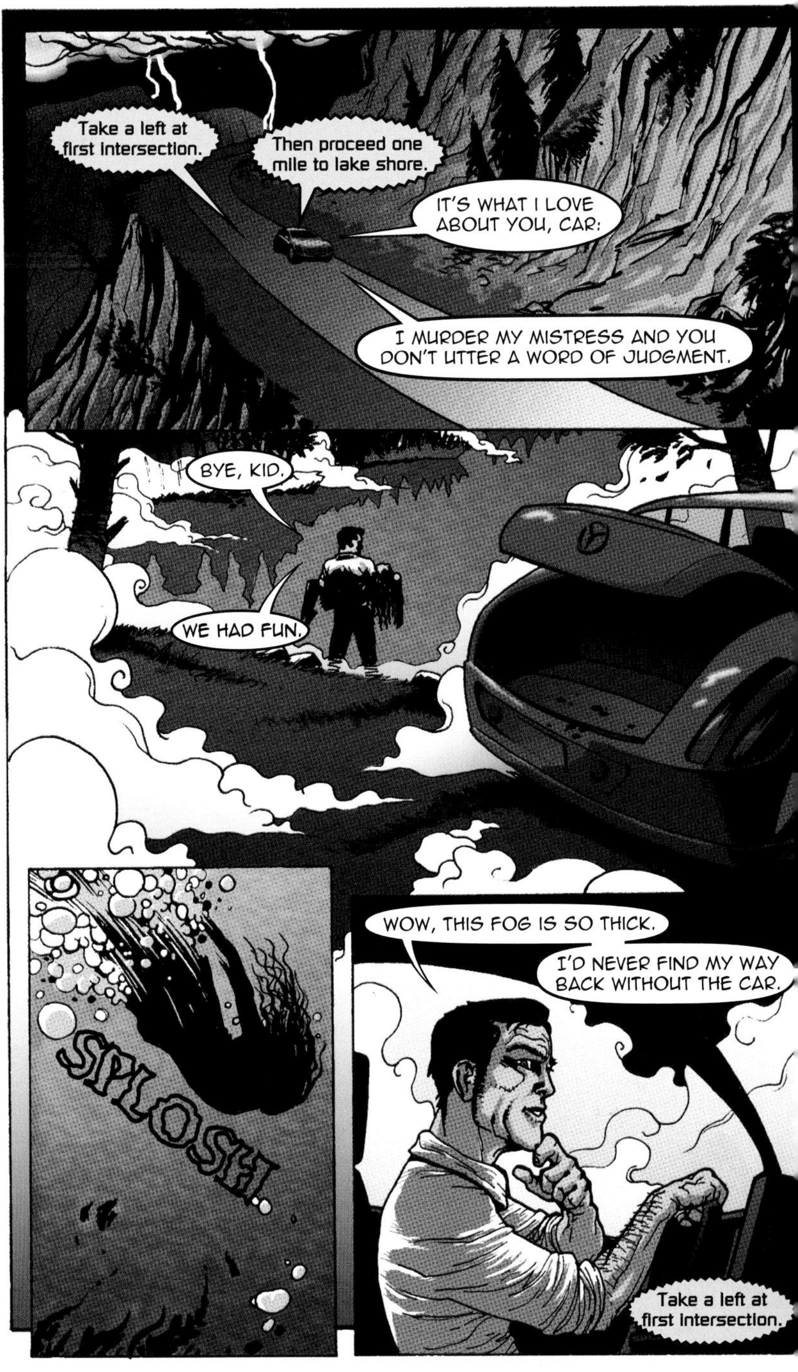
Take a left at first intersection.
Then proceed one mile to lake shore.
IT'S WHAT I LOVE ABOUT YOU, CAR:
I MURDER MY MISTRESS AND YOU DON'T UTTER A WORD OF JUDGMENT.
BYE, KID.
WE HAD FUN.
SPLOSH
WOW, THIS FOG IS SO THICK.
I'D NEVER FIND MY WAY BACK WITHOUT THE CAR.
Take a left at first intersection.

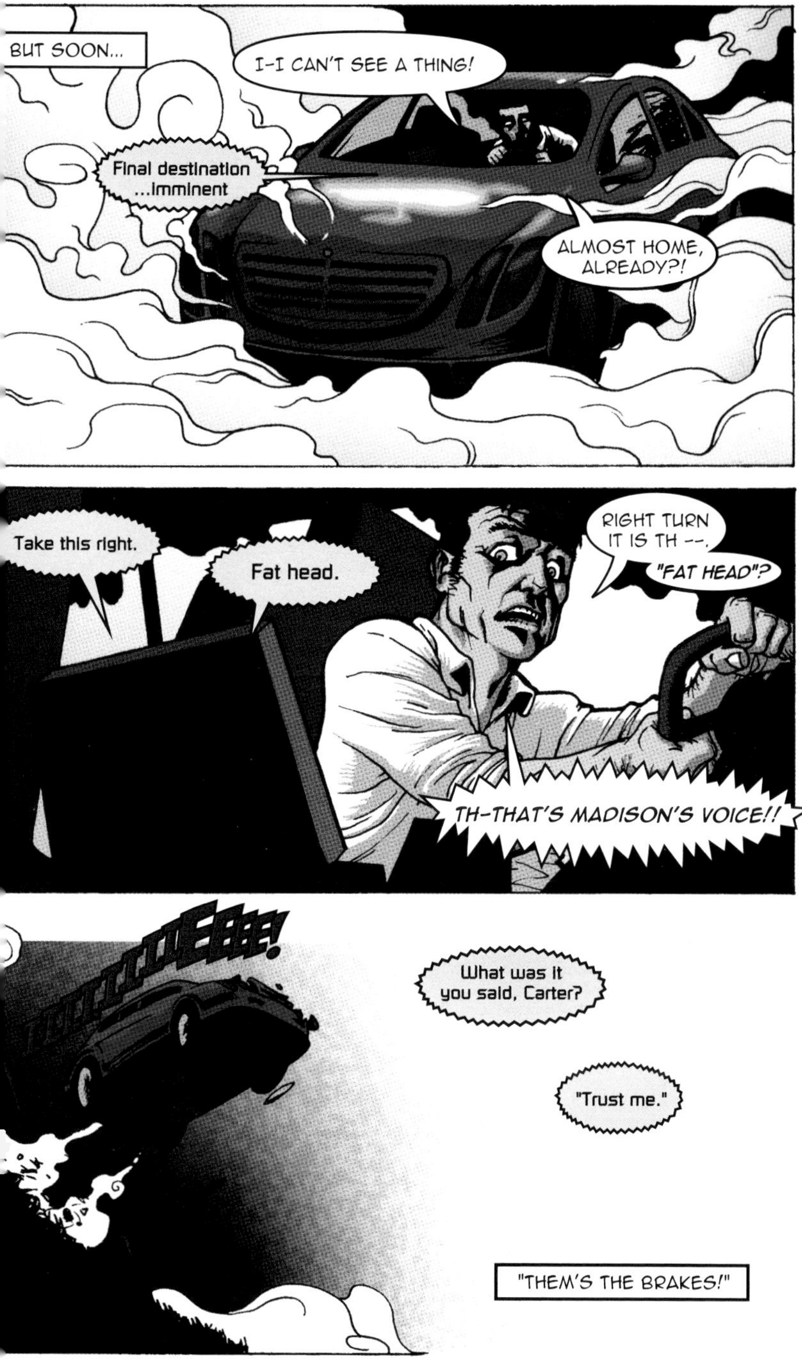

BUT SOON...
I-I CAN'T SEE A THING!
Final destination ...imminent
ALMOST HOME, ALREADY?!
Take this right.
Fat head.
RIGHT TURN IT IS TH --.
"FAT HEAD"?
TH-THAT'S MADISON'S VOICE!!
What was it you said, Carter?
"Trust me."
"THEM'S THE BRAKES!"

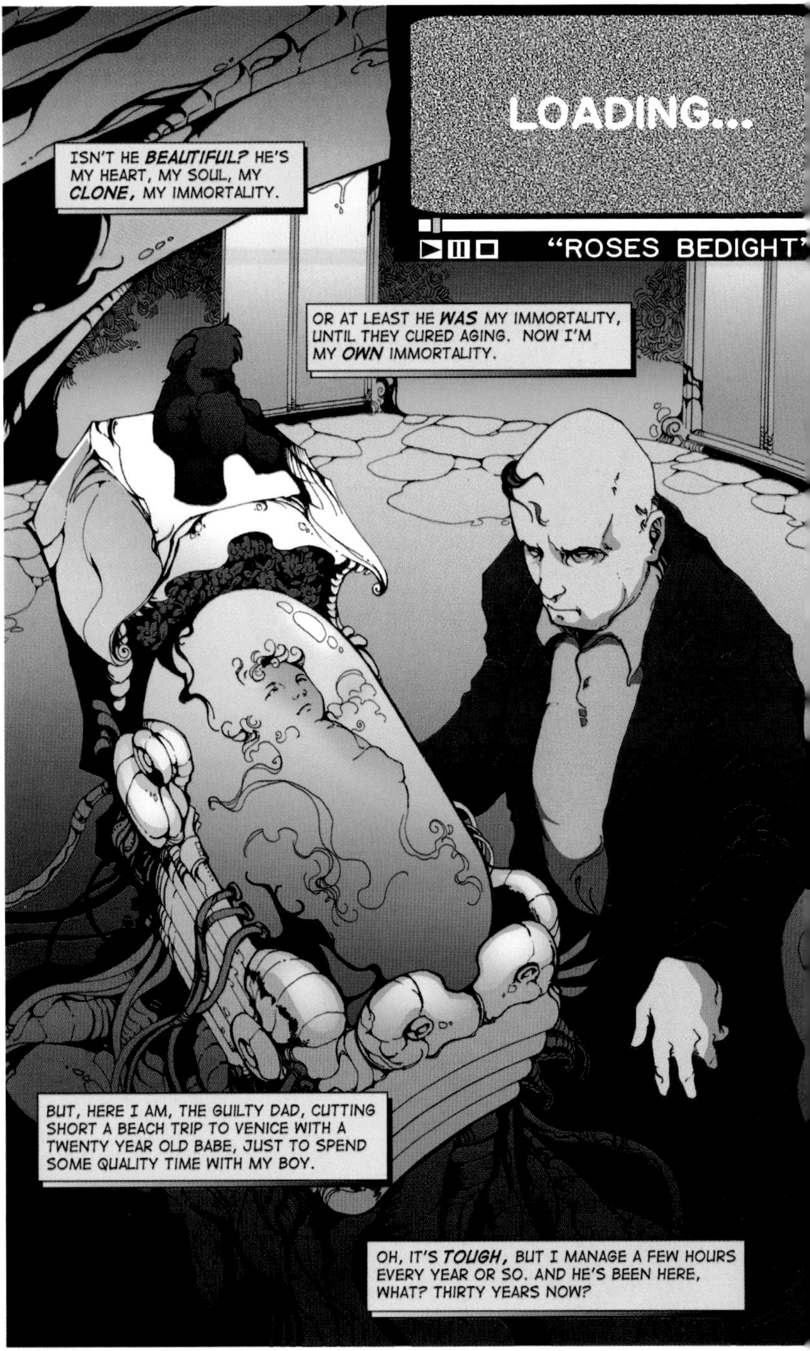
LOADING...
"ROSES BEDIGHT"
ISN'T HE BEAUTIFUL? HE'S MY HEART, MY SOUL, MY CLONE, MY IMMORTALITY.
OR AT LEAST HE WAS MY IMMORTALITY, UNTIL THEY CURED AGING. NOW I'M MY OWN IMMORTALITY.
BUT, HERE I AM, THE GUILTY DAD, CUTTING SHORT A BEACH TRIP TO VENICE WITH A TWENTY YEAR OLD BABE, JUST TO SPEND SOME QUALITY TIME WITH MY BOY.
OH, IT'S TOUGH, BUT I MANAGE A FEW HOURS EVERY YEAR OR SO. AND HE'S BEEN HERE, WHAT? THIRTY YEARS NOW?

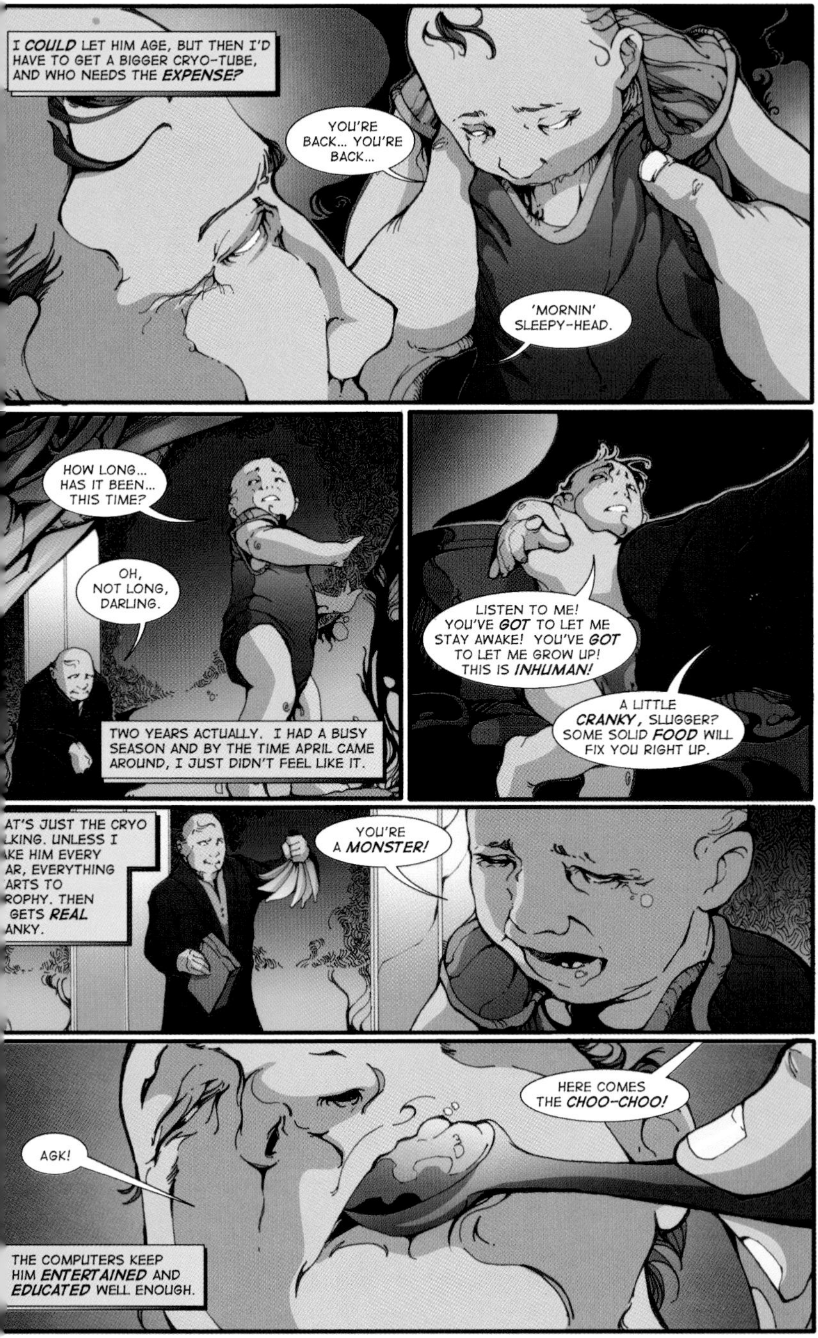

I *COULD* LET HIM AGE, BUT THEN I'D HAVE TO GET A BIGGER CRYO-TUBE, AND WHO NEEDS THE *EXPENSE?*
YOU'RE BACK... YOU'RE BACK...
'MORNIN' SLEEPY-HEAD.
HOW LONG... HAS IT BEEN... THIS TIME?
OH, NOT LONG, DARLING.
TWO YEARS ACTUALLY. I HAD A BUSY SEASON AND BY THE TIME APRIL CAME AROUND, I JUST DIDN'T FEEL LIKE IT.
LISTEN TO ME! YOU'VE *GOT* TO LET ME STAY AWAKE! YOU'VE *GOT* TO LET ME GROW UP! THIS IS *INHUMAN!*
A LITTLE *CRANKY*, SLUGGER? SOME SOLID *FOOD* WILL FIX YOU RIGHT UP.
AT'S JUST THE CRYO LKING. UNLESS I KE HIM EVERY AR, EVERYTHING ARTS TO ROPHY. THEN GETS *REAL* ANKY.
YOU'RE A *MONSTER!*
HERE COMES THE *CHOO-CHOO!*
AGK!
THE COMPUTERS KEEP HIM *ENTERTAINED* AND *EDUCATED* WELL ENOUGH.

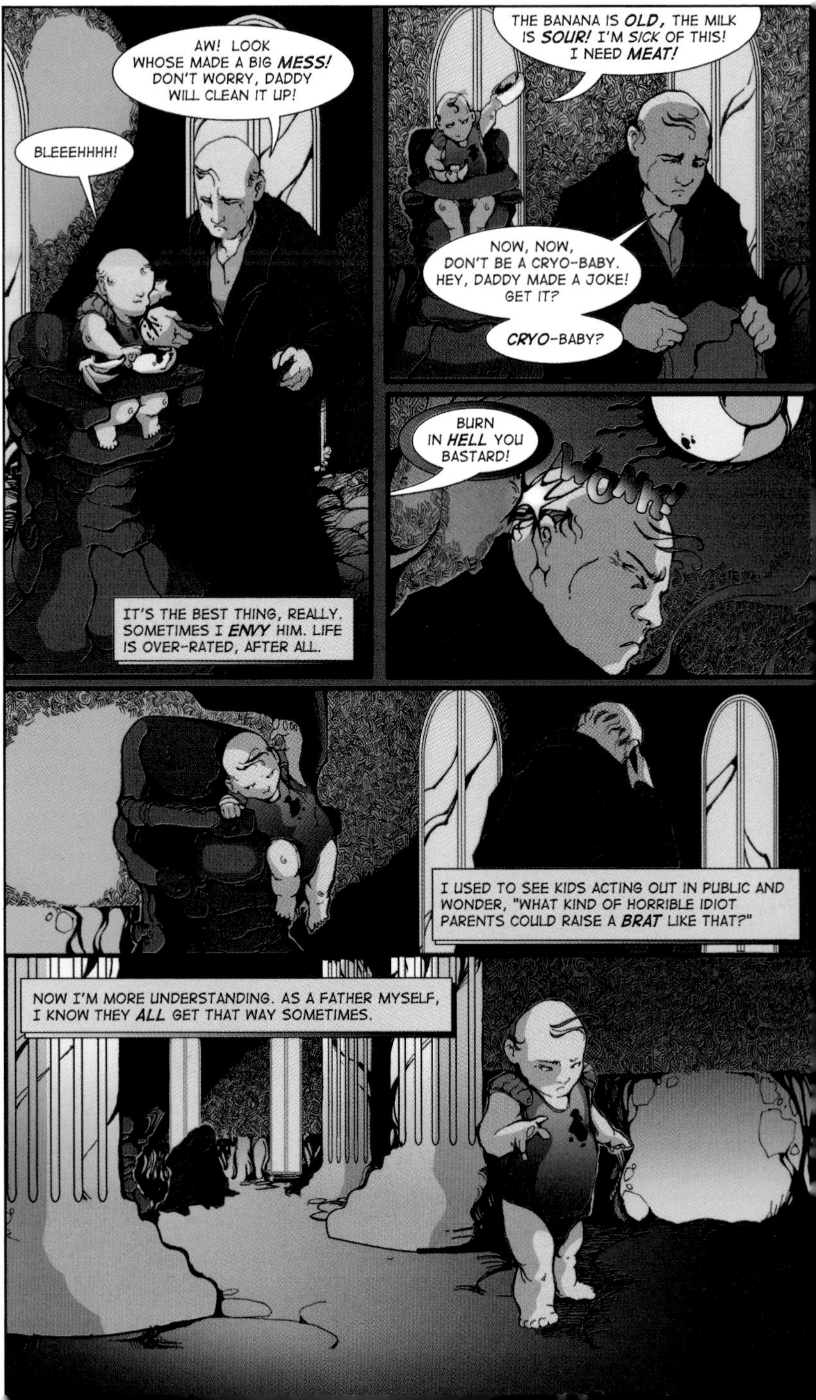
AW! LOOK WHOSE MADE A BIG MESS! DON'T WORRY, DADDY WILL CLEAN IT UP!
BLEEEHHHH!
IT'S THE BEST THING, REALLY. SOMETIMES I ENVY HIM. LIFE IS OVER-RATED, AFTER ALL.
THE BANANA IS OLD, THE MILK IS SOUR! I'M SICK OF THIS! I NEED MEAT!
NOW, NOW, DON'T BE A CRYO-BABY. HEY, DADDY MADE A JOKE! GET IT?
CRYO-BABY?
BURN IN HELL YOU BASTARD!
WONK!
I USED TO SEE KIDS ACTING OUT IN PUBLIC AND WONDER, "WHAT KIND OF HORRIBLE IDIOT PARENTS COULD RAISE A BRAT LIKE THAT?"
NOW I'M MORE UNDERSTANDING. AS A FATHER MYSELF, I KNOW THEY ALL GET THAT WAY SOMETIMES.

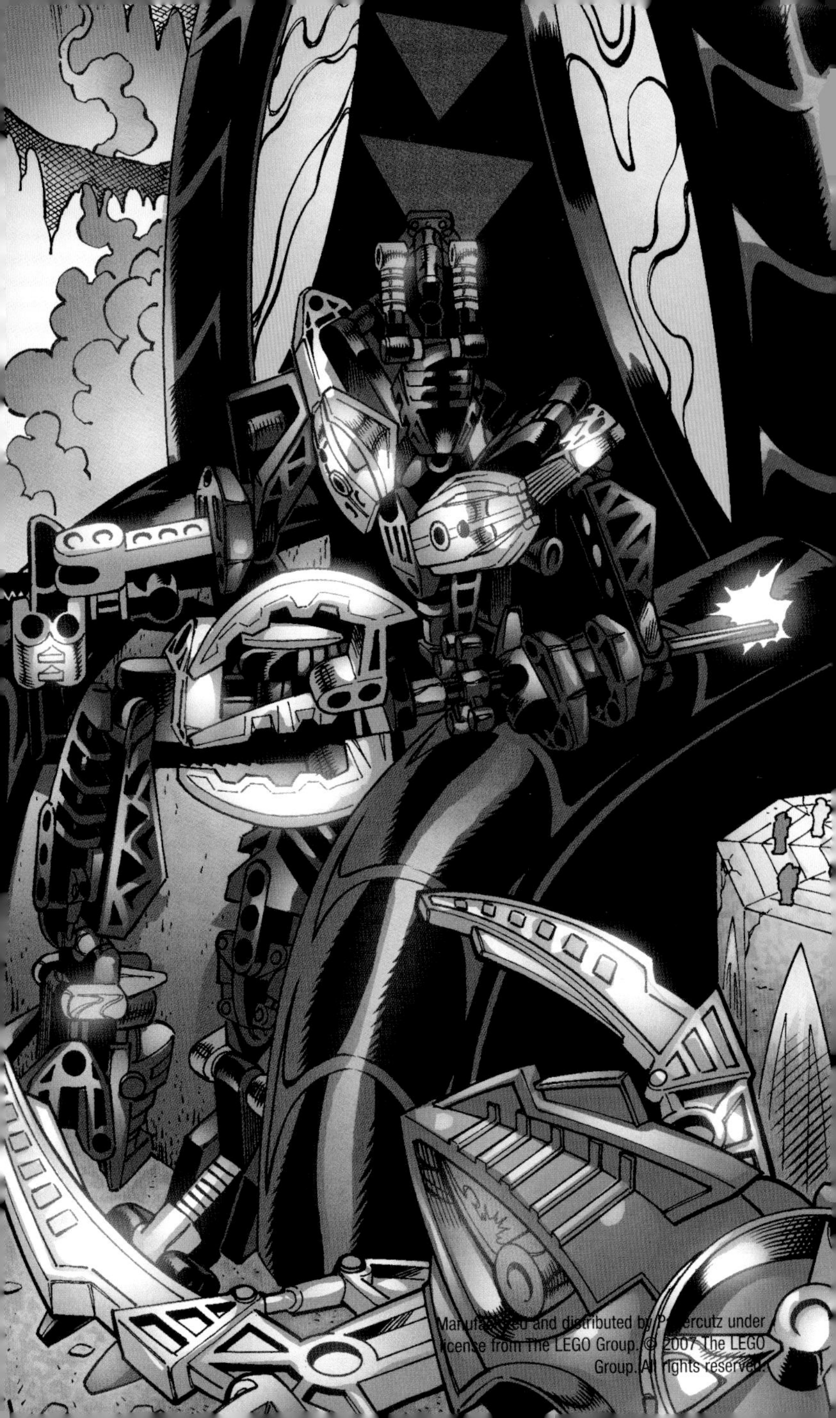

At the start of the new millennium, a new line of toys from LEGO made their dramatic debut. Originally released in six color-coded canisters, each containing a constructible, fully-poseable, articulated character, BIONICLE was an instant hit!

The BIONICLE figures were incredibly intriguing. With their exotic names hinting at a complex history, fans were curious to discover more about these captivating characters. Even now, over six years later, there are still many unanswered questions surrounding every facet of the ever-expanding BIONICLE universe.

A comicbook, written by leading BIONICLE expert and author of most of the BIONICLE novels Greg Farshtey, was created by DC Comics and given away to members of the BIONICLE fan club. The action-packed comics revealed much about these mysterious biomechanical (part biological, part mechanical) beings and the world they inhabited. A world filled with many races, most prominent being the Matoran. A world once protected millennia ago by a Great Spirit known as Mata Nui, who has fallen asleep. A world that has begun to decay as its inhabitants must defend themselves from the evil forces of Makuta.

The first story arc of the comics called "The BIONICLE Chronicles," begins when six heroic beings known as Toa arrive on a tropical-like island which is also named Mata Nui. The Toa may just be the saviors the people of Mata Nui need, if they can avoid fighting with themselves, not to mention the Bohrok and the Rahkshise early comics are incredibly hard-to-find, and many new BIONICLE fans have never seen these all-important early chapters in this epic science fantasy. But soon, those comics will be collected as the first two volumes in the Papercutz series of BIONICLE graphic novels.

These early comics are incredibly hard-to-find, and many new BIONICLE fans have never seen these all-important early chapters in this epic science fantasy. But soon, those comics will be collected as the first two volumes in the Papercutz series of BIONICLE graphic novels.

In the following pages, enjoy a special preview of BIONICLE graphic novel #1...

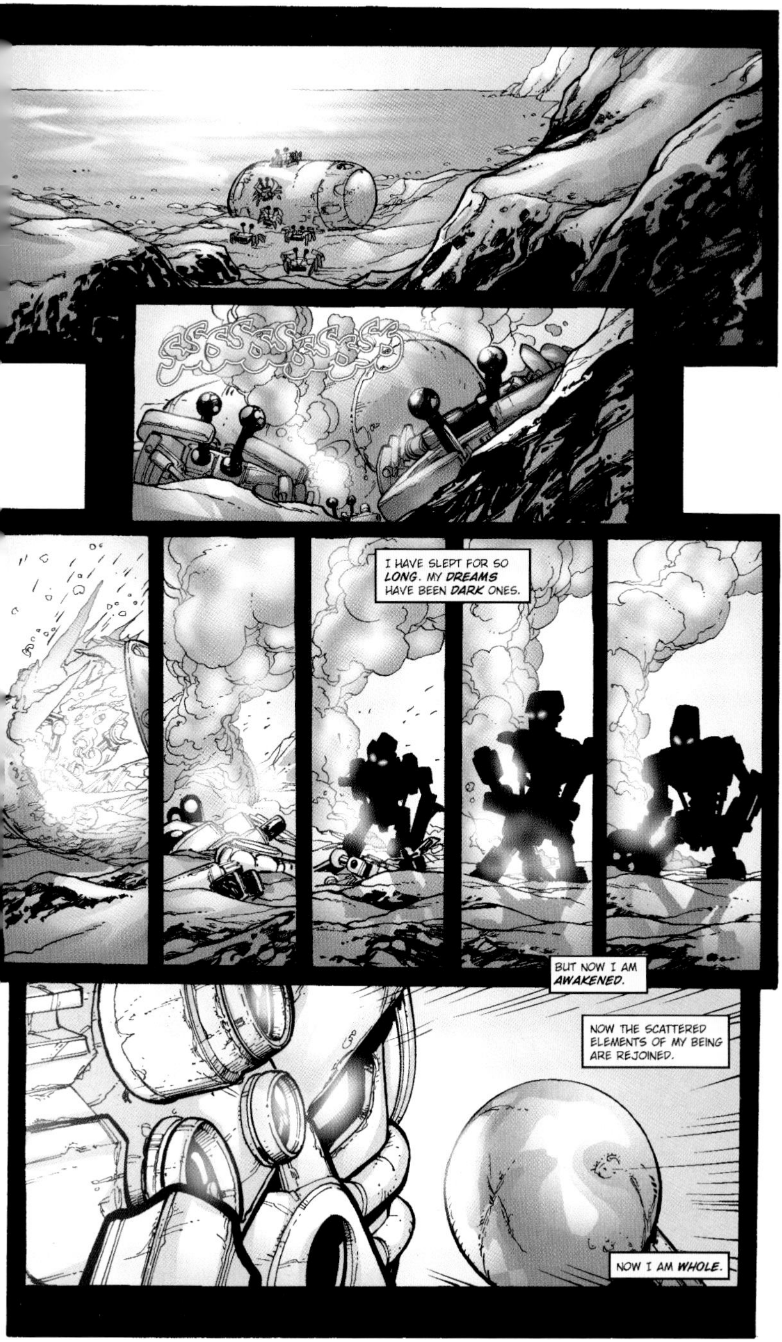
I HAVE SLEPT FOR SO LONG. MY DREAMS HAVE BEEN DARK ONES.
BUT NOW I AM AWAKENED.
NOW THE SCATTERED ELEMENTS OF MY BEING ARE REJOINED.
NOW I AM WHOLE.

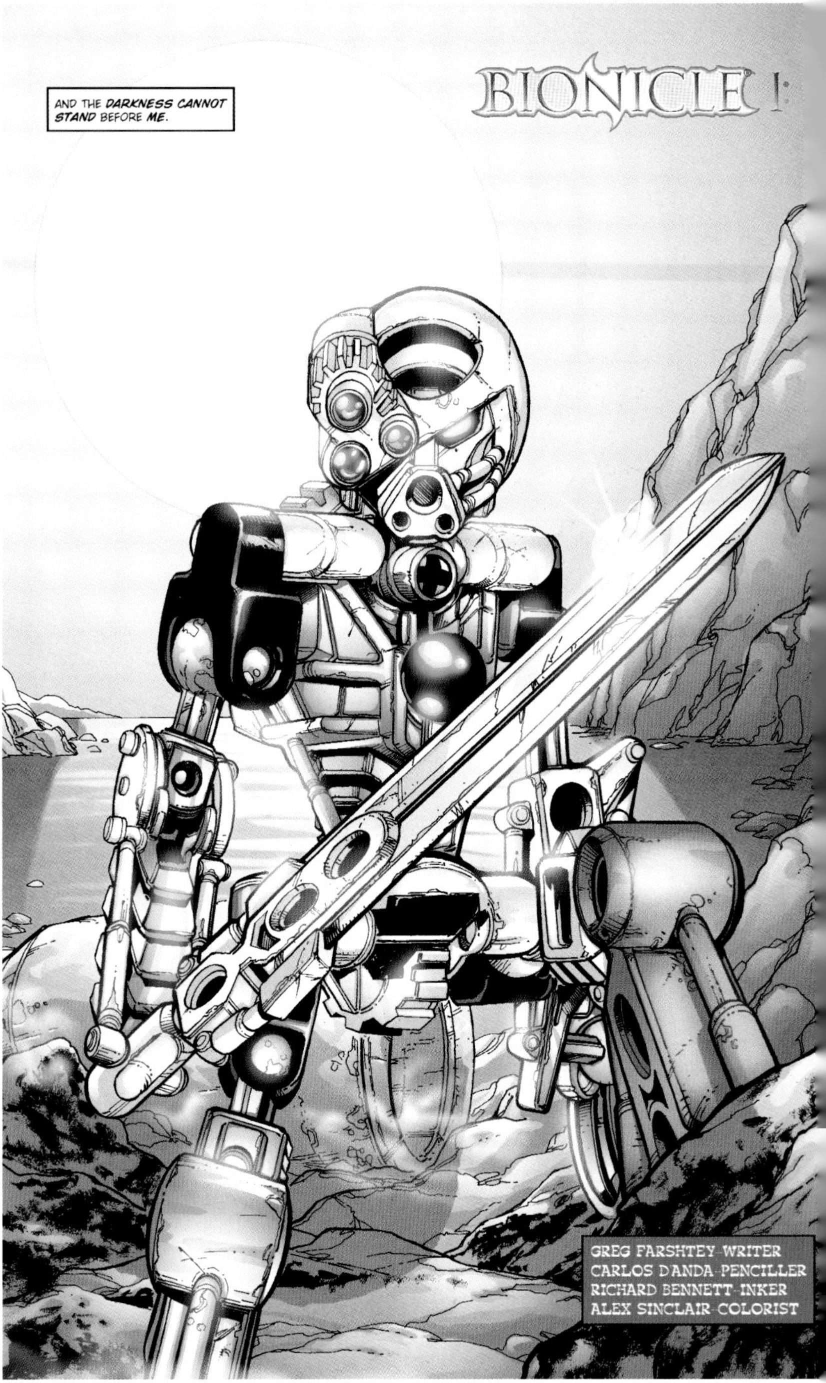

AND THE DARKNESS CANNOT STAND BEFORE ME.
BIONICLE 1:
GREG FARSHTEY-WRITER
CARLOS D'ANDA-PENCILLER
RICHARD BENNETT-INKER
ALEX SINCLAIR-COLORIST

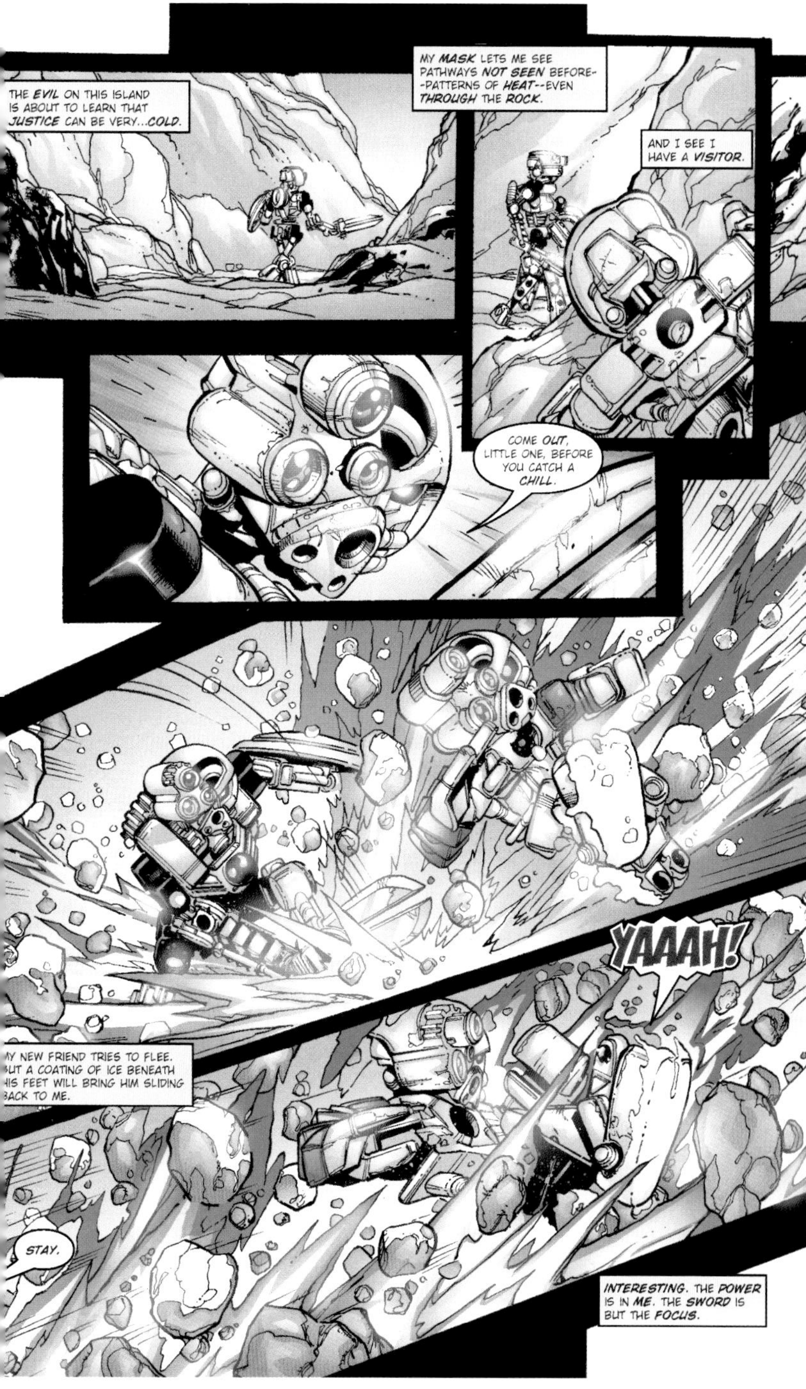
THE EVIL ON THIS ISLAND IS ABOUT TO LEARN THAT JUSTICE CAN BE VERY...COLD.
MY MASK LETS ME SEE PATHWAYS NOT SEEN BEFORE--PATTERNS OF HEAT--EVEN THROUGH THE ROCK.
AND I SEE I HAVE A VISITOR.
COME OUT, LITTLE ONE, BEFORE YOU CATCH A CHILL.
YAAAH!
MY NEW FRIEND TRIES TO FLEE. BUT A COATING OF ICE BENEATH HIS FEET WILL BRING HIM SLIDING BACK TO ME.
STAY.
INTERESTING. THE POWER IS IN ME. THE SWORD IS BUT THE FOCUS.

CLASSICS Illustrated

Featuring Stories by the World's Greatest Authors

Returns in two new series from Papercutz!

The original, best-selling series of comics adaptations of the world's greatest literature, CLASSICS ILLUSTRATED, returns in two new formats--the original, featuring abridged adaptations of classic novels, and CLASSICS ILLUSTRATED DELUXE, featuring longer, more expansive adaptations-from graphic novel publisher Papercutz. "We're very proud to say that Papercutz has received such an enthusiastic reception from librarians and school teachers for its NANCY DREW and HARDY BOYS graphic novels as well as THE LIFE OF POPE JOHN PAUL II...*IN COMICS!*, that it only seemed logical for us to bring back the original CLASSICS ILLUSTRATED comicbook series beloved by parents, educators, and librarians," explained Papercutz Publisher, Terry Nantier. "We can't thank the enlightened librarians and teachers who have supported Papercutz enough. And we're thrilled that they're so excited about CLASSICS ILLUSTRATED."

Upcoming titles include The Invisible Man, Tales from the Brothers Grimm, and Robinson Crusoe.

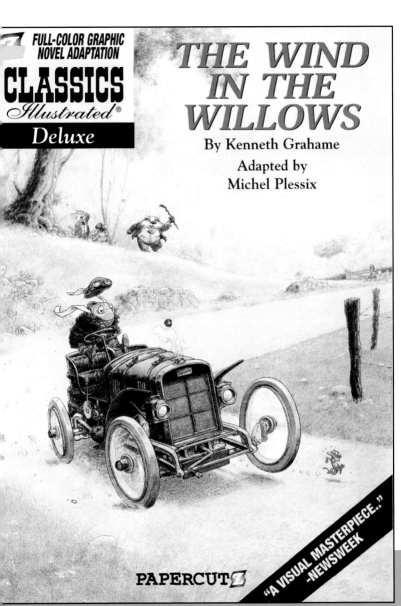

FULL-COLOR GRAPHIC NOVEL ADAPTATION

CLASSICS
Illustrated ®
Deluxe

THE WIND IN THE WILLOWS

By Kenneth Grahame

Adapted by
Michel Plessix

PAPERCUT

"A VISUAL MASTERPIECE."
-NEWSWEEK

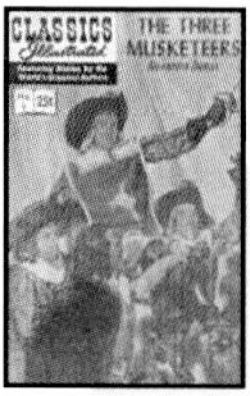
CLASSICS Illustrated
THE THREE MUSKETEERS
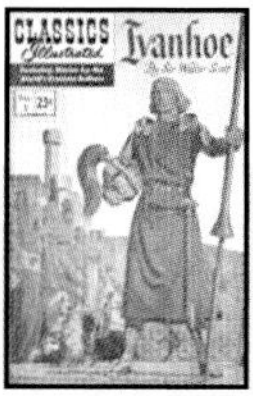
CLASSICS Illustrated
Ivanhoe
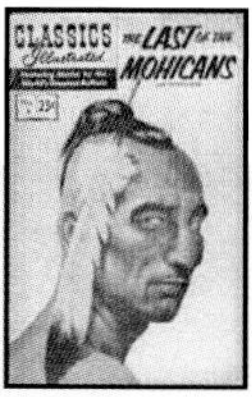
CLASSICS Illustrated
THE LAST OF THE MOHICANS
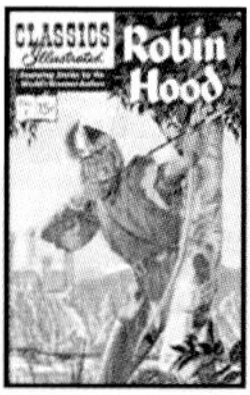
CLASSICS Illustrated
Robin Hood
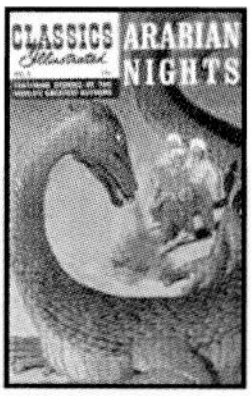
CLASSICS Illustrated
ARABIAN NIGHTS
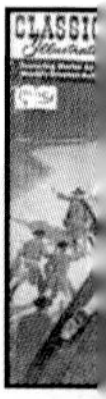

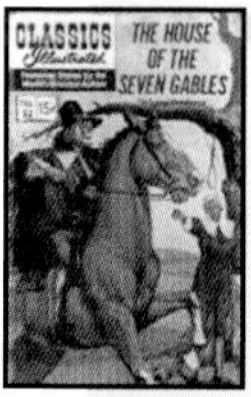
CLASSICS Illustrated
THE HOUSE OF THE SEVEN GABLES

A Short History of CLASSICS ILLUSTRATED...

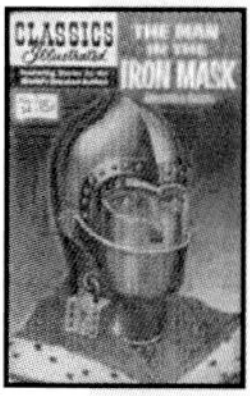
CLASSICS Illustrated
THE MAN IN THE IRON MASK

William B. Jones Jr. is the author of Classics Illustrated: A Cultural History, which offers a comprehensive overview of the original comic-book series and the writers, artists, editors, and publishers behind-the-scenes. With Mr. Jones Jr.'s kind permission, here's a very short overview of the history of CLASSICS ILLUSTRATED adapted from his 2005 essay on Albert Kanter.

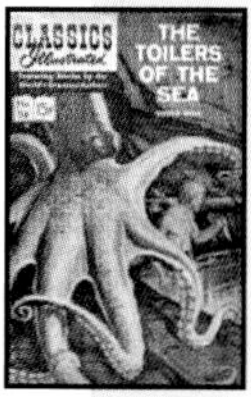
CLASSICS Illustrated
THE TOILERS OF THE SEA

CLASSICS ILLUSTRATED was the creation of Albert Lewis Kanter, a visionary publisher, who from 1941 to 1971, introduced young readers worldwide to the realms of literature, history, folklore, mythology, and science in over 200 titles in such comicbook series as CLASSICS ILLUSTRATED and CLASSICS ILLUSTRATED JUNIOR. Kanter, inspired by the success of the first comicbooks published in the early 30s and late 40s, believed he

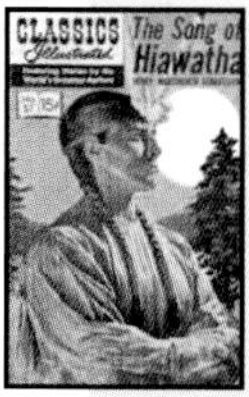
CLASSICS Illustrated
The Song of Hiawatha

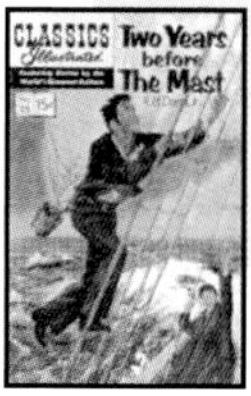
CLASSICS Illustrated
Two Years before The Mast
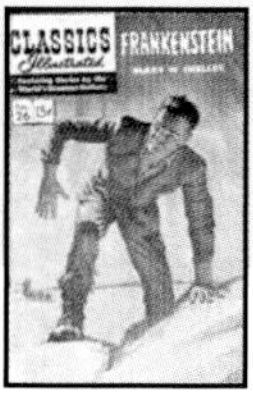
CLASSICS Illustrated
FRANKENSTEIN
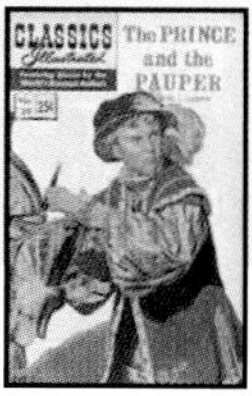
CLASSICS Illustrated
The PRINCE and the PAUPER
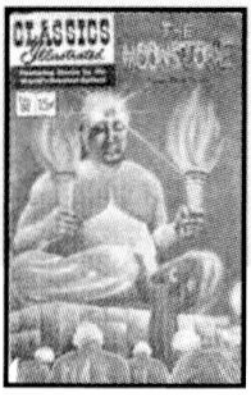
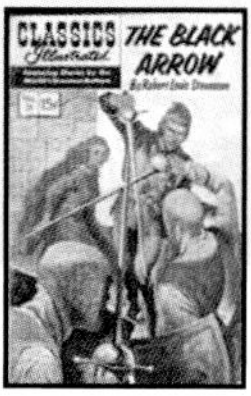
CLASSICS Illustrated
THE BLACK ARROW
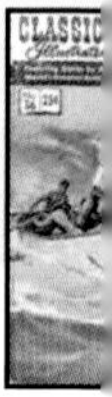

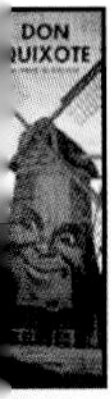
DON
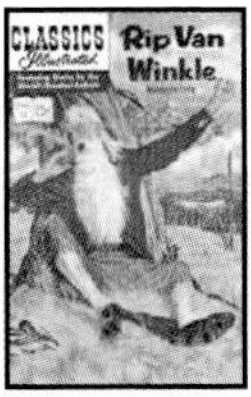
CLASSICS Illustrated
Rip Van Winkle
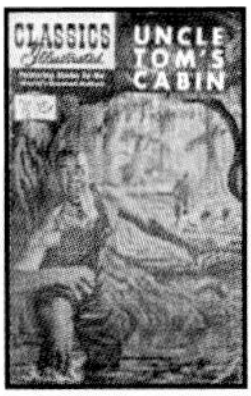
CLASSICS Illustrated
UNCLE TOM'S CABIN
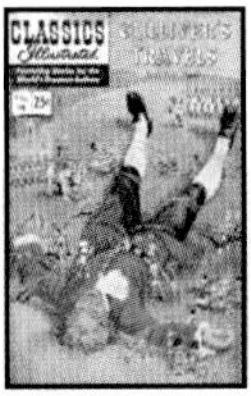
CLASSICS Illustrated
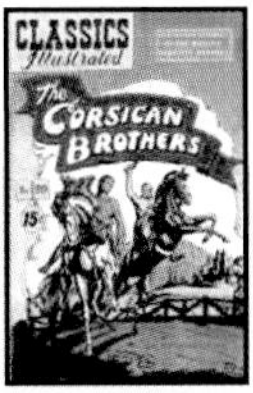
CLASSICS Illustrated
The CORSICAN BROTHERS
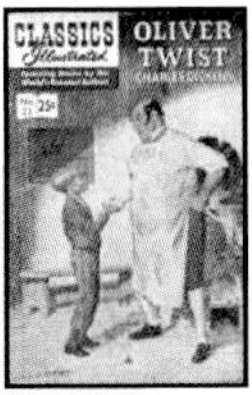
CLASSICS Illustrated
OLIVER TWIST
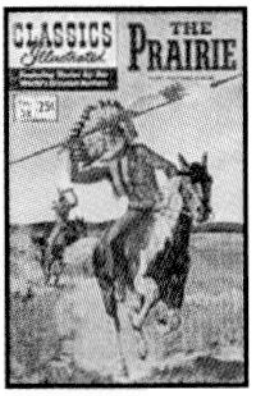
CLASSICS Illustrated
THE PRAIRIE

could use the same medium to introduce young readers to the world of great literature. CLASSIC COMICS (later changed to CLASSICS ILLUSTRATED in 1947) was launched in 1941, and soon the comicbook adaptations of Shakespeare, Stevenson, Twain, Verne, and other authors, were being used in schools and endorsed by educators.

CLASSICS ILLUSTRATED was translated and distributed in countries such as Canada, Great Britain, the Netherlands, Greece, Brazil, Mexico, and Australia. The genial publisher was hailed abroad as "Papa Klassiker." By the beginning of the 1960s, CLASSICS ILLUSTRATED was the largest childrens publication in the world. The original CLASSICS ILLUSTRATED series adapted into comics 169 titles; among these were Frankenstein, 20,000 Leagues Under the Sea, Treasure Island, Julius Caesar, and Faust.

Albert L. Kanter died, March 17, 1973, leaving behind a rich legacy for the millions of readers whose imaginations were awakened by CLASSICS ILLUSTRATED.

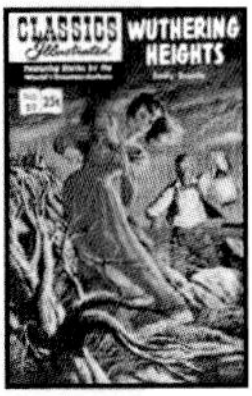
CLASSICS Illustrated
WUTHERING HEIGHTS
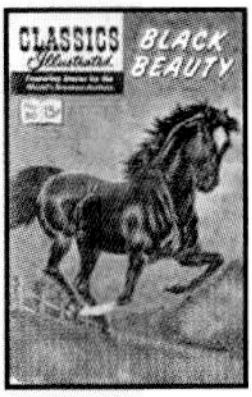
CLASSICS Illustrated
BLACK BEAUTY
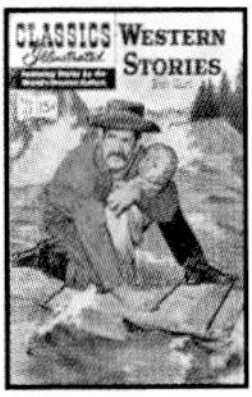
CLASSICS Illustrated
WESTERN STORIES

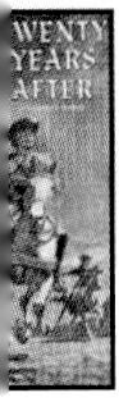
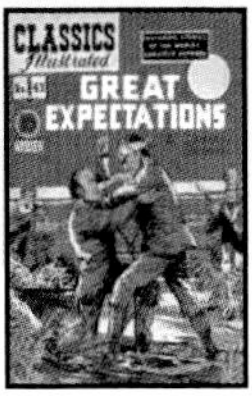
CLASSICS Illustrated
GREAT EXPECTATIONS
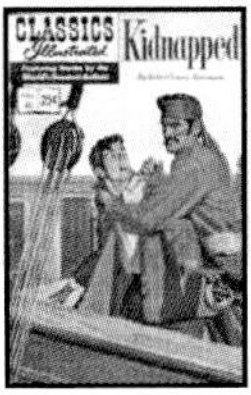
CLASSICS Illustrated
Kidnapped
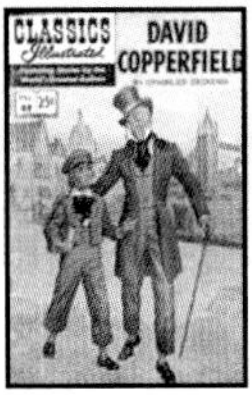
CLASSICS Illustrated
DAVID COPPERFIELD
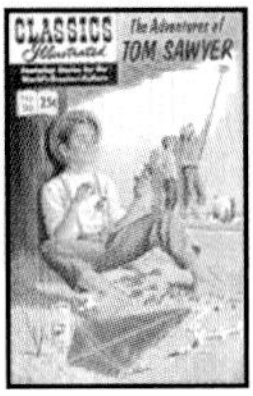
CLASSICS Illustrated
TOM SAWYER
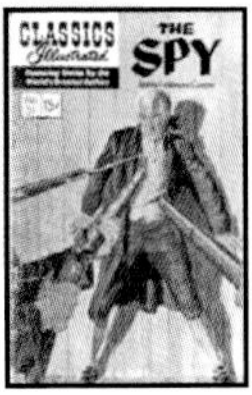
CLASSICS Illustrated
THE SPY

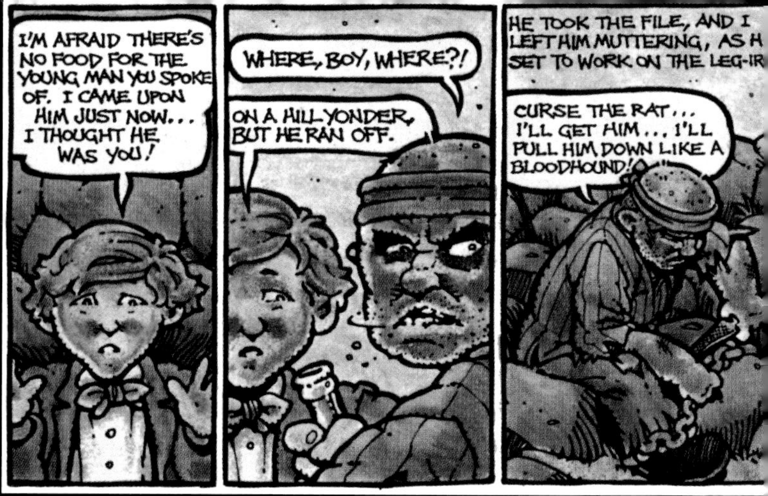
I'M AFRAID THERE'S NO FOOD FOR THE YOUNG MAN YOU SPOKE OF. I CAME UPON HIM JUST NOW... I THOUGHT HE WAS YOU!
WHERE, BOY, WHERE?!
ON A HILL YONDER, BUT HE RAN OFF.
HE TOOK THE FILE, AND I LEFT HIM MUTTERING, AS H
SET TO WORK ON THE LEG-IR
CURSE THE RAT... I'LL GET HIM... I'LL PULL HIM DOWN LIKE A BLOODHOUND!

CLASSICS ILLUSTRATED was re-launched in 1990 in graphic novel/book form by the Berkley Publishing Group and First Publishing, Inc. featuring all-new adaptations by such top graphic novelists as Rick Geary, Bill Sienkiewicz, Kyle Baker, Gahan Wilson, and others. "First had the right idea, they just came out about 15 years too soon. Now bookstores are ready for graphic novels such as these," Jim explains. Many of these excellent adaptations have been acquired by Papercutz and will make up the new series of CLASSICS ILLUSTRATED titles.

The first volume of the new CLASSICS ILLUSTRATED series presents graphic novelist Rick Geary's adaptation of "Great Expectations" by Charles Dickens. The bittersweet tale of one boy's adolescence, and of the choices he makes to shape his destiny. Into an engrossing mystery, Dickens weaves a heartfelt inquiry into morals and virtues-as the orphan Pip, the convict Magwitch, the beautiful Estella, the bitter Miss Havisham, the goodhearted Biddy, the kind Joe and other memorable characters entwine in a battle of human nature. Rick Geary's delightful illustrations capture the newfound awe and frustrations of young Pip as he comes of age, and begins to understand the opportunities that life presents.

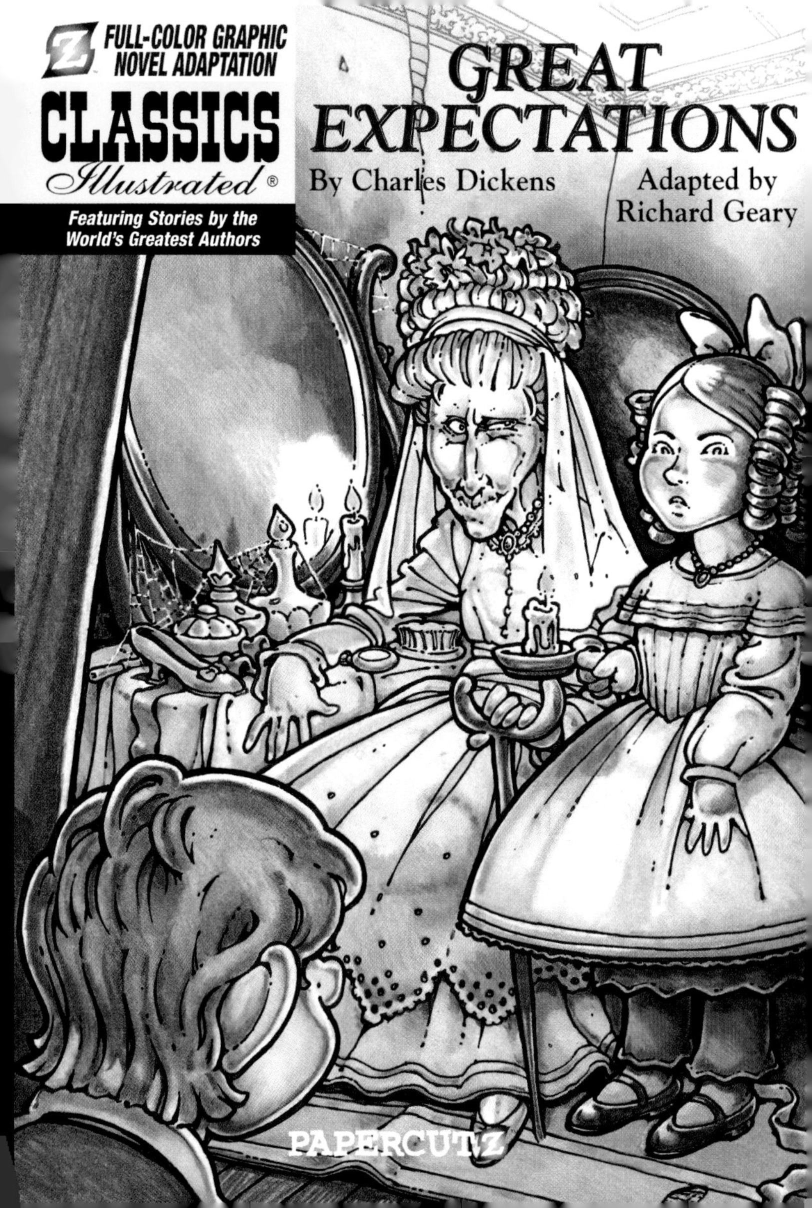

FULL-COLOR GRAPHIC NOVEL ADAPTATION
CLASSICS Illustrated®
Featuring Stories by the World's Greatest Authors
GREAT EXPECTATIONS
By Charles Dickens
Adapted by Richard Geary
PAPERCUTZ

Here are two pages of CLASSICS ILLUSTRATED #1 "Great Expectation
by Charles Dickens, as adapted by Rick Geary.

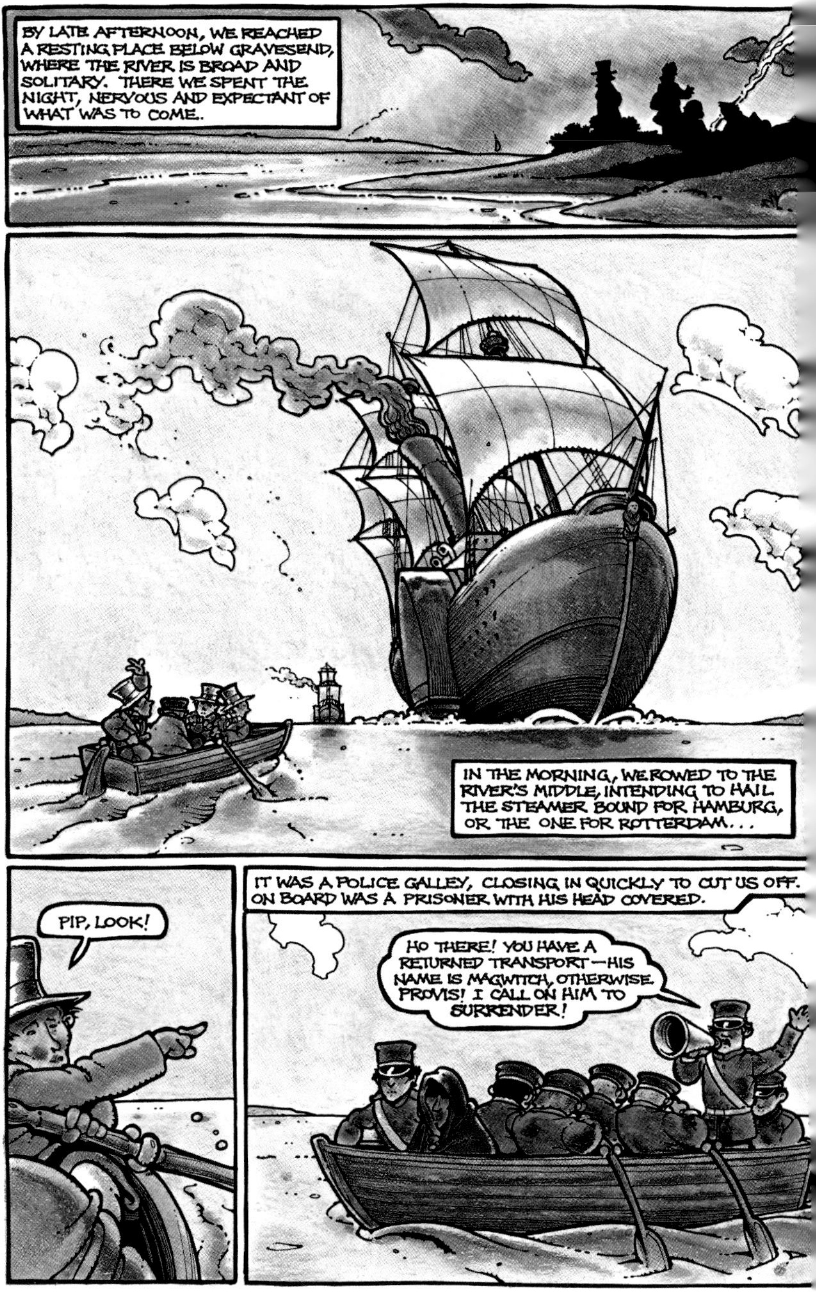
BY LATE AFTERNOON, WE REACHED A RESTING PLACE BELOW GRAVESEND, WHERE THE RIVER IS BROAD AND SOLITARY. THERE WE SPENT THE NIGHT, NERVOUS AND EXPECTANT OF WHAT WAS TO COME.
IN THE MORNING, WE ROWED TO THE RIVER'S MIDDLE, INTENDING TO HAIL THE STEAMER BOUND FOR HAMBURG, OR THE ONE FOR ROTTERDAM...
PIP, LOOK!
IT WAS A POLICE GALLEY, CLOSING IN QUICKLY TO CUT US OFF. ON BOARD WAS A PRISONER WITH HIS HEAD COVERED.
HO THERE! YOU HAVE A RETURNED TRANSPORT—HIS NAME IS MAGWITCH, OTHERWISE PROVIS! I CALL ON HIM TO SURRENDER!

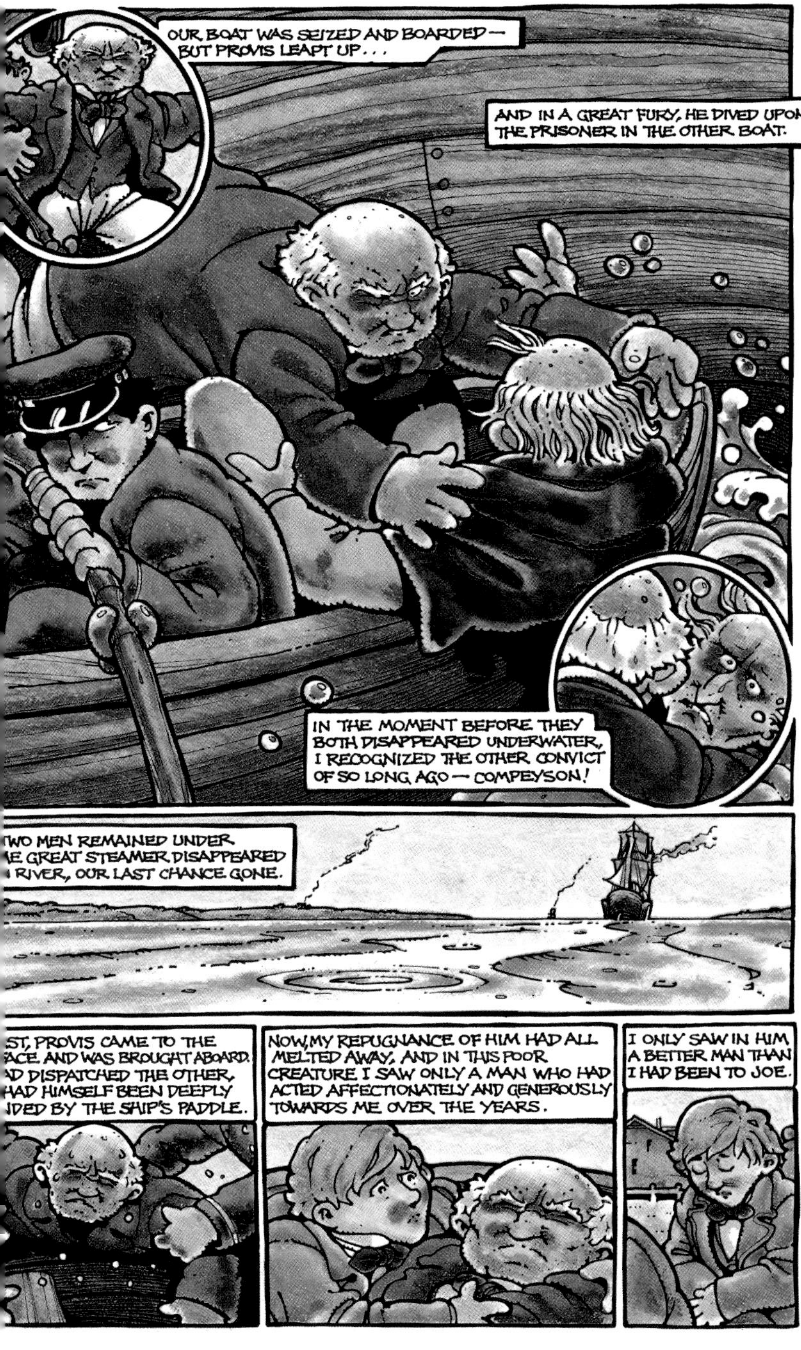
OUR BOAT WAS SEIZED AND BOARDED — BUT PROVIS LEAPT UP . . .
AND IN A GREAT FURY, HE DIVED UPON THE PRISONER IN THE OTHER BOAT.
IN THE MOMENT BEFORE THEY BOTH DISAPPEARED UNDERWATER, I RECOGNIZED THE OTHER CONVICT OF SO LONG AGO — COMPEYSON!
TWO MEN REMAINED UNDER
E GREAT STEAMER DISAPPEARED
RIVER, OUR LAST CHANCE GONE.
ST, PROVIS CAME TO THE
ACE AND WAS BROUGHT ABOARD.
D DISPATCHED THE OTHER,
HAD HIMSELF BEEN DEEPLY
DED BY THE SHIP'S PADDLE.
NOW, MY REPUGNANCE OF HIM HAD ALL MELTED AWAY, AND IN THIS POOR CREATURE I SAW ONLY A MAN WHO HAD ACTED AFFECTIONATELY AND GENEROUSLY TOWARDS ME OVER THE YEARS.
I ONLY SAW IN HIM A BETTER MAN THAN I HAD BEEN TO JOE.

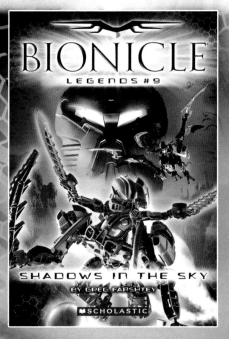

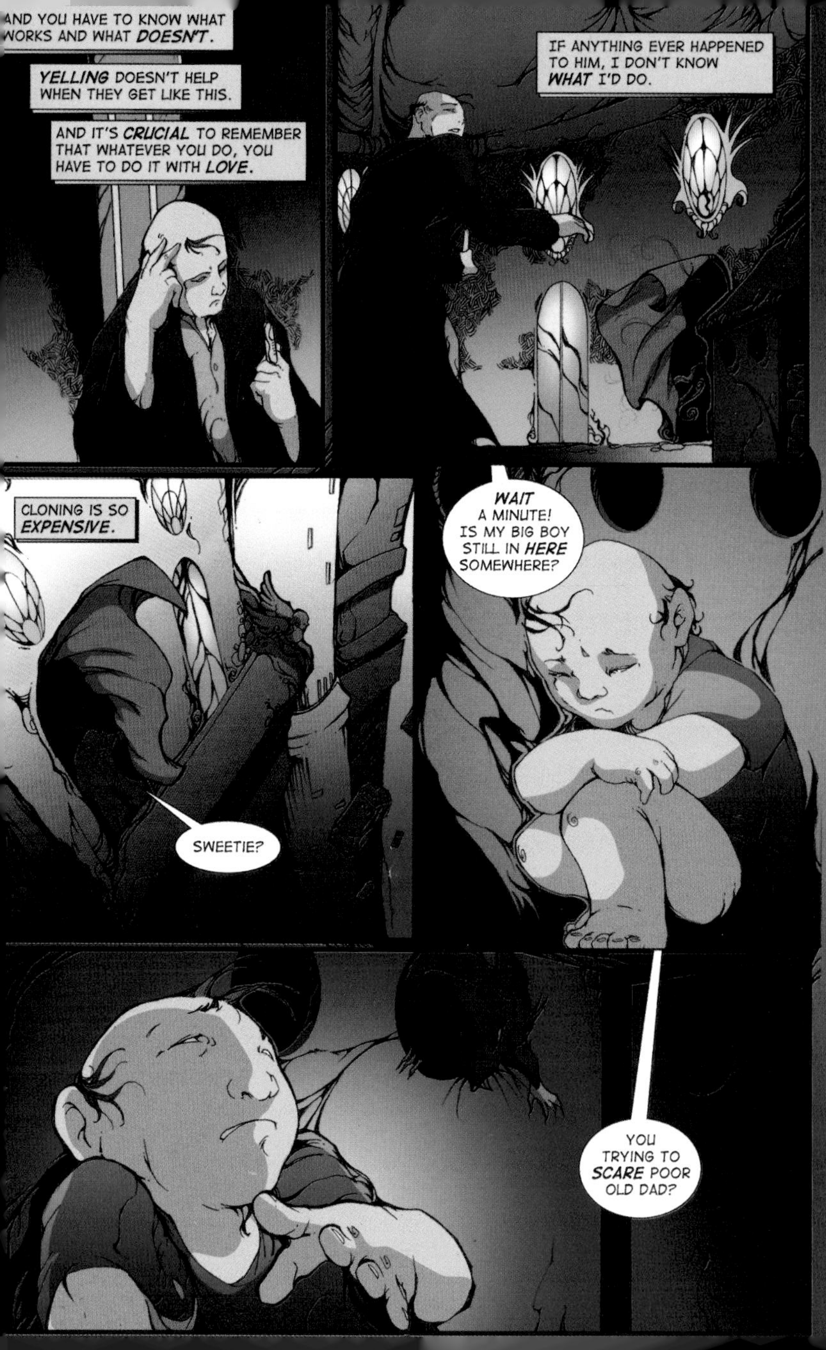
AND YOU HAVE TO KNOW WHAT WORKS AND WHAT DOESN'T.
YELLING DOESN'T HELP WHEN THEY GET LIKE THIS.
AND IT'S CRUCIAL TO REMEMBER THAT WHATEVER YOU DO, YOU HAVE TO DO IT WITH LOVE.
IF ANYTHING EVER HAPPENED TO HIM, I DON'T KNOW WHAT I'D DO.
CLONING IS SO EXPENSIVE.
SWEETIE?
WAIT A MINUTE! IS MY BIG BOY STILL IN HERE SOMEWHERE?
YOU TRYING TO SCARE POOR OLD DAD?

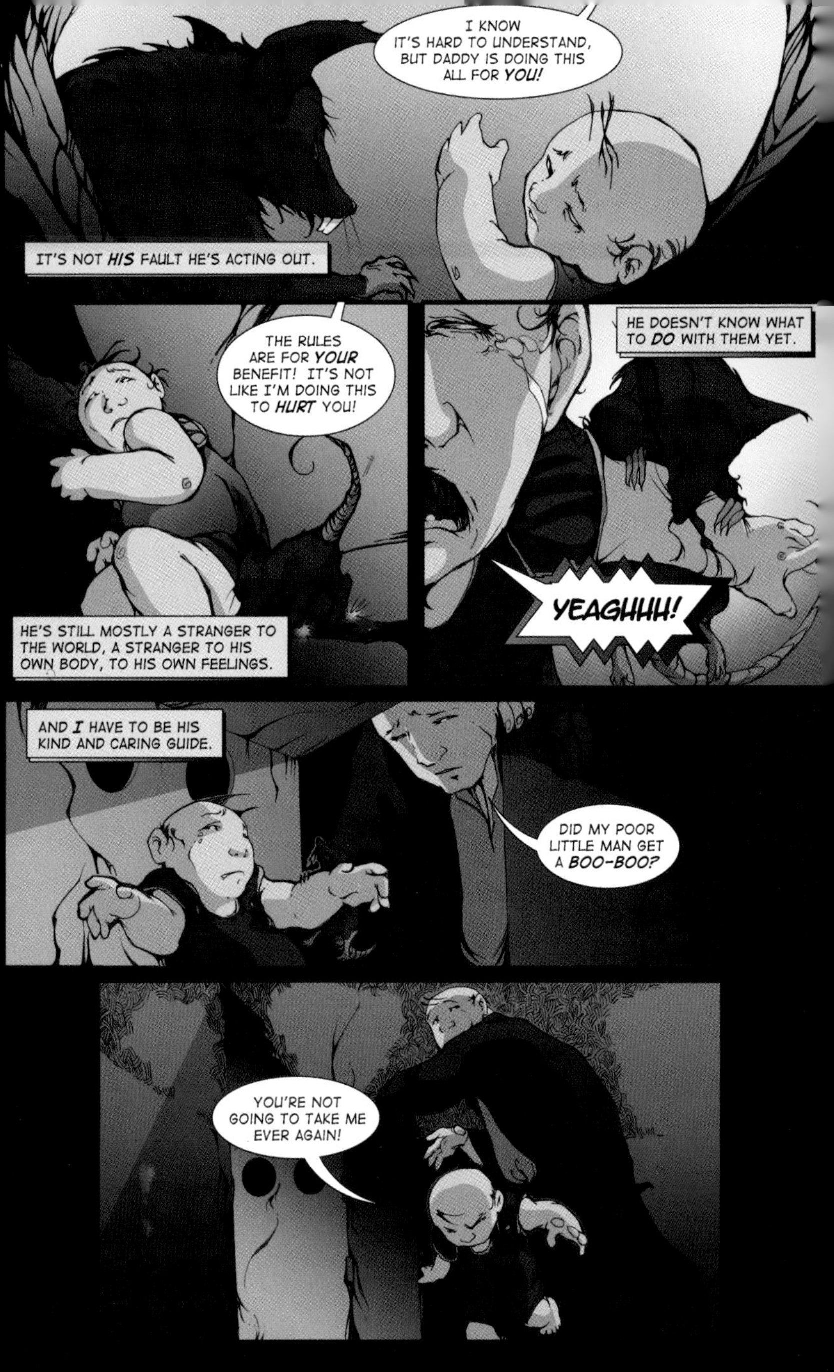
I KNOW IT'S HARD TO UNDERSTAND, BUT DADDY IS DOING THIS ALL FOR YOU!
IT'S NOT HIS FAULT HE'S ACTING OUT.
THE RULES ARE FOR YOUR BENEFIT! IT'S NOT LIKE I'M DOING THIS TO HURT YOU!
HE'S STILL MOSTLY A STRANGER TO THE WORLD, A STRANGER TO HIS OWN BODY, TO HIS OWN FEELINGS.
HE DOESN'T KNOW WHAT TO DO WITH THEM YET.
YEAGHHH!
AND I HAVE TO BE HIS KIND AND CARING GUIDE.
DID MY POOR LITTLE MAN GET A BOO-BOO?
YOU'RE NOT GOING TO TAKE ME EVER AGAIN!

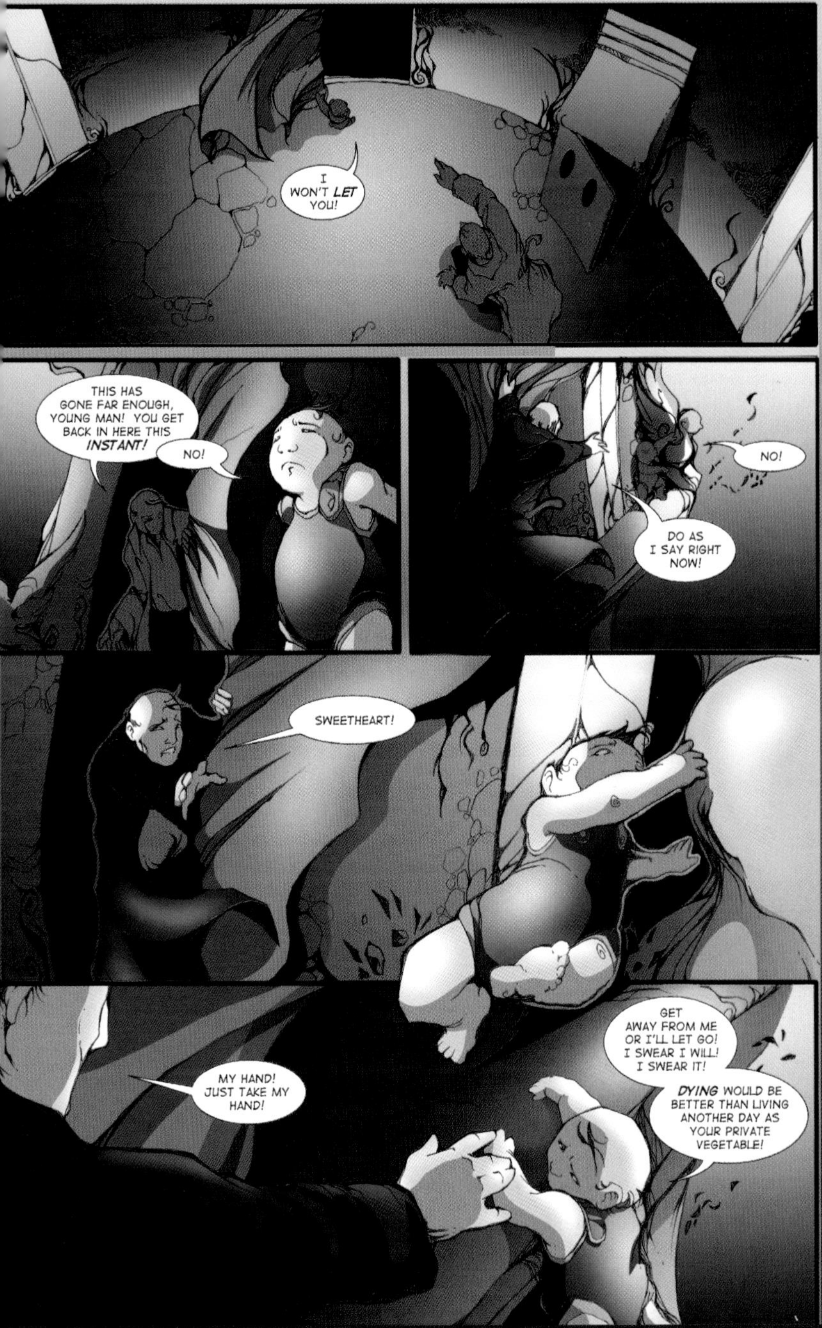

I WON'T LET YOU!
THIS HAS GONE FAR ENOUGH, YOUNG MAN! YOU GET BACK IN HERE THIS INSTANT!
NO!
NO!
DO AS I SAY RIGHT NOW!
SWEETHEART!
GET AWAY FROM ME OR I'LL LET GO! I SWEAR I WILL! I SWEAR IT!
DYING WOULD BE BETTER THAN LIVING ANOTHER DAY AS YOUR PRIVATE VEGETABLE!
MY HAND! JUST TAKE MY HAND!

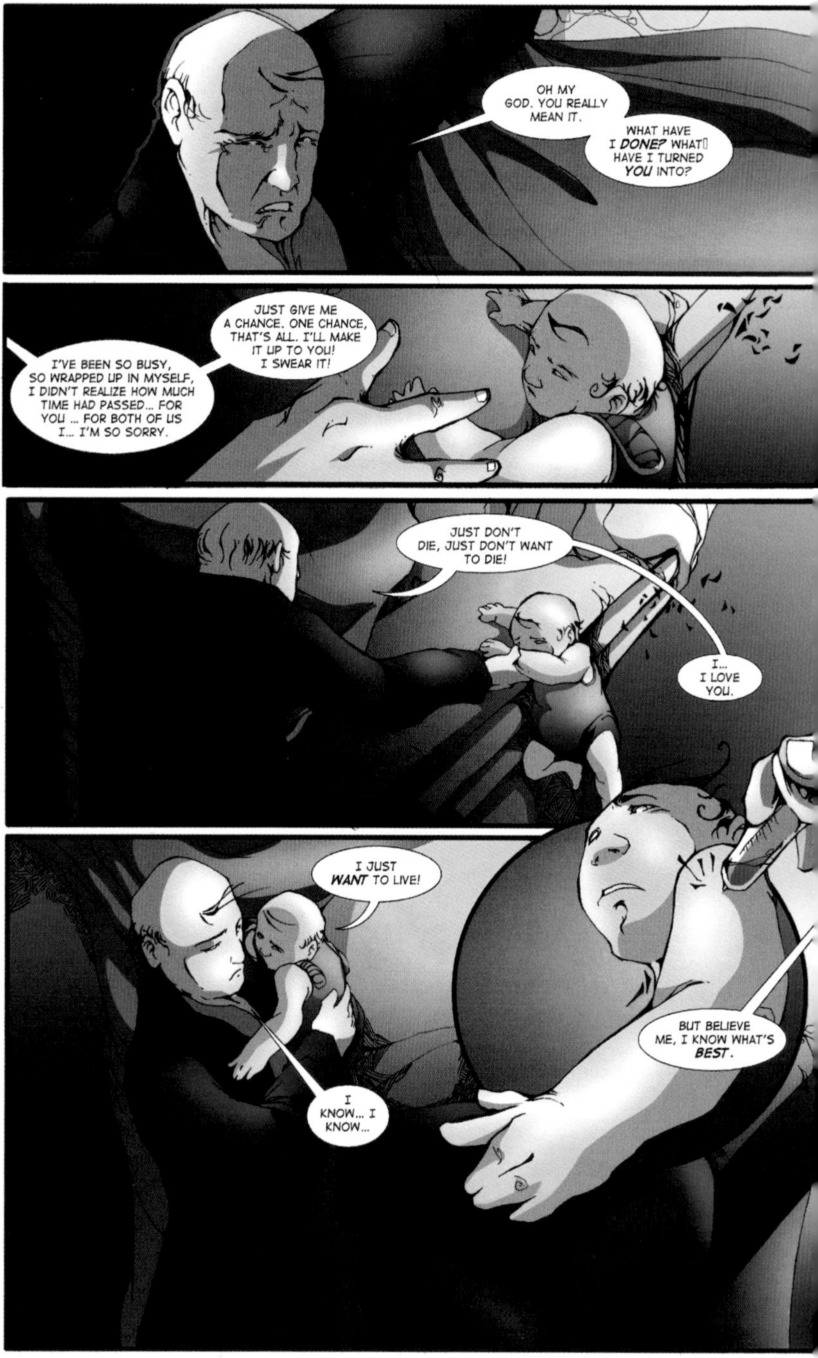

OH MY GOD. YOU REALLY MEAN IT.
WHAT HAVE I DONE? WHAT HAVE I TURNED YOU INTO?
I'VE BEEN SO BUSY, SO WRAPPED UP IN MYSELF, I DIDN'T REALIZE HOW MUCH TIME HAD PASSED... FOR YOU ... FOR BOTH OF US I... I'M SO SORRY.
JUST GIVE ME A CHANCE. ONE CHANCE, THAT'S ALL. I'LL MAKE IT UP TO YOU! I SWEAR IT!
JUST DON'T DIE, JUST DON'T WANT TO DIE!
I... I LOVE YOU.
I JUST WANT TO LIVE!
I KNOW... I KNOW...
BUT BELIEVE ME, I KNOW WHAT'S BEST.

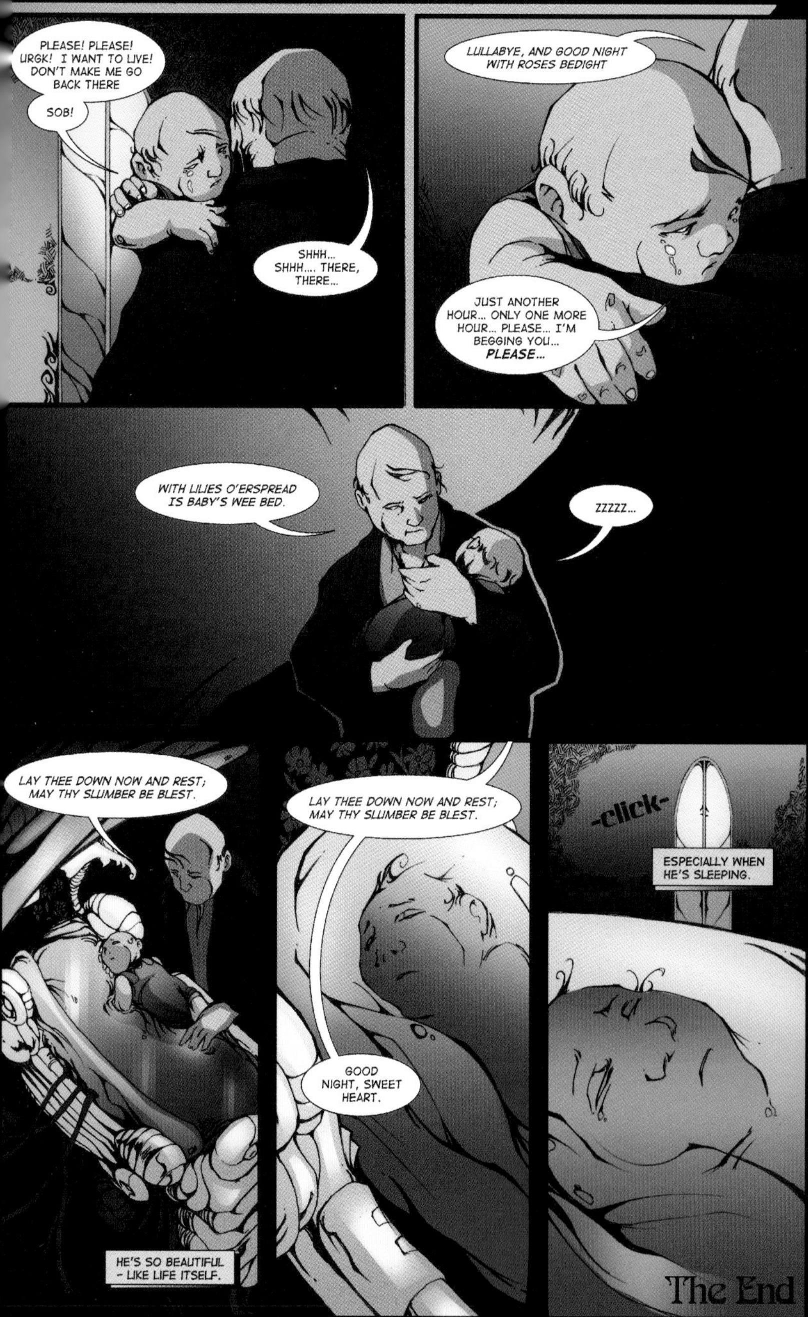
PLEASE! PLEASE! URGK! I WANT TO LIVE! DON'T MAKE ME GO BACK THERE
SOB!
SHHH... SHHH.... THERE, THERE...
LULLABYE, AND GOOD NIGHT WITH ROSES BEDIGHT
JUST ANOTHER HOUR... ONLY ONE MORE HOUR... PLEASE... I'M BEGGING YOU... PLEASE...
WITH LILIES O'ERSPREAD IS BABY'S WEE BED.
ZZZZZ...
LAY THEE DOWN NOW AND REST; MAY THY SLUMBER BE BLEST.
HE'S SO BEAUTIFUL - LIKE LIFE ITSELF.
LAY THEE DOWN NOW AND REST; MAY THY SLUMBER BE BLEST.
GOOD NIGHT, SWEET HEART.
-click-
ESPECIALLY WHEN HE'S SLEEPING.
The End

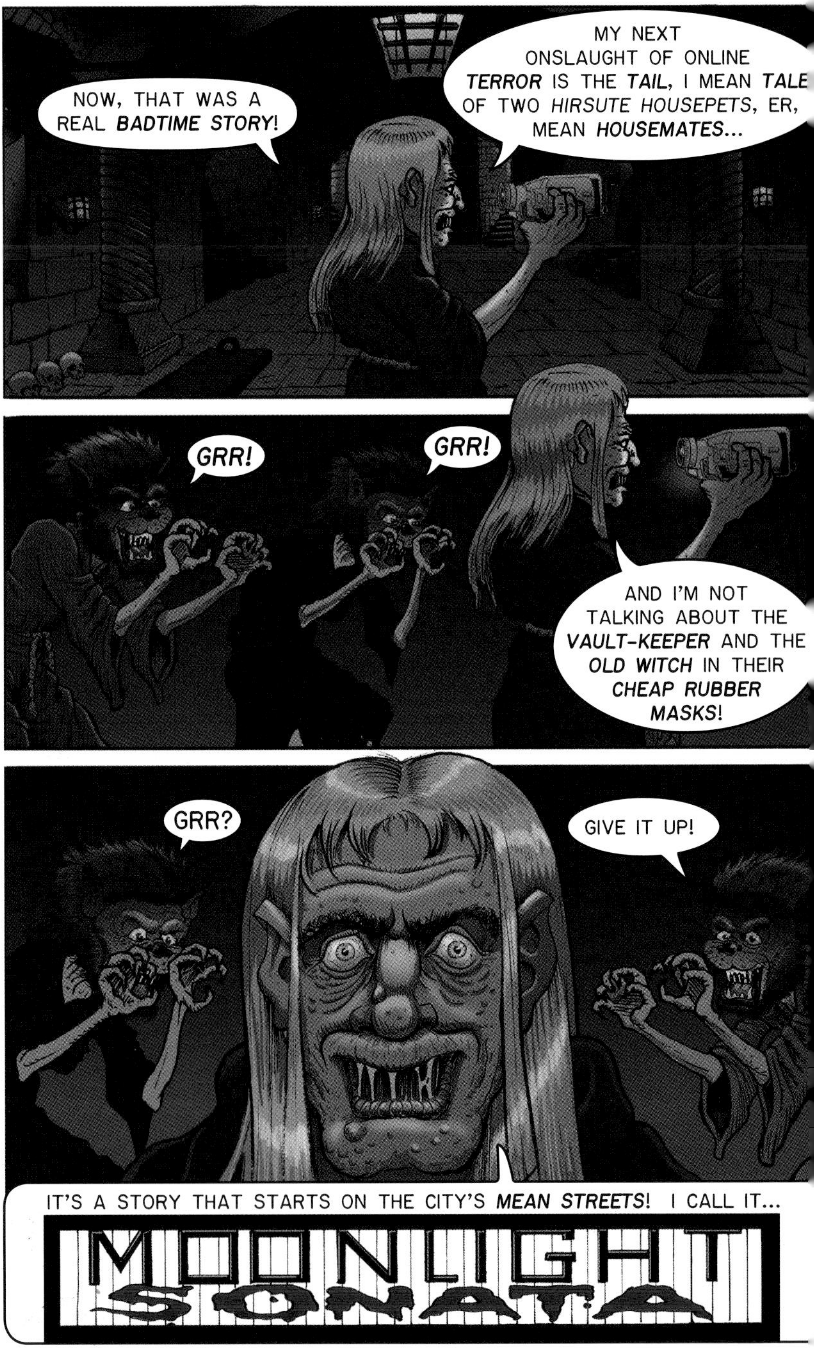
NOW, THAT WAS A REAL BADTIME STORY!
MY NEXT ONSLAUGHT OF ONLINE TERROR IS THE TAIL, I MEAN TALE OF TWO HIRSUTE HOUSEPETS, ER, MEAN HOUSEMATES...
GRR!
GRR!
AND I'M NOT TALKING ABOUT THE VAULT-KEEPER AND THE OLD WITCH IN THEIR CHEAP RUBBER MASKS!
GRR?
GIVE IT UP!
IT'S A STORY THAT STARTS ON THE CITY'S MEAN STREETS! I CALL IT...
MOONLIGHT SONATA

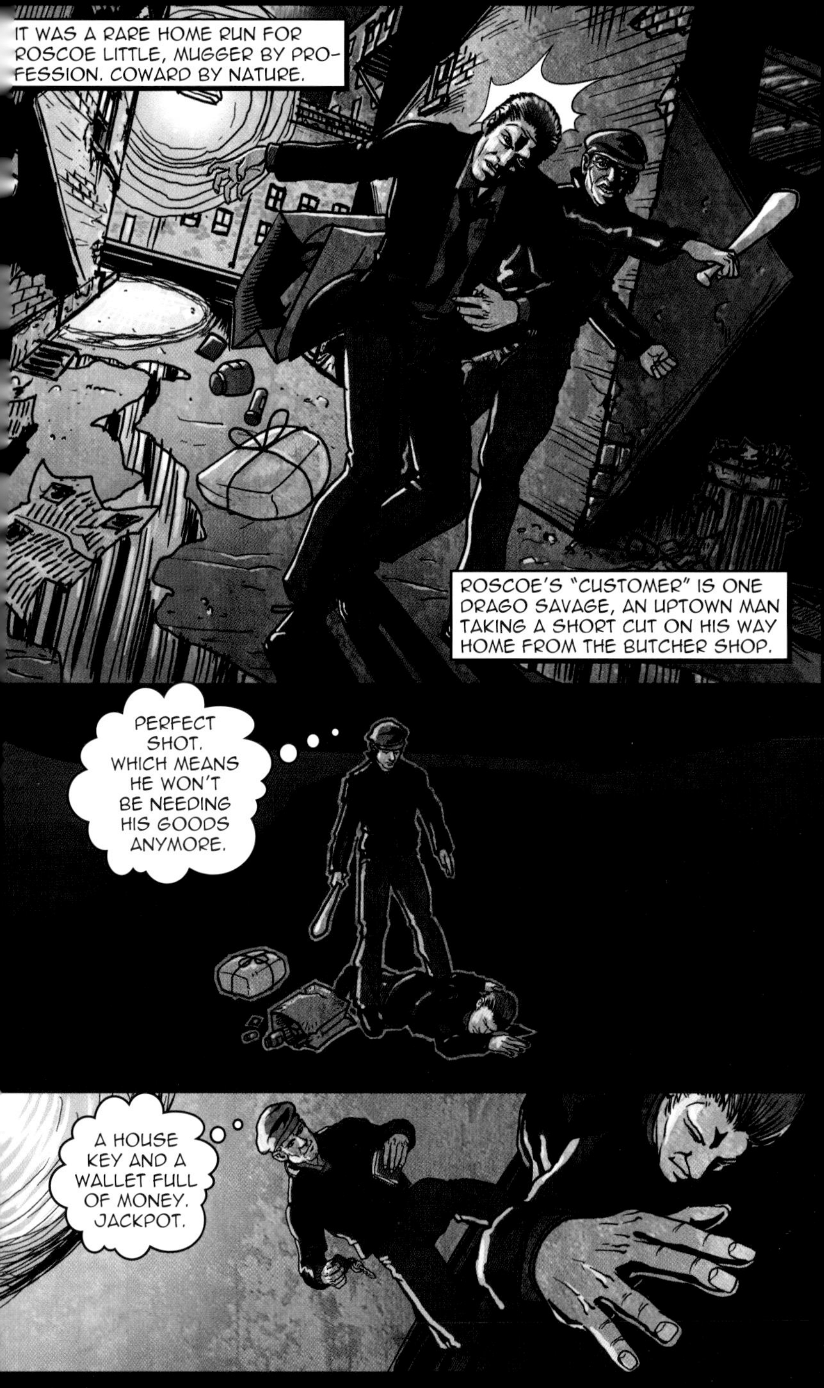
IT WAS A RARE HOME RUN FOR ROSCOE LITTLE, MUGGER BY PRO-FESSION. COWARD BY NATURE.
ROSCOE'S "CUSTOMER" IS ONE DRAGO SAVAGE, AN UPTOWN MAN TAKING A SHORT CUT ON HIS WAY HOME FROM THE BUTCHER SHOP.
PERFECT SHOT. WHICH MEANS HE WON'T BE NEEDING HIS GOODS ANYMORE.
A HOUSE KEY AND A WALLET FULL OF MONEY. JACKPOT.

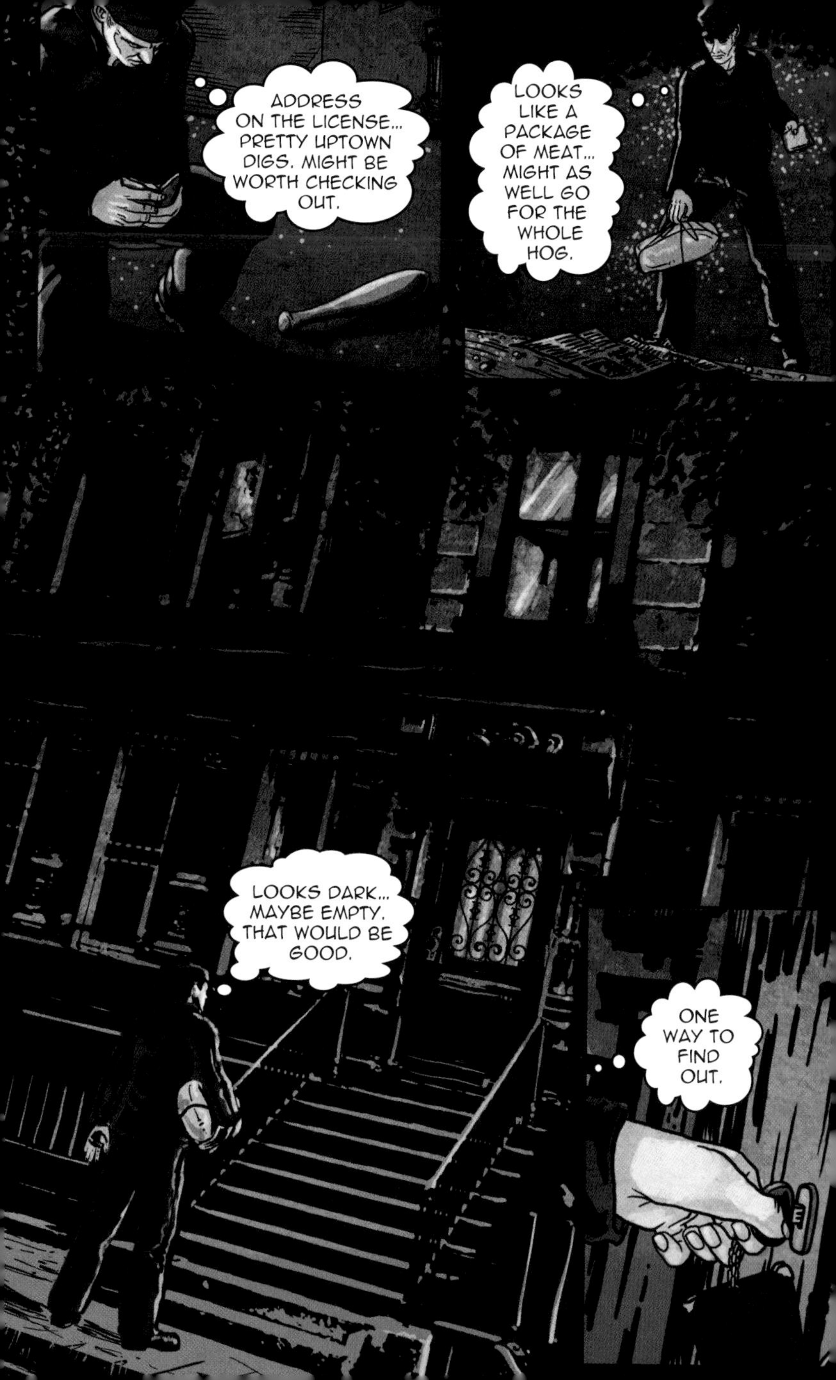
ADDRESS ON THE LICENSE... PRETTY UPTOWN DIGS. MIGHT BE WORTH CHECKING OUT.
LOOKS LIKE A PACKAGE OF MEAT... MIGHT AS WELL GO FOR THE WHOLE HOG.
LOOKS DARK... MAYBE EMPTY. THAT WOULD BE GOOD.
ONE WAY TO FIND OUT.

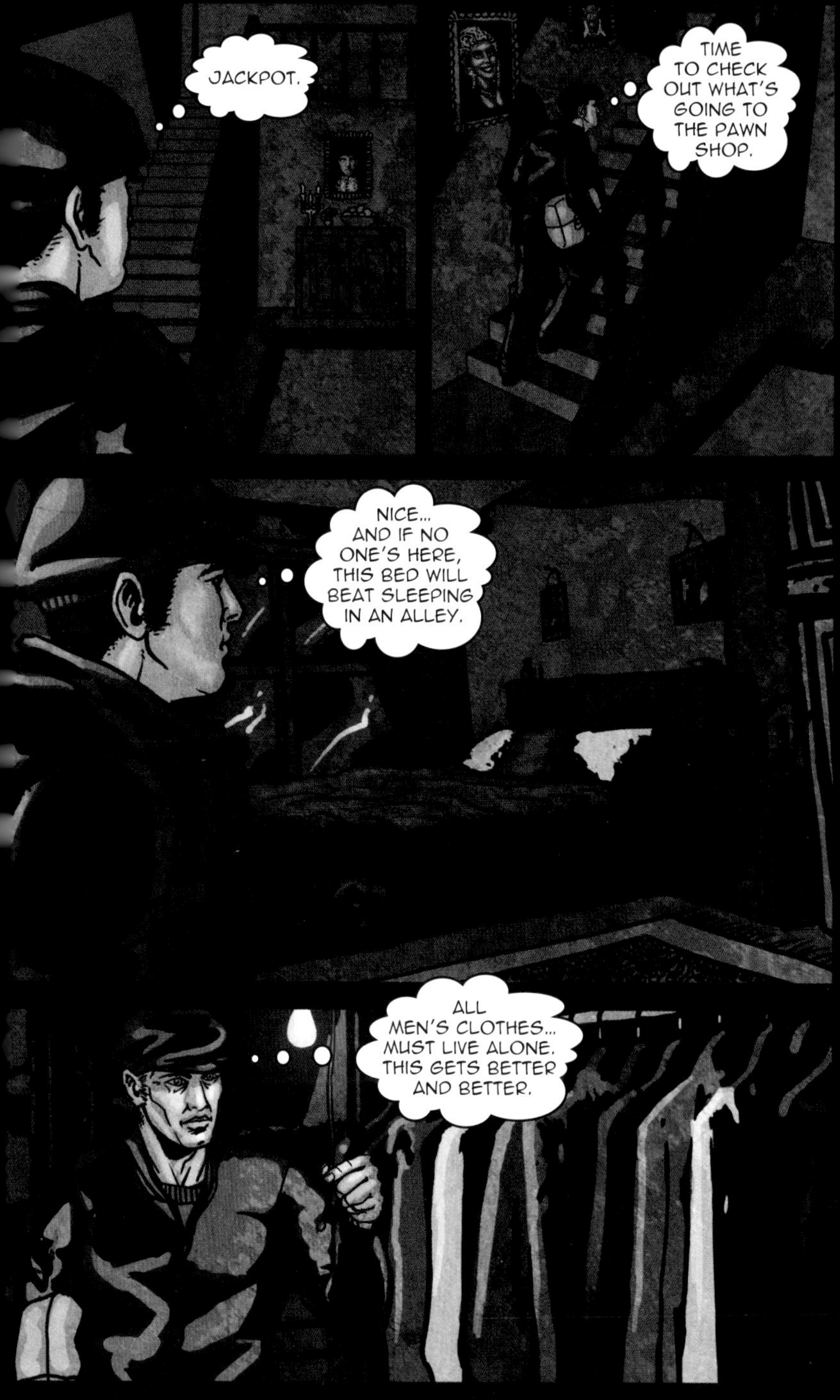
JACKPOT.
TIME TO CHECK OUT WHAT'S GOING TO THE PAWN SHOP.
NICE... AND IF NO ONE'S HERE, THIS BED WILL BEAT SLEEPING IN AN ALLEY.
ALL MEN'S CLOTHES... MUST LIVE ALONE. THIS GETS BETTER AND BETTER.

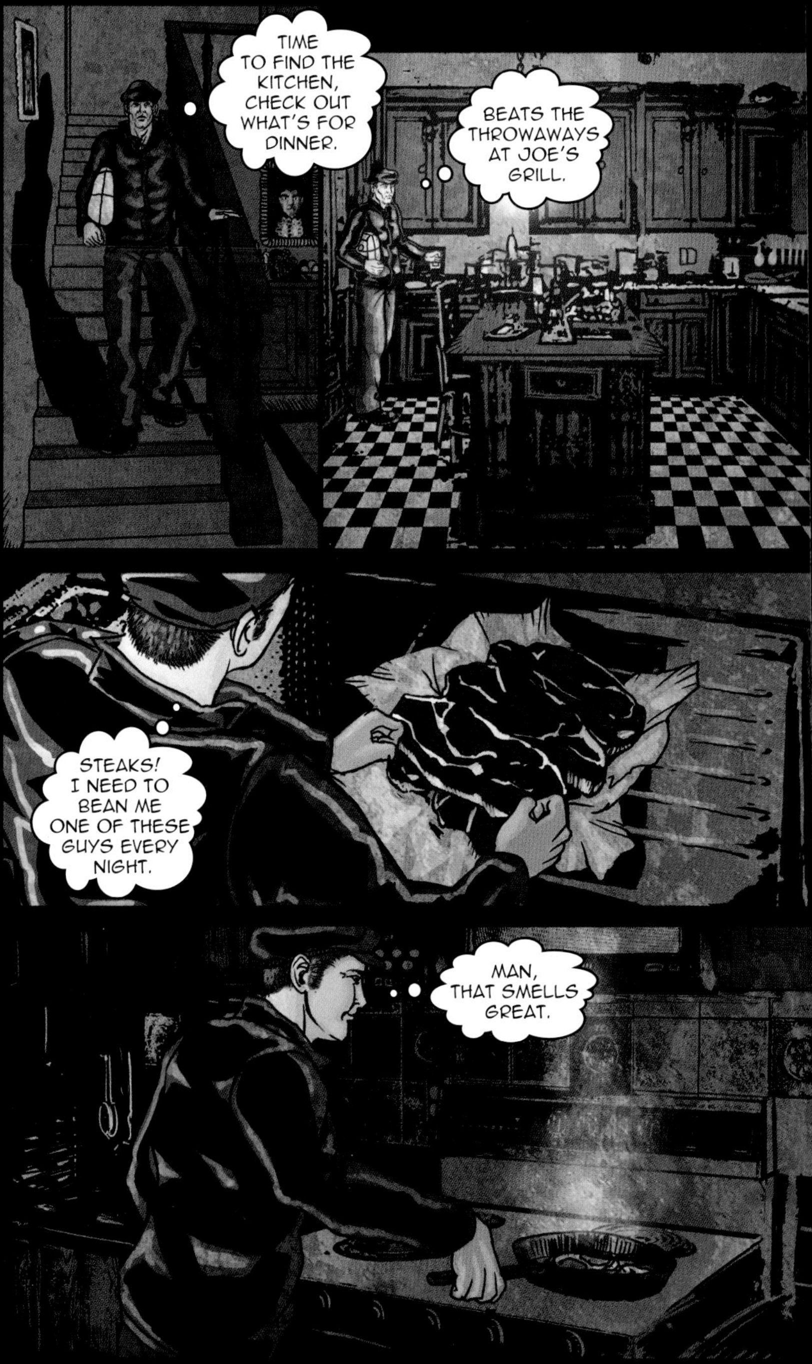
TIME TO FIND THE KITCHEN, CHECK OUT WHAT'S FOR DINNER.
BEATS THE THROWAWAYS AT JOE'S GRILL.
STEAKS! I NEED TO BEAN ME ONE OF THESE GUYS EVERY NIGHT.
MAN, THAT SMELLS GREAT.

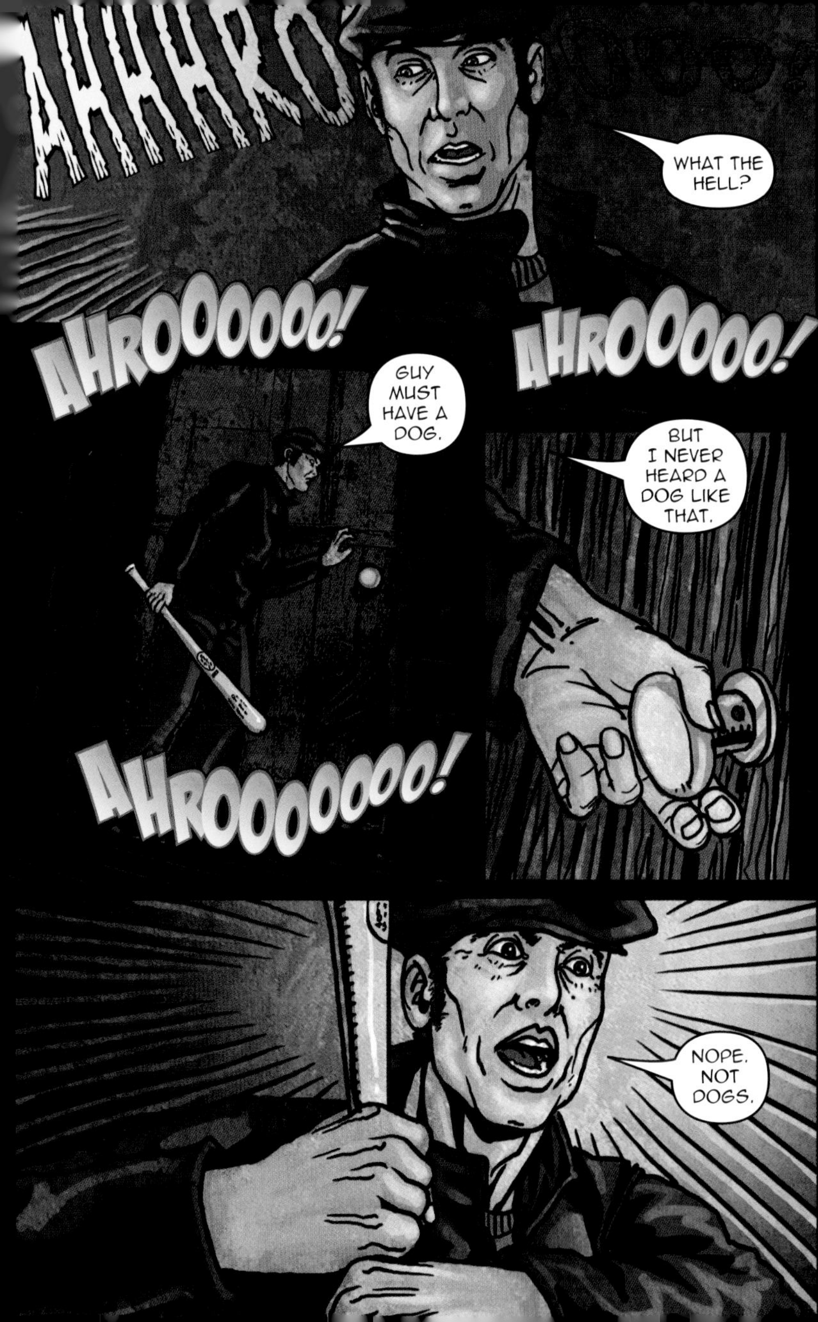
AHHRO
WHAT THE HELL?
AHROOOOOO!
AHROOOOO!
GUY MUST HAVE A DOG.
BUT I NEVER HEARD A DOG LIKE THAT.
AHROOOOOOO!
NOPE. NOT DOGS.

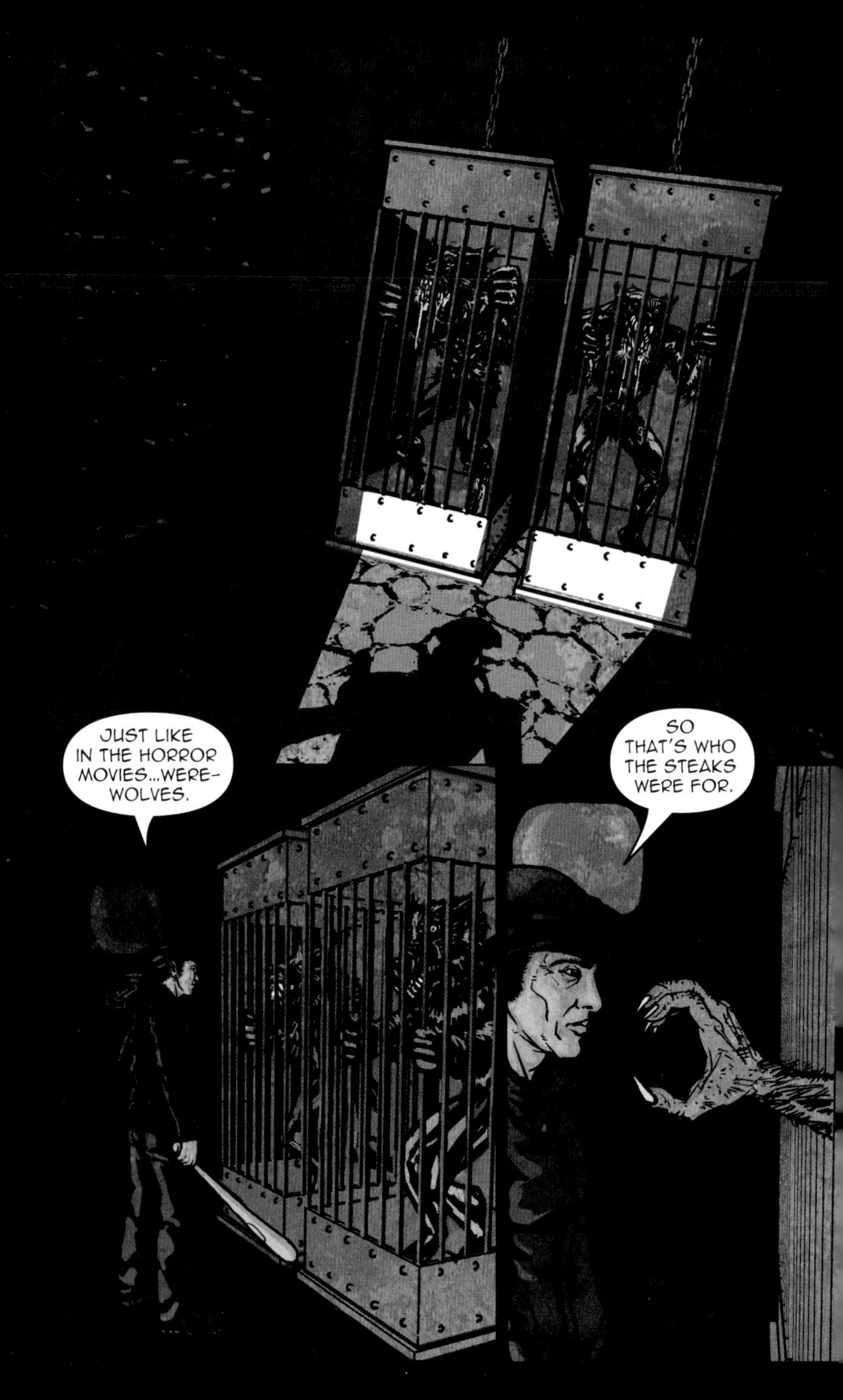
JUST LIKE IN THE HORROR MOVIES...WERE-WOLVES.
SO THAT'S WHO THE STEAKS WERE FOR.

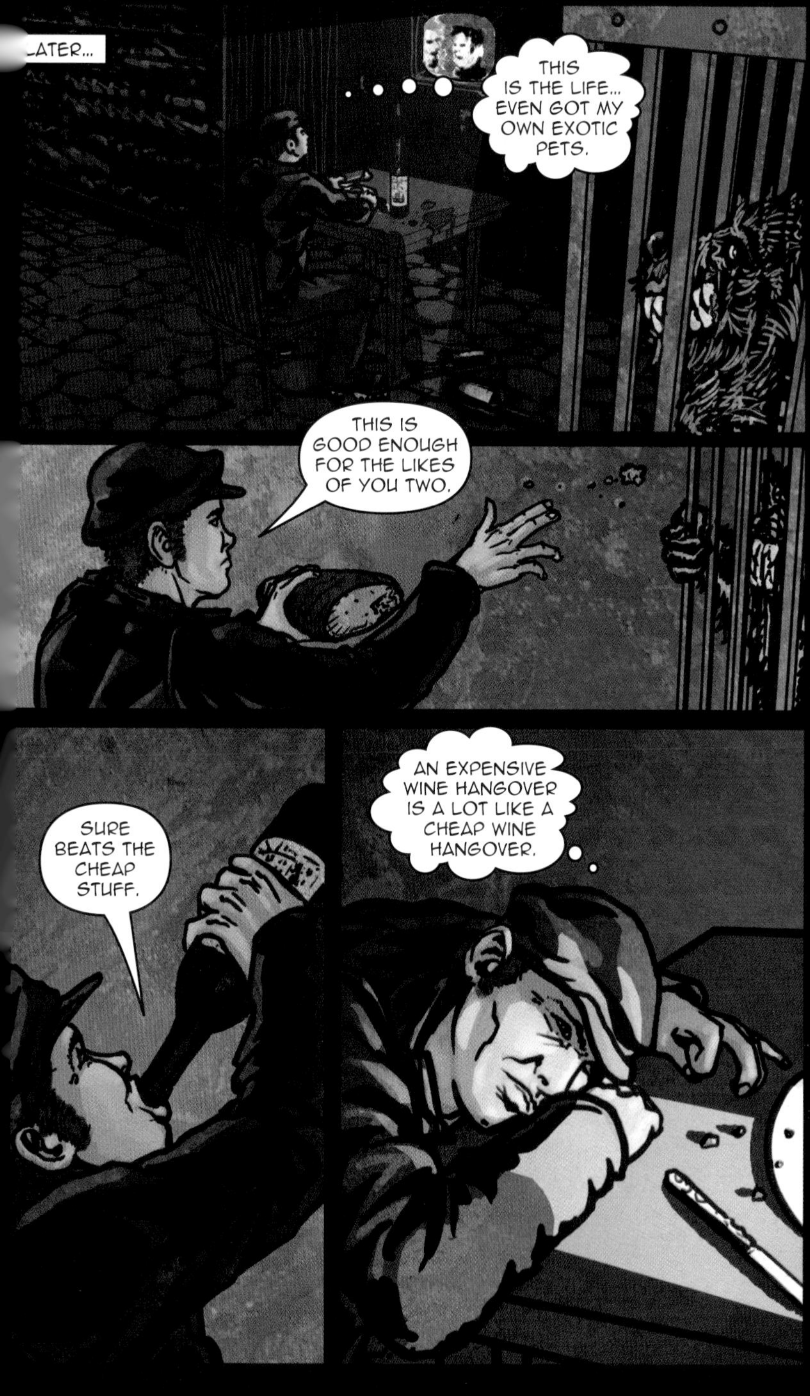
LATER...
THIS IS THE LIFE... EVEN GOT MY OWN EXOTIC PETS.
THIS IS GOOD ENOUGH FOR THE LIKES OF YOU TWO.
SURE BEATS THE CHEAP STUFF.
AN EXPENSIVE WINE HANGOVER IS A LOT LIKE A CHEAP WINE HANGOVER.

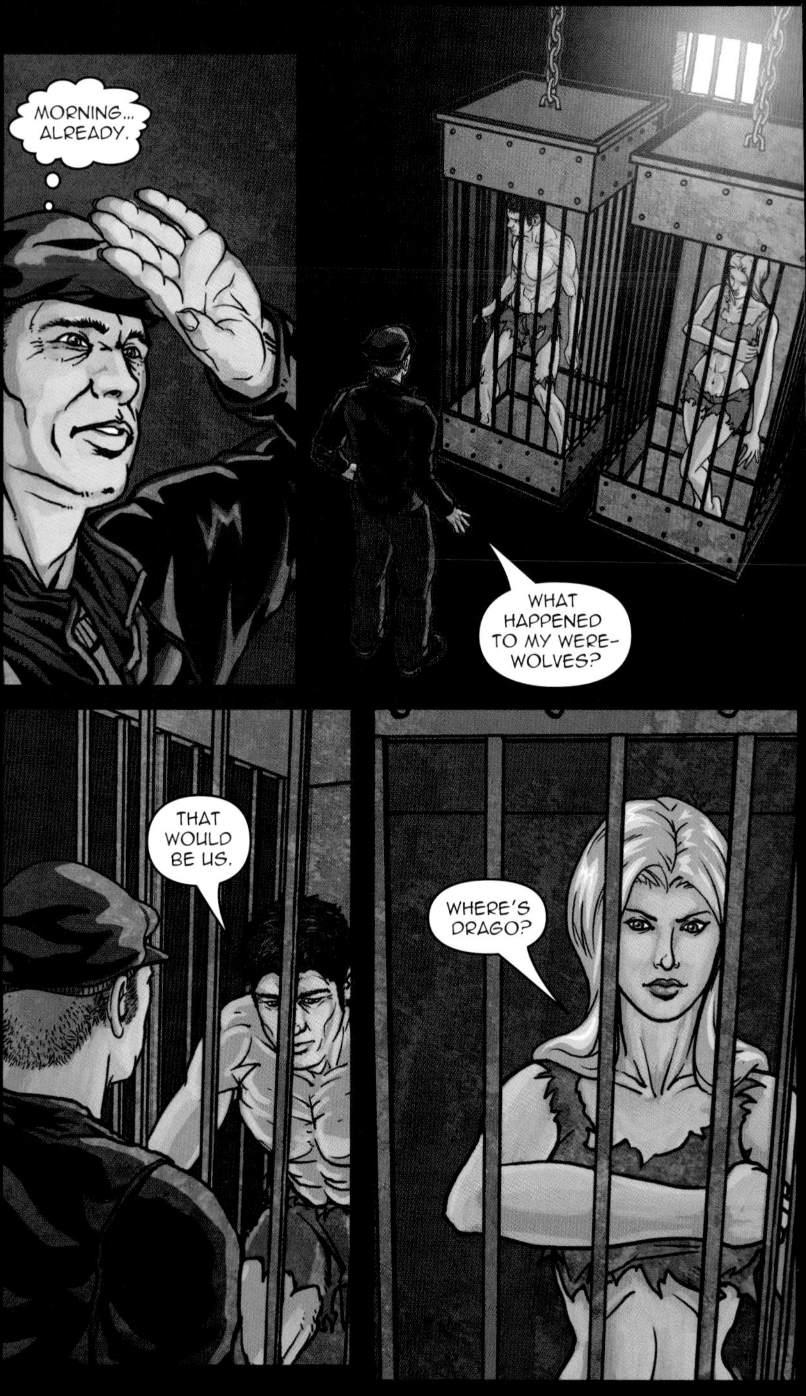
MORNING... ALREADY.
WHAT HAPPENED TO MY WERE-WOLVES?
THAT WOULD BE US.
WHERE'S DRAGO?

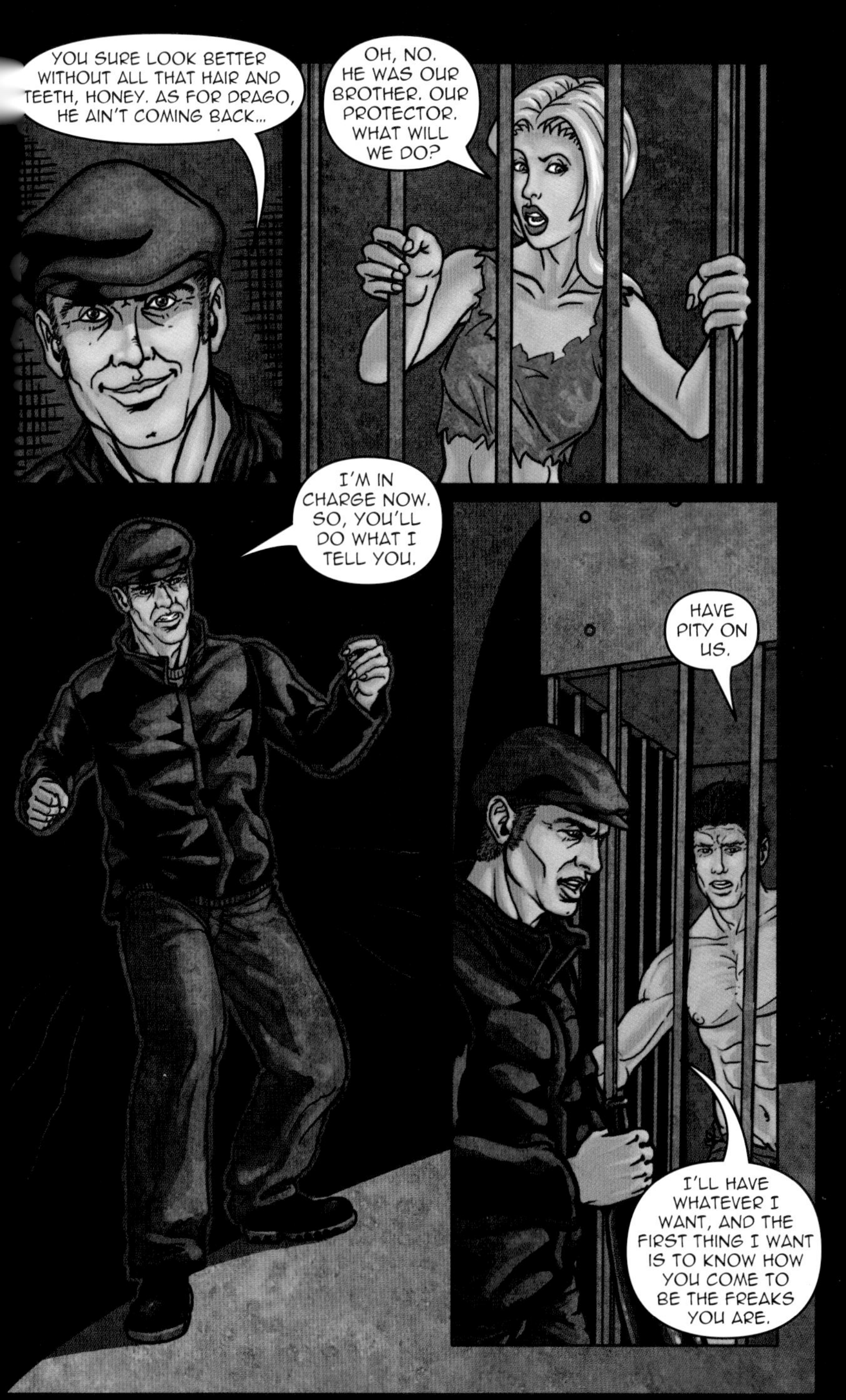
YOU SURE LOOK BETTER WITHOUT ALL THAT HAIR AND TEETH, HONEY. AS FOR DRAGO, HE AIN'T COMING BACK...
OH, NO. HE WAS OUR BROTHER. OUR PROTECTOR. WHAT WILL WE DO?
I'M IN CHARGE NOW. SO, YOU'LL DO WHAT I TELL YOU.
HAVE PITY ON US.
I'LL HAVE WHATEVER I WANT, AND THE FIRST THING I WANT IS TO KNOW HOW YOU COME TO BE THE FREAKS YOU ARE.

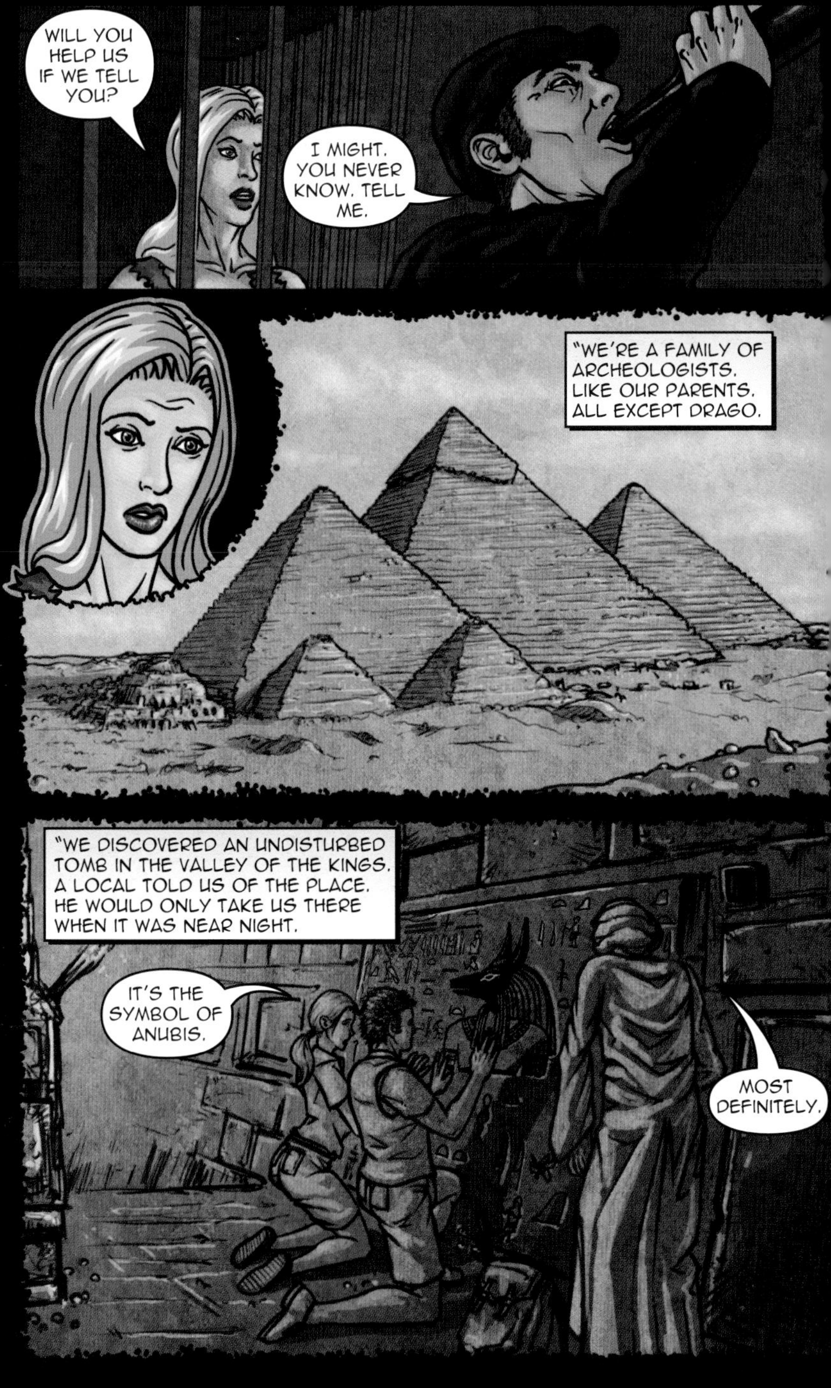
WILL YOU HELP US IF WE TELL YOU?
I MIGHT. YOU NEVER KNOW. TELL ME.
"WE'RE A FAMILY OF ARCHEOLOGISTS. LIKE OUR PARENTS. ALL EXCEPT DRAGO.
"WE DISCOVERED AN UNDISTURBED TOMB IN THE VALLEY OF THE KINGS. A LOCAL TOLD US OF THE PLACE. HE WOULD ONLY TAKE US THERE WHEN IT WAS NEAR NIGHT.
IT'S THE SYMBOL OF ANUBIS.
MOST DEFINITELY.

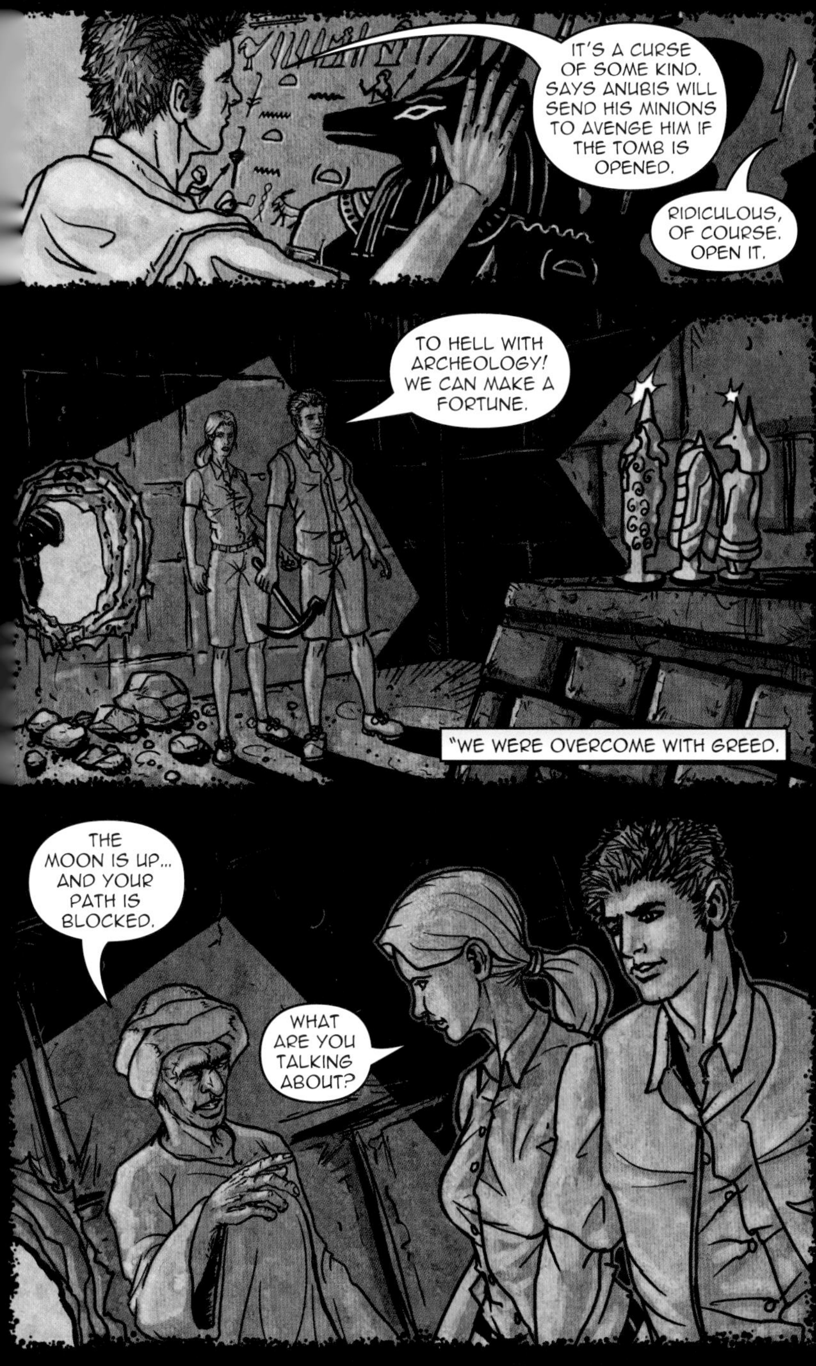
IT'S A CURSE OF SOME KIND. SAYS ANUBIS WILL SEND HIS MINIONS TO AVENGE HIM IF THE TOMB IS OPENED.
RIDICULOUS, OF COURSE. OPEN IT.
TO HELL WITH ARCHEOLOGY! WE CAN MAKE A FORTUNE.
"WE WERE OVERCOME WITH GREED.
THE MOON IS UP... AND YOUR PATH IS BLOCKED.
WHAT ARE YOU TALKING ABOUT?

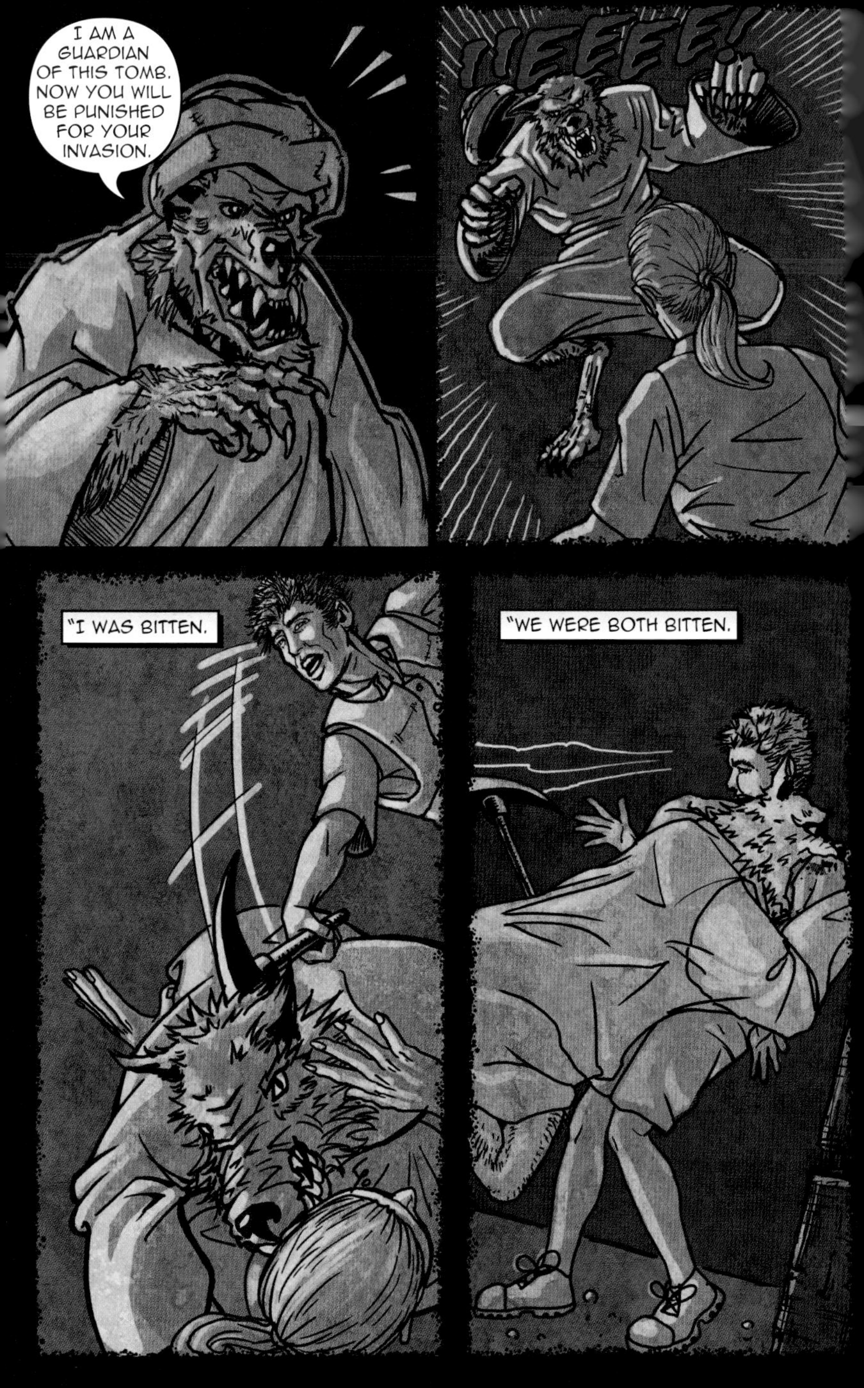
I AM A GUARDIAN OF THIS TOMB. NOW YOU WILL BE PUNISHED FOR YOUR INVASION.
!!EEEEE!
"I WAS BITTEN.
"WE WERE BOTH BITTEN.

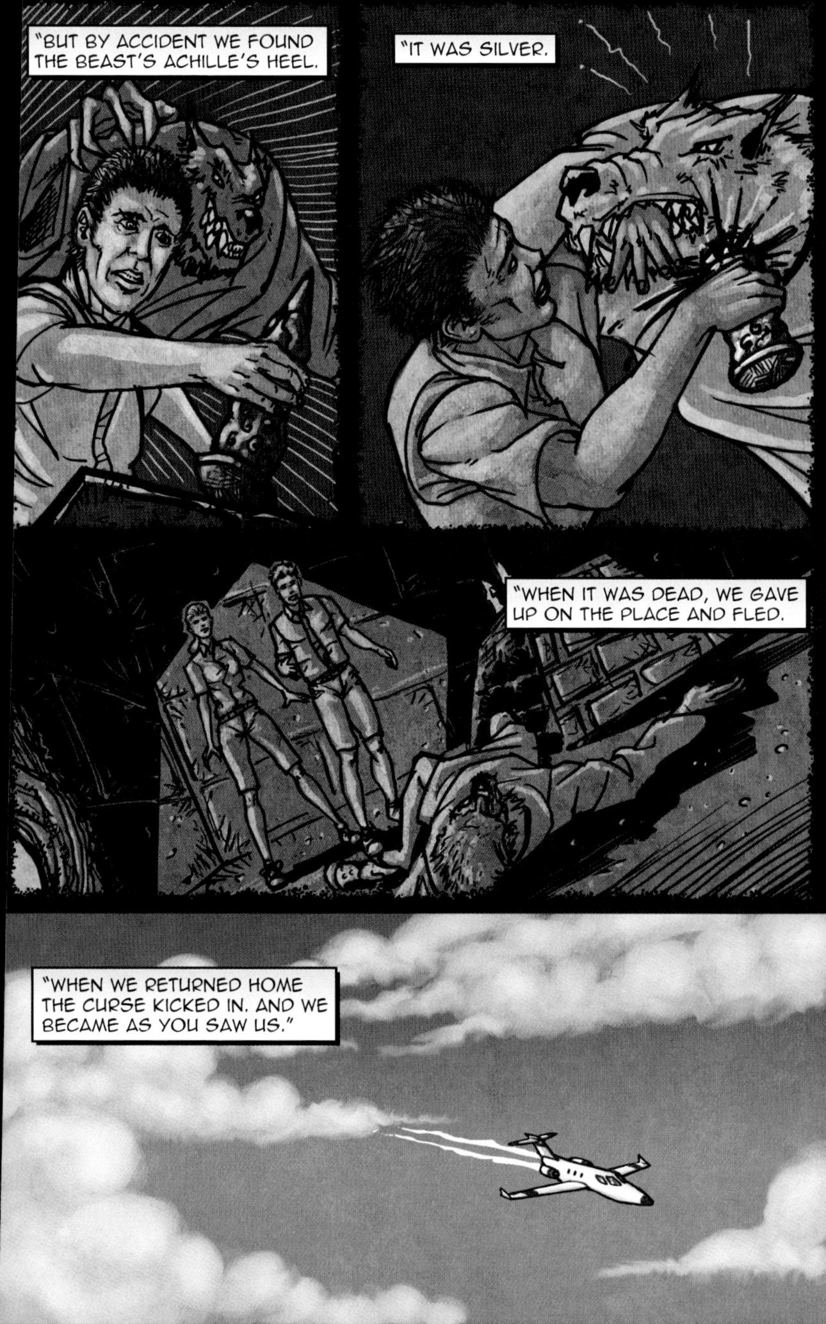
"BUT BY ACCIDENT WE FOUND THE BEAST'S ACHILLE'S HEEL.
"IT WAS SILVER.
"WHEN IT WAS DEAD, WE GAVE UP ON THE PLACE AND FLED.
"WHEN WE RETURNED HOME THE CURSE KICKED IN. AND WE BECAME AS YOU SAW US."

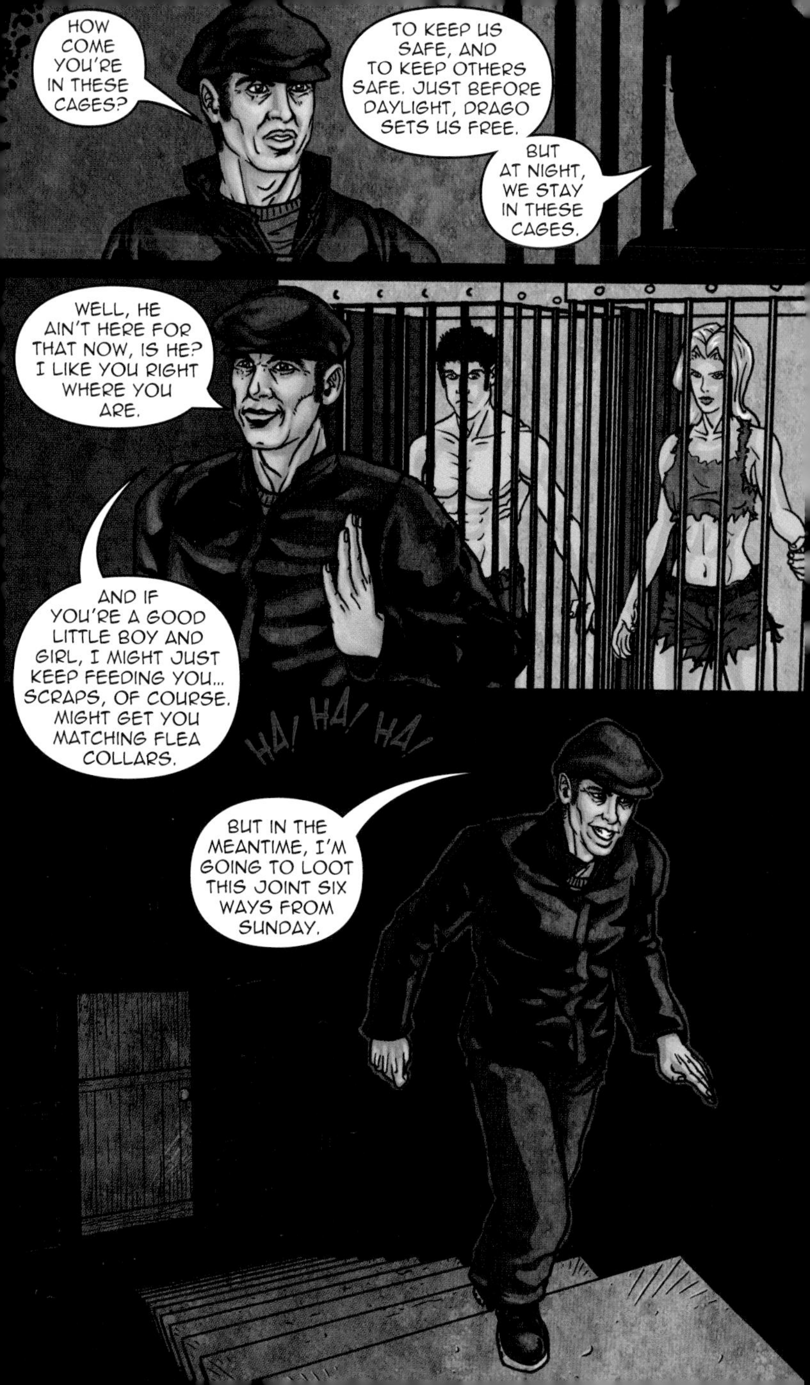
HOW COME YOU'RE IN THESE CAGES?
TO KEEP US SAFE, AND TO KEEP OTHERS SAFE. JUST BEFORE DAYLIGHT, DRAGO SETS US FREE.
BUT AT NIGHT, WE STAY IN THESE CAGES.
WELL, HE AIN'T HERE FOR THAT NOW, IS HE? I LIKE YOU RIGHT WHERE YOU ARE.
AND IF YOU'RE A GOOD LITTLE BOY AND GIRL, I MIGHT JUST KEEP FEEDING YOU... SCRAPS, OF COURSE. MIGHT GET YOU MATCHING FLEA COLLARS.
HA! HA! HA!
BUT IN THE MEANTIME, I'M GOING TO LOOT THIS JOINT SIX WAYS FROM SUNDAY.

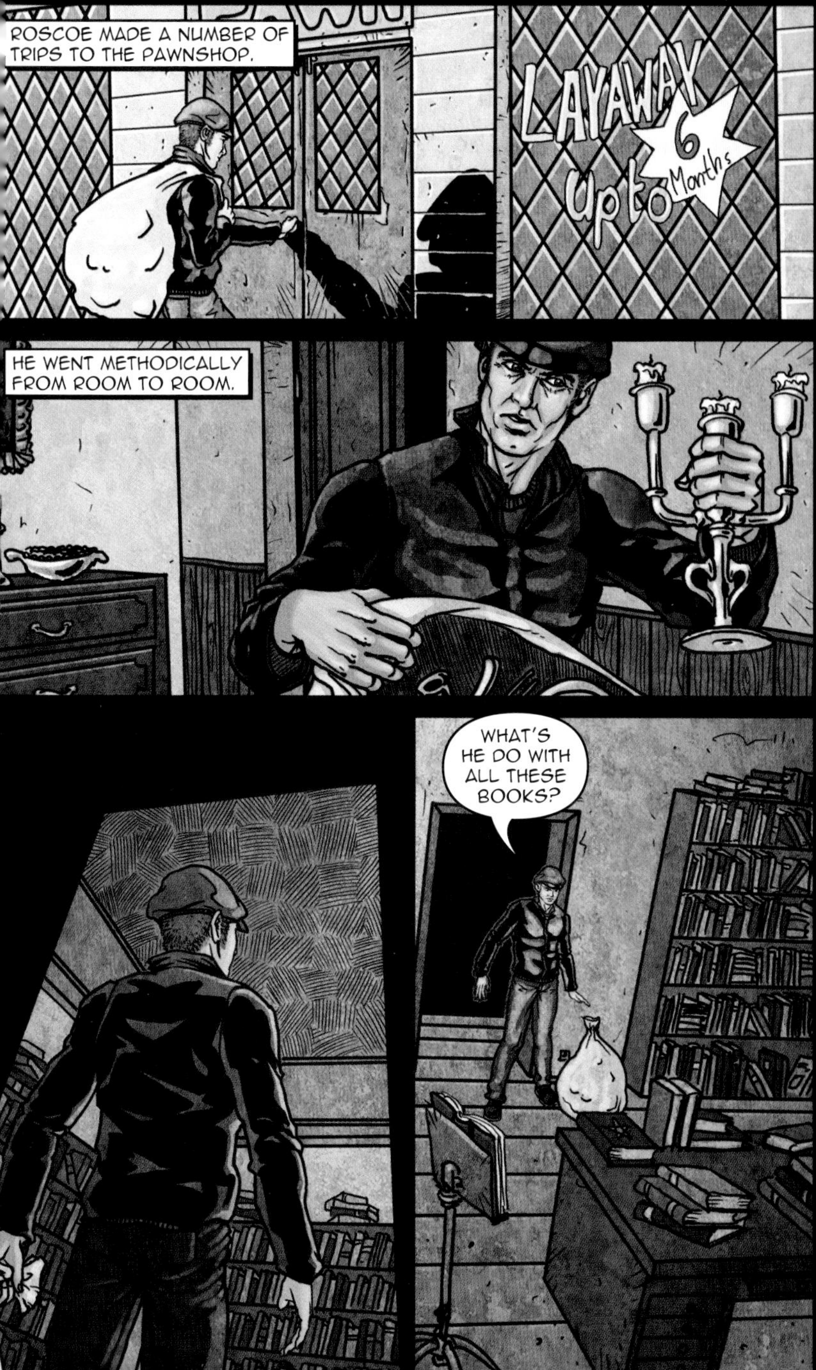
ROSCOE MADE A NUMBER OF TRIPS TO THE PAWNSHOP.
LAYAWAY Up to 6 Months
HE WENT METHODICALLY FROM ROOM TO ROOM.
WHAT'S HE DO WITH ALL THESE BOOKS?

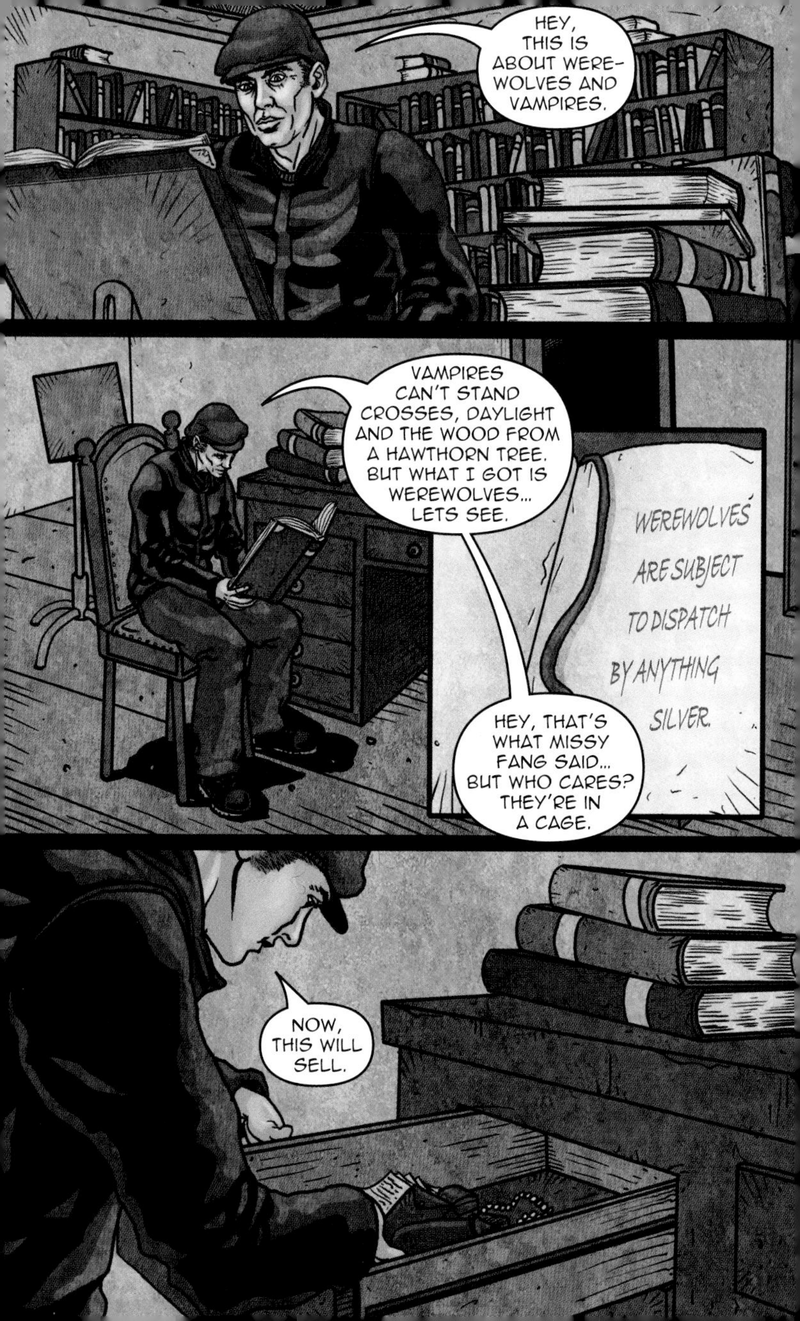
HEY, THIS IS ABOUT WERE-WOLVES AND VAMPIRES.
VAMPIRES CAN'T STAND CROSSES, DAYLIGHT AND THE WOOD FROM A HAWTHORN TREE. BUT WHAT I GOT IS WEREWOLVES... LETS SEE.
WEREWOLVES ARE SUBJECT TO DISPATCH BY ANYTHING SILVER.
HEY, THAT'S WHAT MISSY FANG SAID... BUT WHO CARES? THEY'RE IN A CAGE.
NOW, THIS WILL SELL.

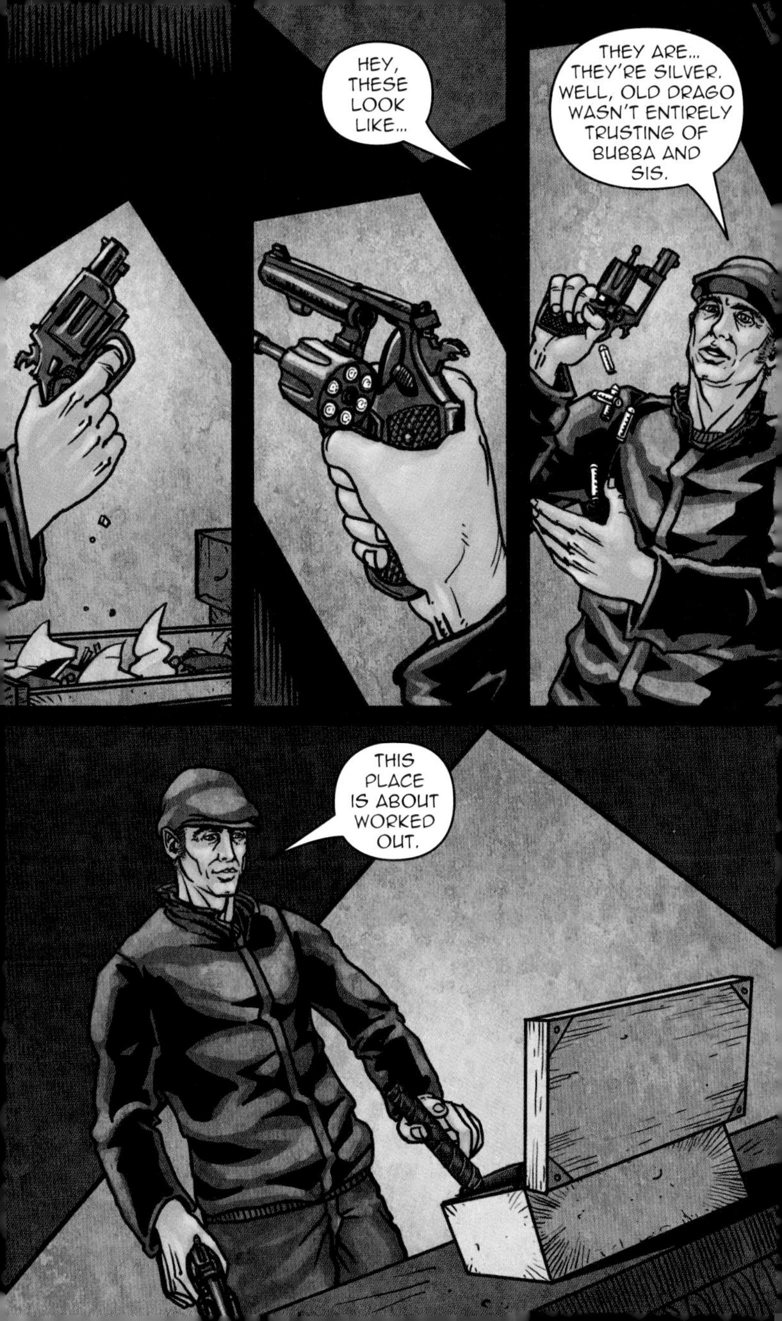
HEY, THESE LOOK LIKE...
THEY ARE... THEY'RE SILVER. WELL, OLD DRAGO WASN'T ENTIRELY TRUSTING OF BUBBA AND SIS.
THIS PLACE IS ABOUT WORKED OUT.

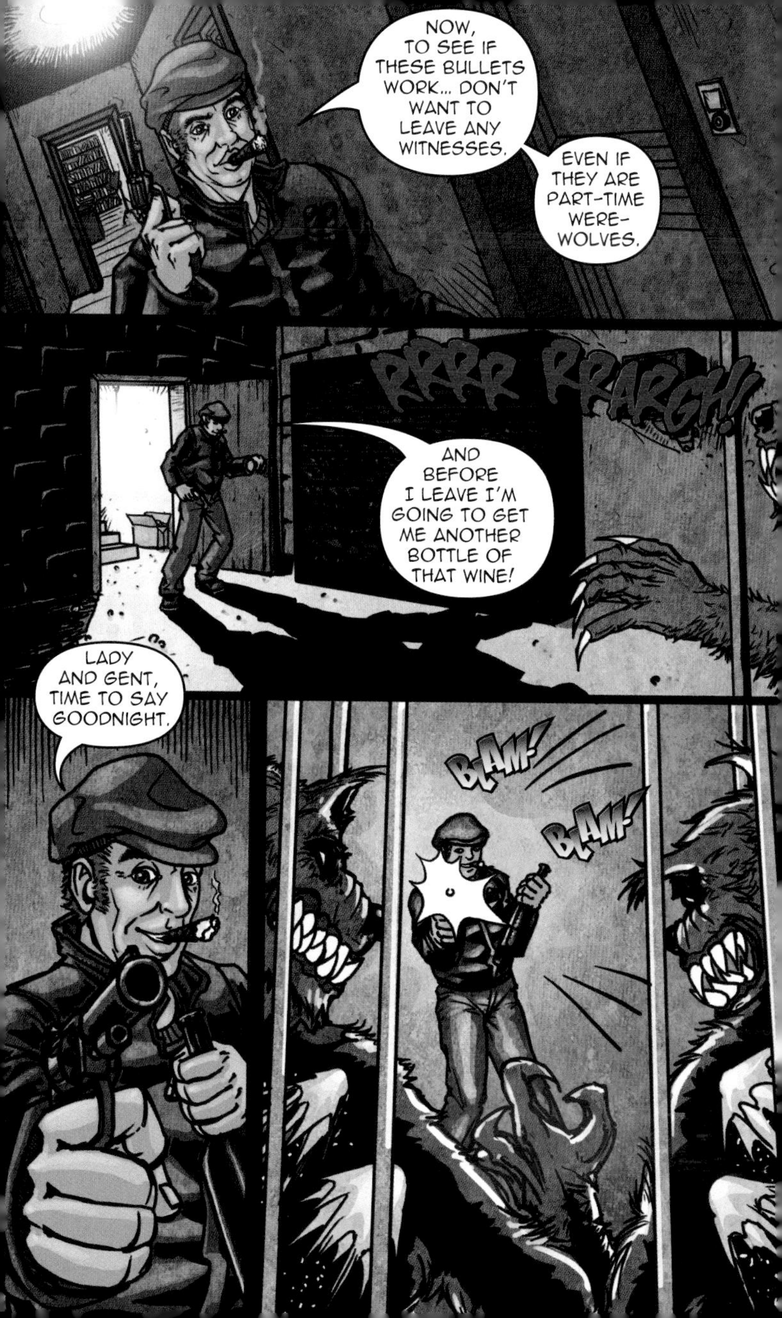
NOW, TO SEE IF THESE BULLETS WORK... DON'T WANT TO LEAVE ANY WITNESSES.
EVEN IF THEY ARE PART-TIME WERE-WOLVES.
RRRR RRARGH!!
AND BEFORE I LEAVE I'M GOING TO GET ME ANOTHER BOTTLE OF THAT WINE!
LADY AND GENT, TIME TO SAY GOODNIGHT.
BLAM!
BLAM!

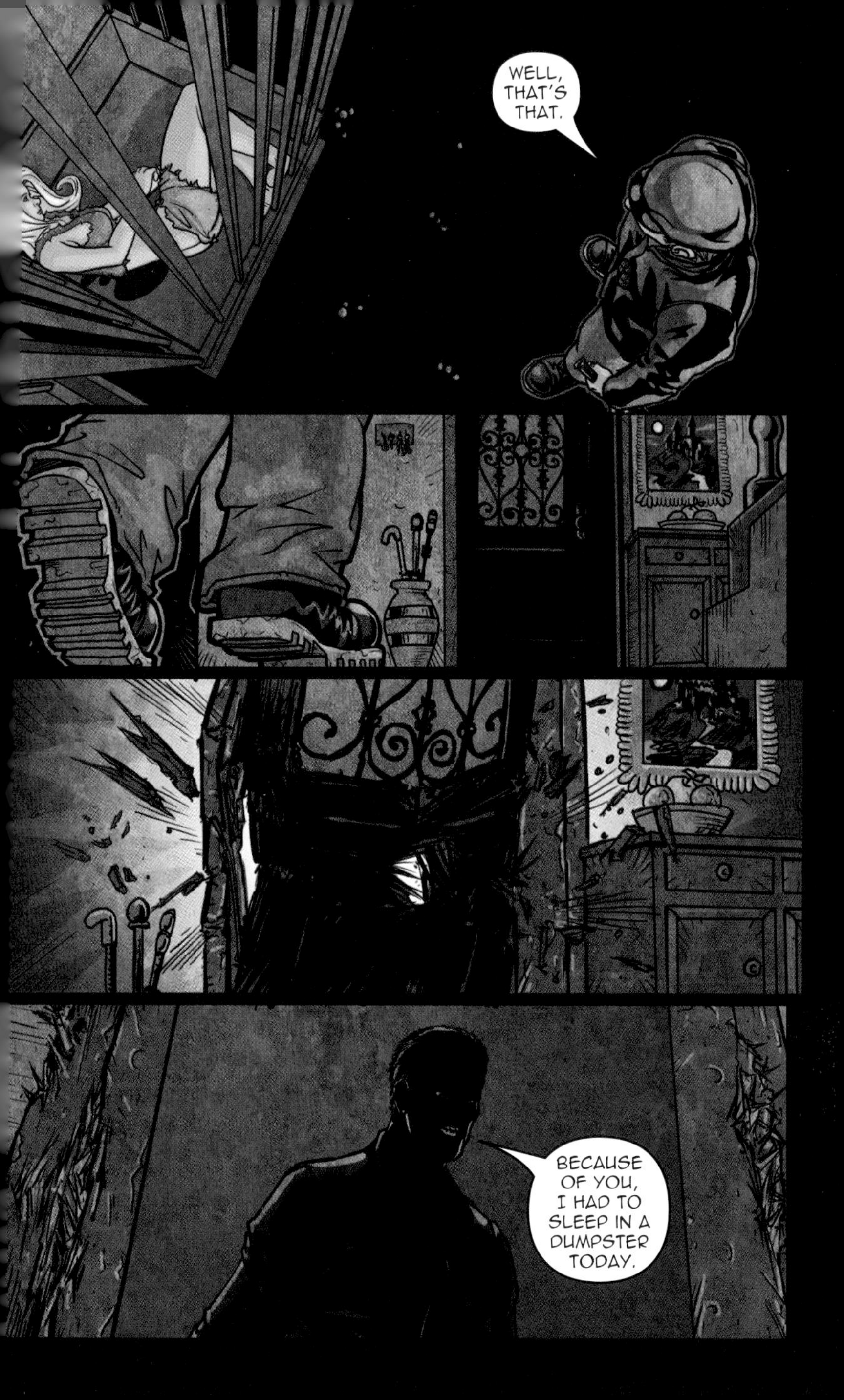
WELL, THAT'S THAT.
BECAUSE OF YOU, I HAD TO SLEEP IN A DUMPSTER TODAY.

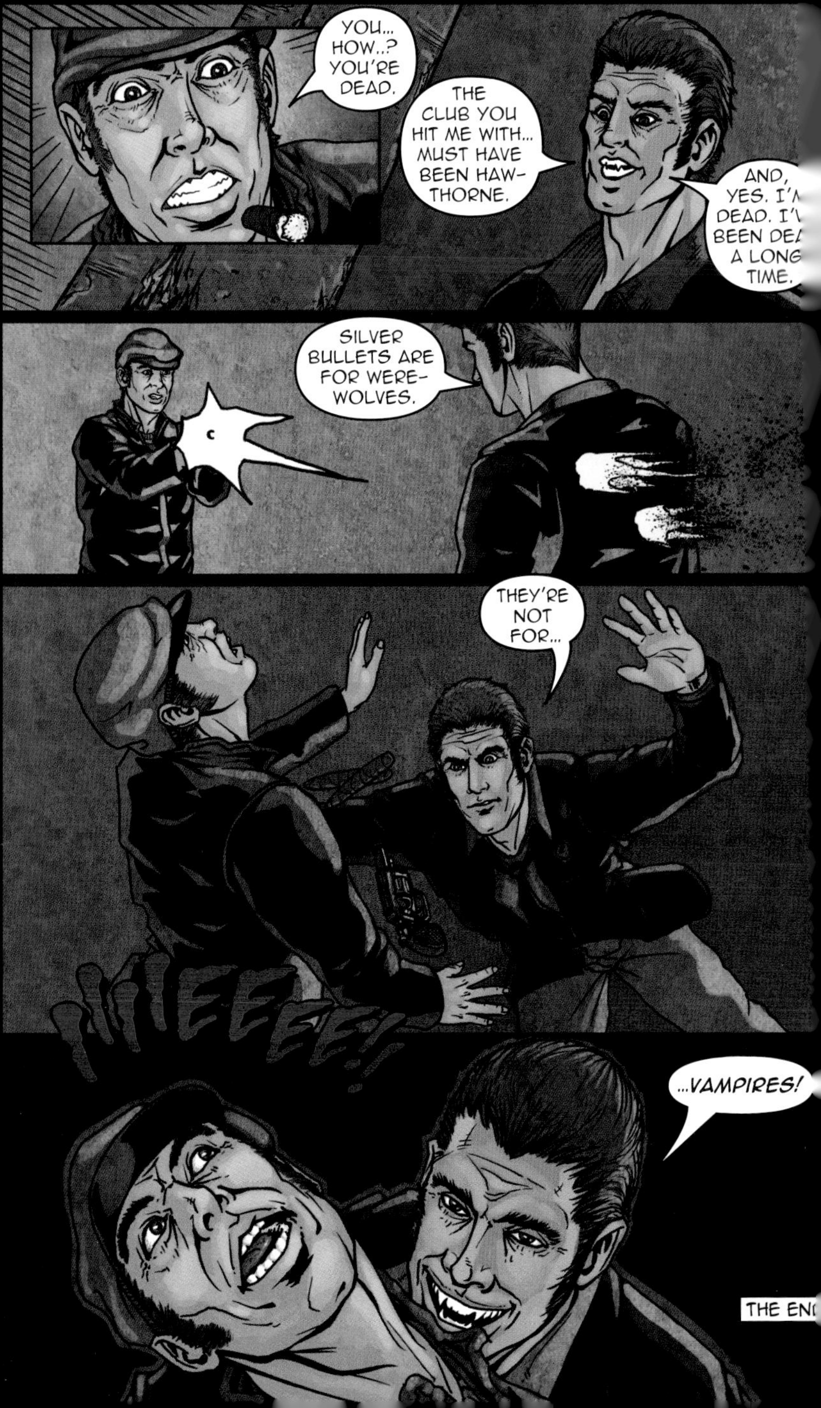
YOU... HOW..? YOU'RE DEAD.
THE CLUB YOU HIT ME WITH... MUST HAVE BEEN HAW-THORNE.
AND, YES. I'M DEAD. I'VE BEEN DEAD A LONG TIME.
SILVER BULLETS ARE FOR WERE-WOLVES.
THEY'RE NOT FOR...
WHEEEEE!
...VAMPIRES!
THE END

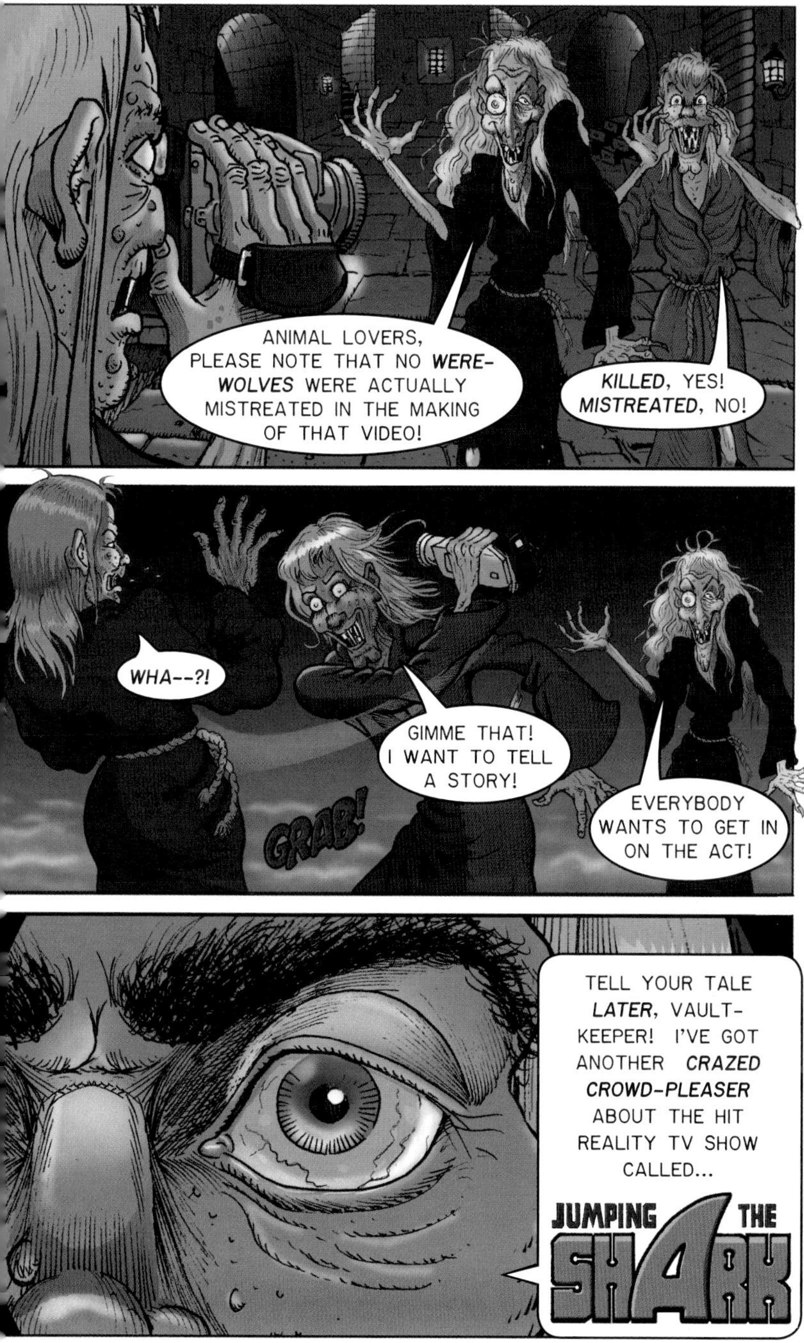

ANIMAL LOVERS, PLEASE NOTE THAT NO *WERE-WOLVES* WERE ACTUALLY MISTREATED IN THE MAKING OF THAT VIDEO!
KILLED, YES! *MISTREATED*, NO!
WHA--?!
GIMME THAT! I WANT TO TELL A STORY!
GRAB!
EVERYBODY WANTS TO GET IN ON THE ACT!
TELL YOUR TALE *LATER*, VAULT-KEEPER! I'VE GOT ANOTHER *CRAZED CROWD-PLEASER* ABOUT THE HIT REALITY TV SHOW CALLED...
JUMPING THE SHARK

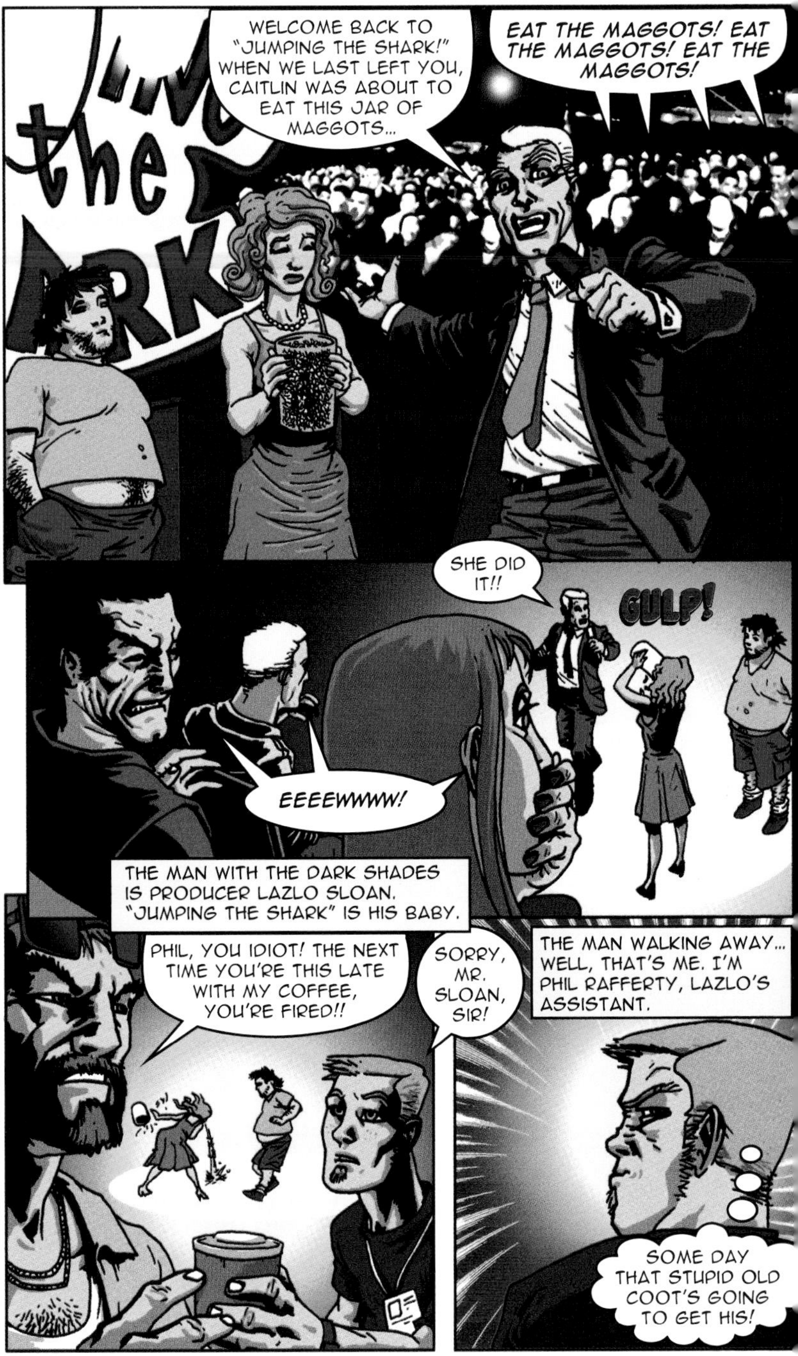
WELCOME BACK TO "JUMPING THE SHARK!" WHEN WE LAST LEFT YOU, CAITLIN WAS ABOUT TO EAT THIS JAR OF MAGGOTS...
EAT THE MAGGOTS! EAT THE MAGGOTS! EAT THE MAGGOTS!
SHE DID IT!!
GULP!
EEEEWWWW!
THE MAN WITH THE DARK SHADES IS PRODUCER LAZLO SLOAN. "JUMPING THE SHARK" IS HIS BABY.
PHIL, YOU IDIOT! THE NEXT TIME YOU'RE THIS LATE WITH MY COFFEE, YOU'RE FIRED!!
SORRY, MR. SLOAN, SIR!
THE MAN WALKING AWAY... WELL, THAT'S ME. I'M PHIL RAFFERTY, LAZLO'S ASSISTANT.
SOME DAY THAT STUPID OLD COOT'S GOING TO GET HIS!

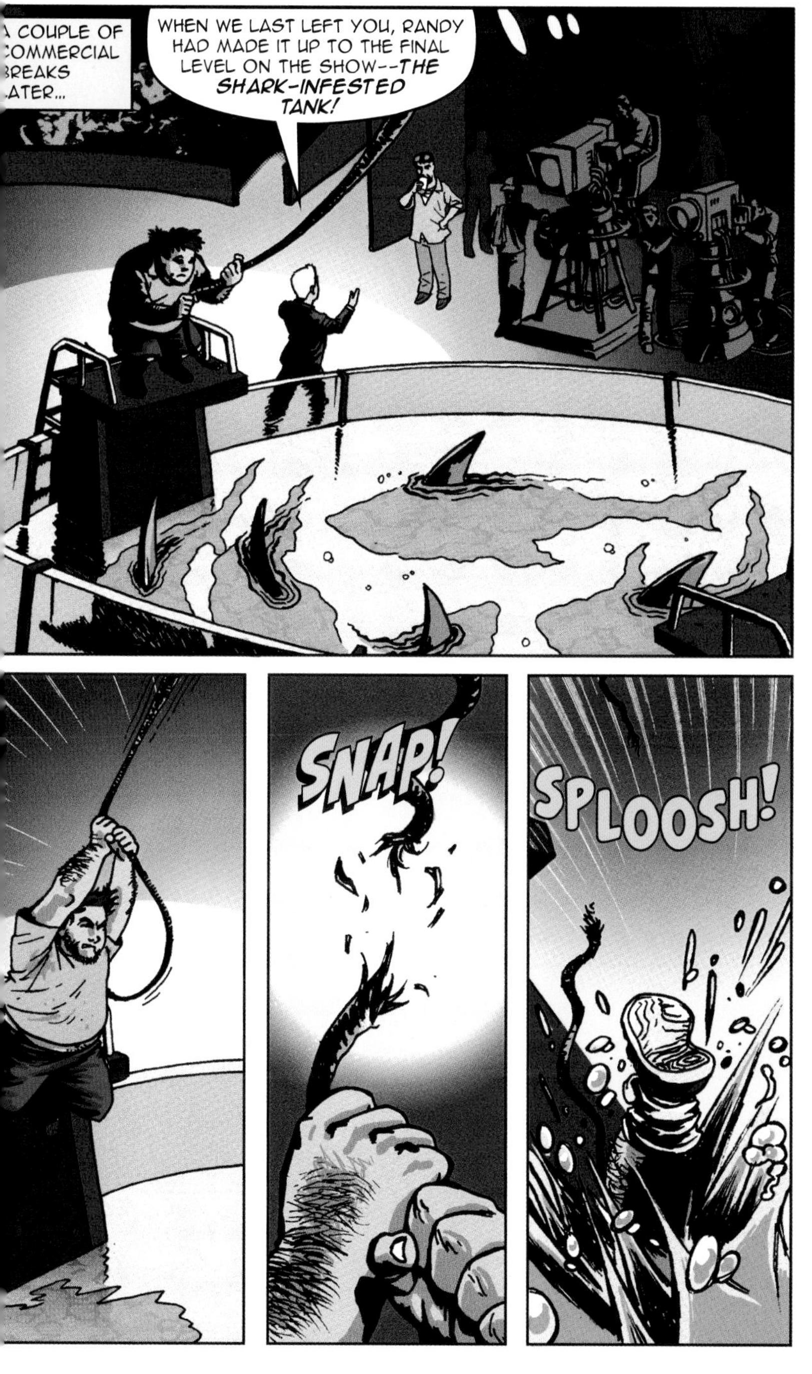
A COUPLE OF COMMERCIAL BREAKS LATER...
WHEN WE LAST LEFT YOU, RANDY HAD MADE IT UP TO THE FINAL LEVEL ON THE SHOW--THE SHARK-INFESTED TANK!
SNAP!
SPLOOSH!

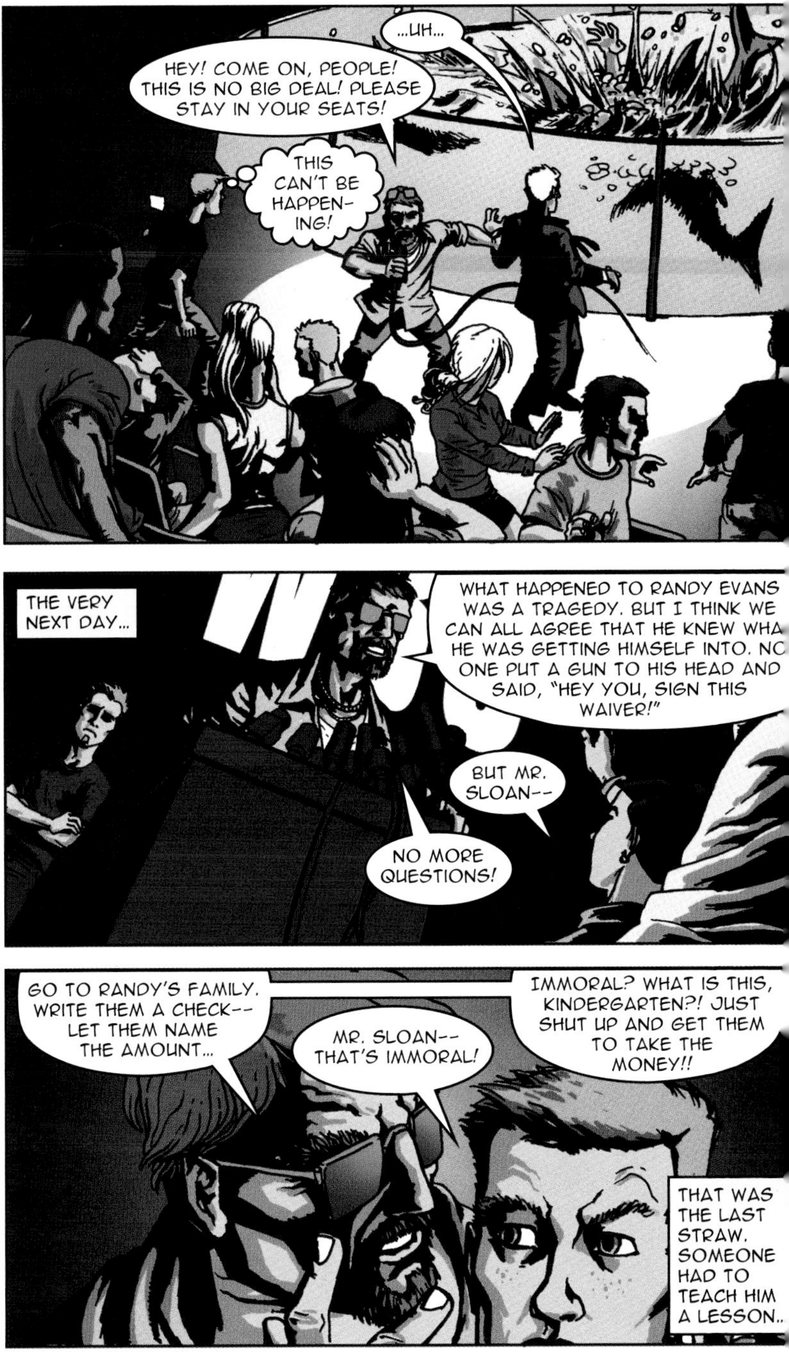

HEY! COME ON, PEOPLE! THIS IS NO BIG DEAL! PLEASE STAY IN YOUR SEATS!
...UH...
THIS CAN'T BE HAPPEN-ING!
THE VERY NEXT DAY...
WHAT HAPPENED TO RANDY EVANS WAS A TRAGEDY. BUT I THINK WE CAN ALL AGREE THAT HE KNEW WHA HE WAS GETTING HIMSELF INTO. NO ONE PUT A GUN TO HIS HEAD AND SAID, "HEY YOU, SIGN THIS WAIVER!"
BUT MR. SLOAN--
NO MORE QUESTIONS!
GO TO RANDY'S FAMILY. WRITE THEM A CHECK-- LET THEM NAME THE AMOUNT...
MR. SLOAN-- THAT'S IMMORAL!
IMMORAL? WHAT IS THIS, KINDERGARTEN?! JUST SHUT UP AND GET THEM TO TAKE THE MONEY!!
THAT WAS THE LAST STRAW. SOMEONE HAD TO TEACH HIM A LESSON..

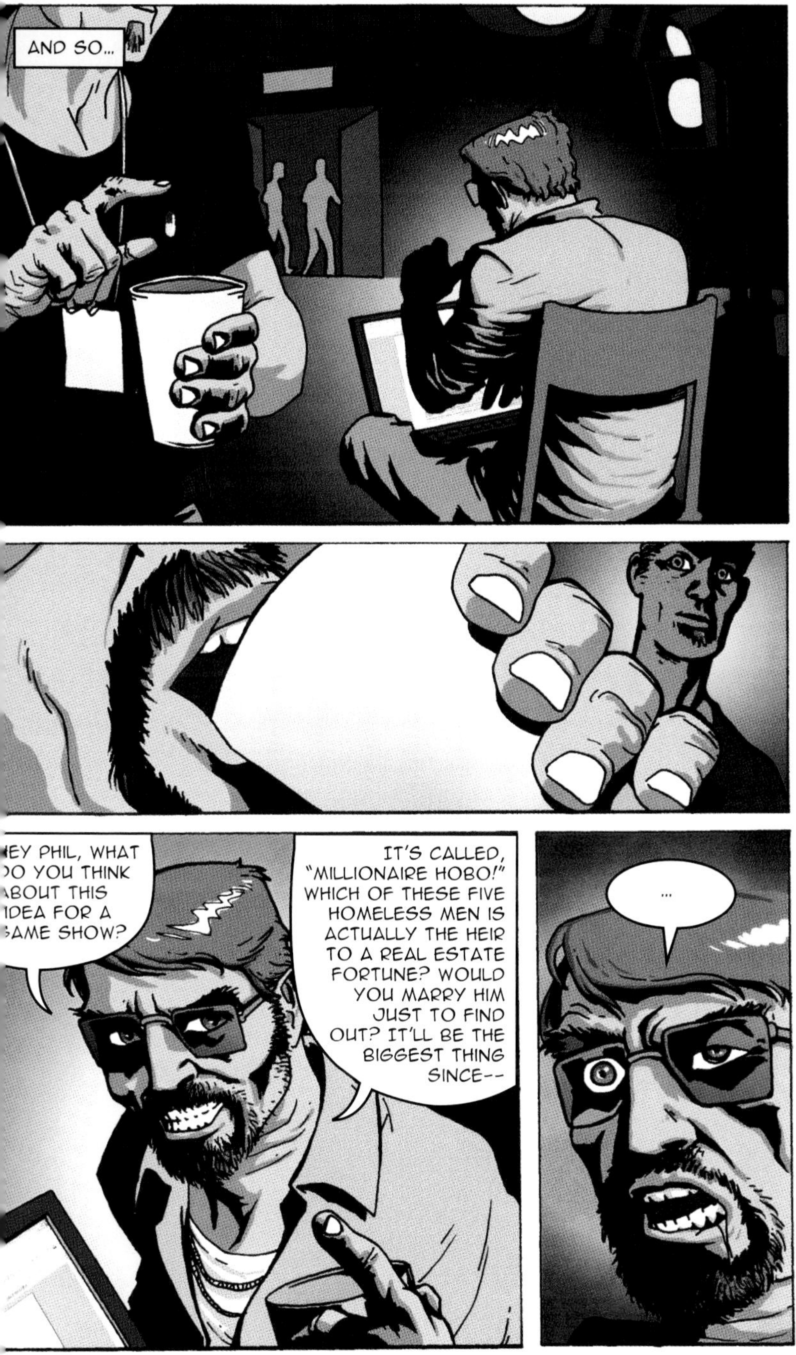
AND SO...
EY PHIL, WHAT O YOU THINK BOUT THIS IDEA FOR A AME SHOW?
IT'S CALLED, "MILLIONAIRE HOBO!" WHICH OF THESE FIVE HOMELESS MEN IS ACTUALLY THE HEIR TO A REAL ESTATE FORTUNE? WOULD YOU MARRY HIM JUST TO FIND OUT? IT'LL BE THE BIGGEST THING SINCE--
...

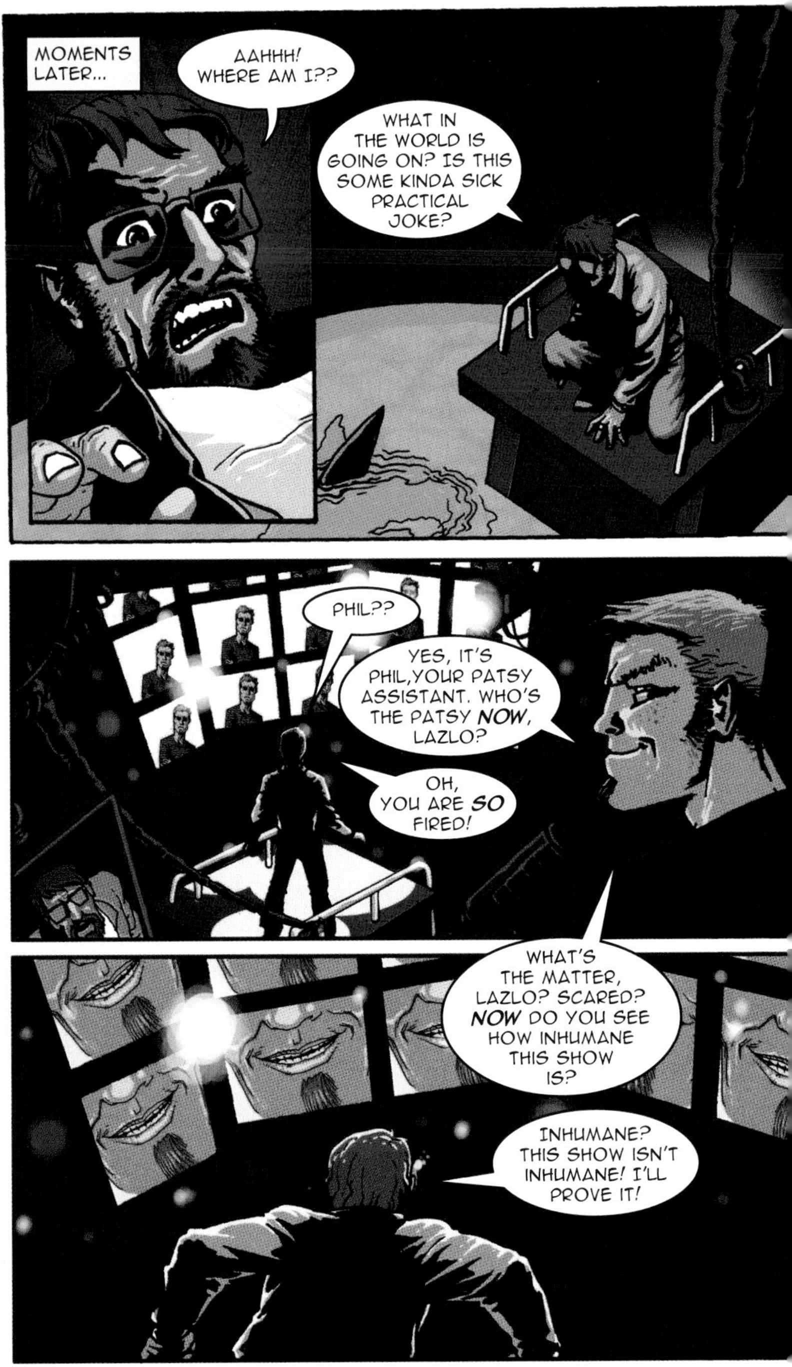
MOMENTS LATER...
AAHHH! WHERE AM I??
WHAT IN THE WORLD IS GOING ON? IS THIS SOME KINDA SICK PRACTICAL JOKE?
PHIL??
YES, IT'S PHIL,YOUR PATSY ASSISTANT. WHO'S THE PATSY NOW, LAZLO?
OH, YOU ARE SO FIRED!
WHAT'S THE MATTER, LAZLO? SCARED? NOW DO YOU SEE HOW INHUMANE THIS SHOW IS?
INHUMANE? THIS SHOW ISN'T INHUMANE! I'LL PROVE IT!

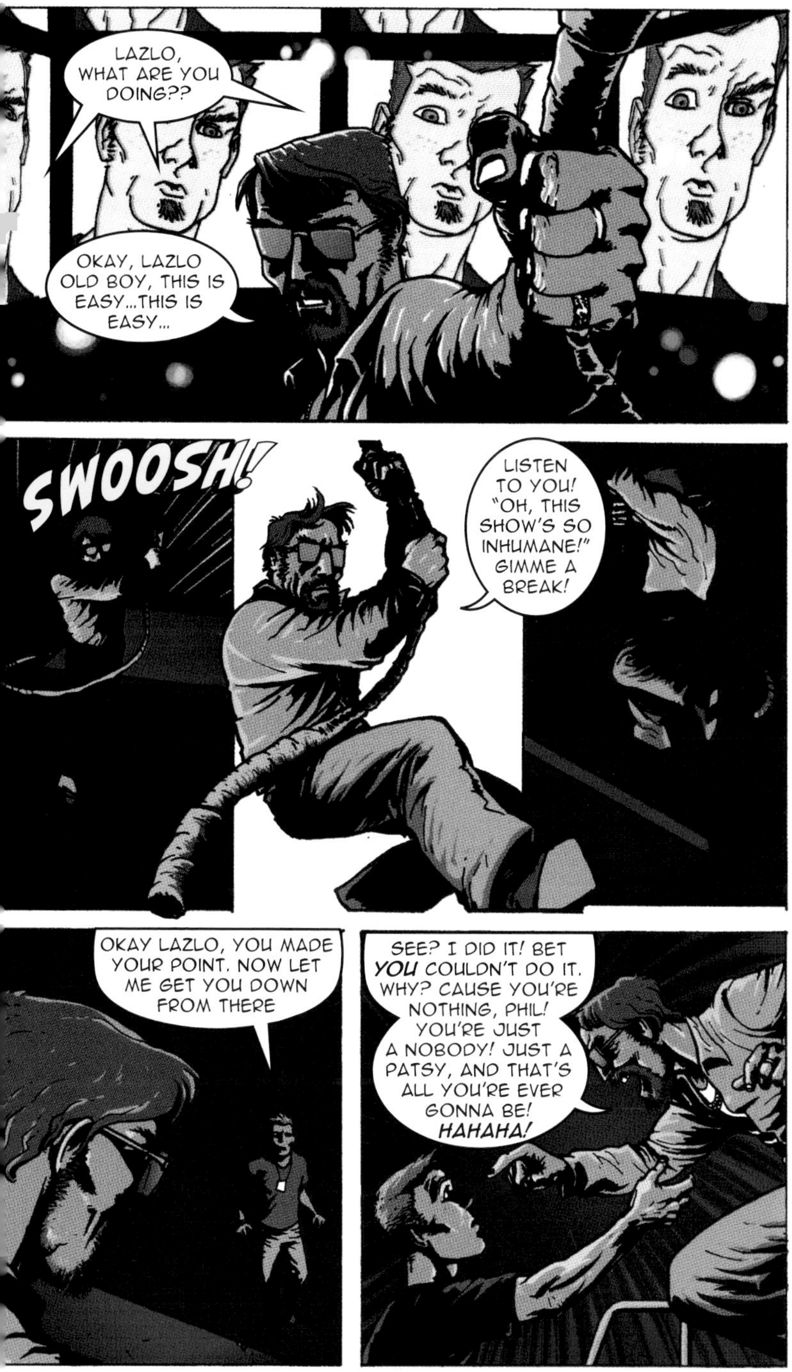
LAZLO, WHAT ARE YOU DOING??
OKAY, LAZLO OLD BOY, THIS IS EASY...THIS IS EASY...
SWOOSH!
LISTEN TO YOU! "OH, THIS SHOW'S SO INHUMANE!" GIMME A BREAK!
OKAY LAZLO, YOU MADE YOUR POINT. NOW LET ME GET YOU DOWN FROM THERE
SEE? I DID IT! BET *YOU* COULDN'T DO IT. WHY? CAUSE YOU'RE NOTHING, PHIL! YOU'RE JUST A NOBODY! JUST A PATSY, AND THAT'S ALL YOU'RE EVER GONNA BE! ***HAHAHA!***

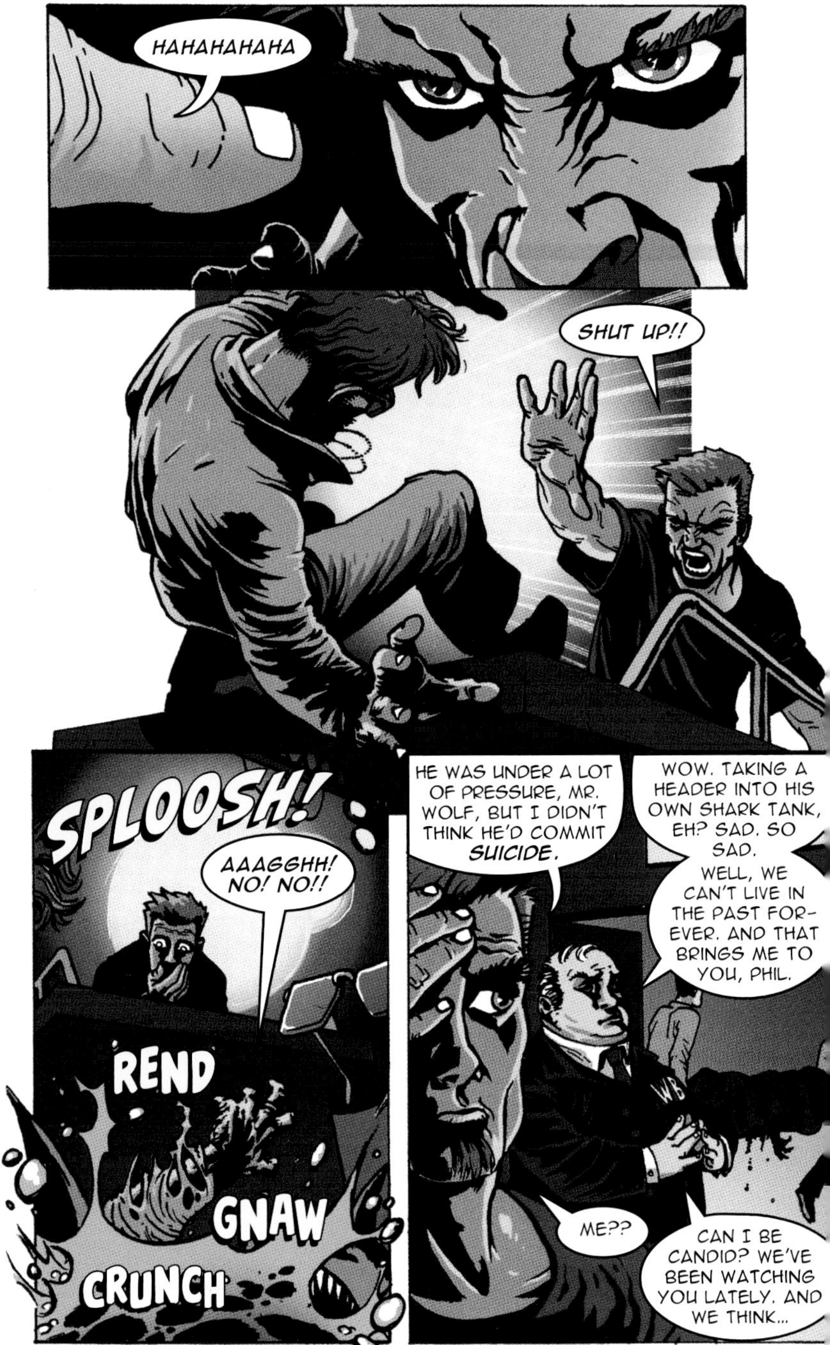
HAHAHAHAHA
SHUT UP!!
SPLOOSH!
AAAGGHH! NO! NO!!
REND
GNAW
CRUNCH
HE WAS UNDER A LOT OF PRESSURE, MR. WOLF, BUT I DIDN'T THINK HE'D COMMIT SUICIDE.
WOW. TAKING A HEADER INTO HIS OWN SHARK TANK, EH? SAD. SO SAD.
WELL, WE CAN'T LIVE IN THE PAST FOREVER. AND THAT BRINGS ME TO YOU, PHIL.
ME??
CAN I BE CANDID? WE'VE BEEN WATCHING YOU LATELY. AND WE THINK...

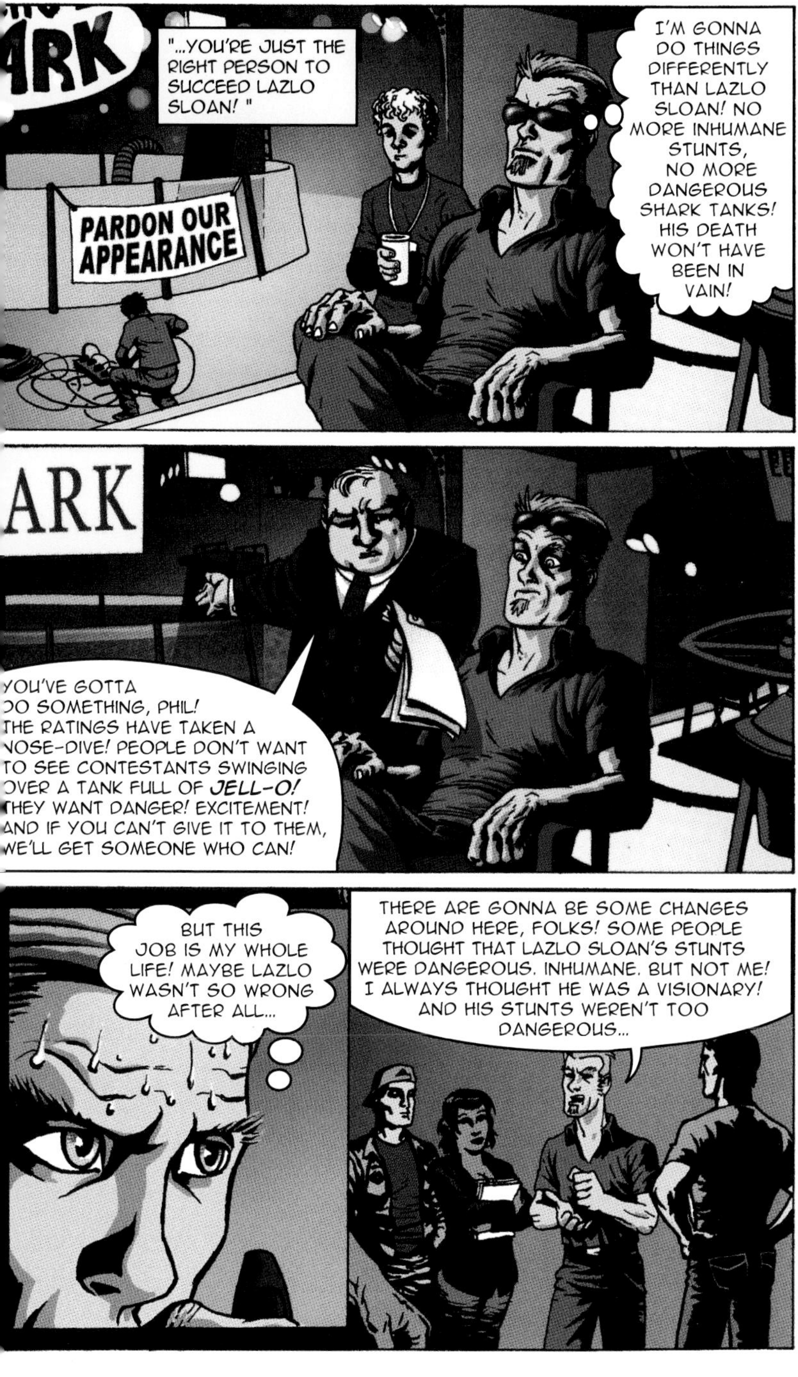
ARK
"...YOU'RE JUST THE RIGHT PERSON TO SUCCEED LAZLO SLOAN! "
I'M GONNA DO THINGS DIFFERENTLY THAN LAZLO SLOAN! NO MORE INHUMANE STUNTS, NO MORE DANGEROUS SHARK TANKS! HIS DEATH WON'T HAVE BEEN IN VAIN!
PARDON OUR APPEARANCE
ARK
YOU'VE GOTTA DO SOMETHING, PHIL! THE RATINGS HAVE TAKEN A NOSE-DIVE! PEOPLE DON'T WANT TO SEE CONTESTANTS SWINGING OVER A TANK FULL OF JELL-O! THEY WANT DANGER! EXCITEMENT! AND IF YOU CAN'T GIVE IT TO THEM, WE'LL GET SOMEONE WHO CAN!
BUT THIS JOB IS MY WHOLE LIFE! MAYBE LAZLO WASN'T SO WRONG AFTER ALL...
THERE ARE GONNA BE SOME CHANGES AROUND HERE, FOLKS! SOME PEOPLE THOUGHT THAT LAZLO SLOAN'S STUNTS WERE DANGEROUS. INHUMANE. BUT NOT ME! I ALWAYS THOUGHT HE WAS A VISIONARY! AND HIS STUNTS WEREN'T TOO DANGEROUS...

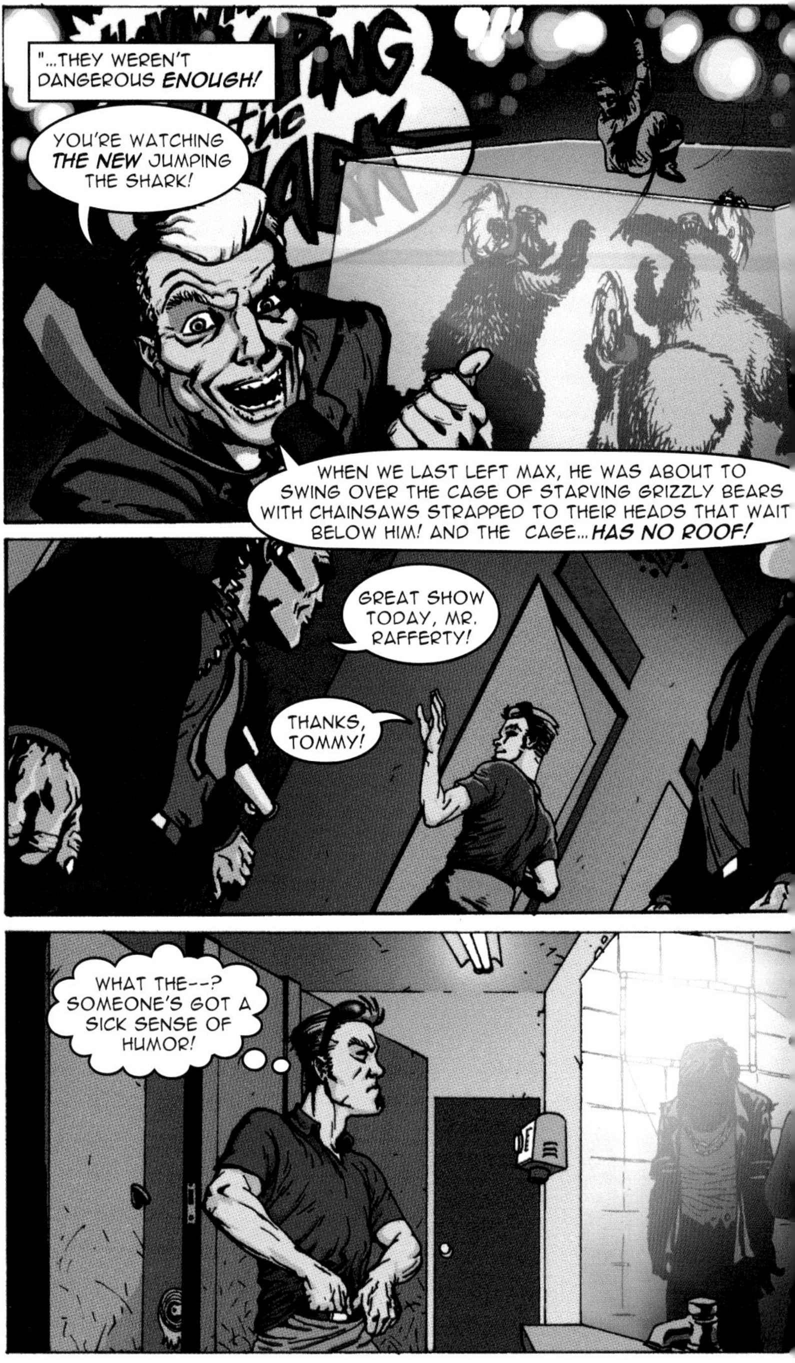
"...THEY WEREN'T DANGEROUS *ENOUGH!*
YOU'RE WATCHING *THE NEW* JUMPING THE SHARK!
WHEN WE LAST LEFT MAX, HE WAS ABOUT TO SWING OVER THE CAGE OF STARVING GRIZZLY BEARS WITH CHAINSAWS STRAPPED TO THEIR HEADS THAT WAIT BELOW HIM! AND THE CAGE... *HAS NO ROOF!*
GREAT SHOW TODAY, MR. RAFFERTY!
THANKS, TOMMY!
WHAT THE--? SOMEONE'S GOT A SICK SENSE OF HUMOR!

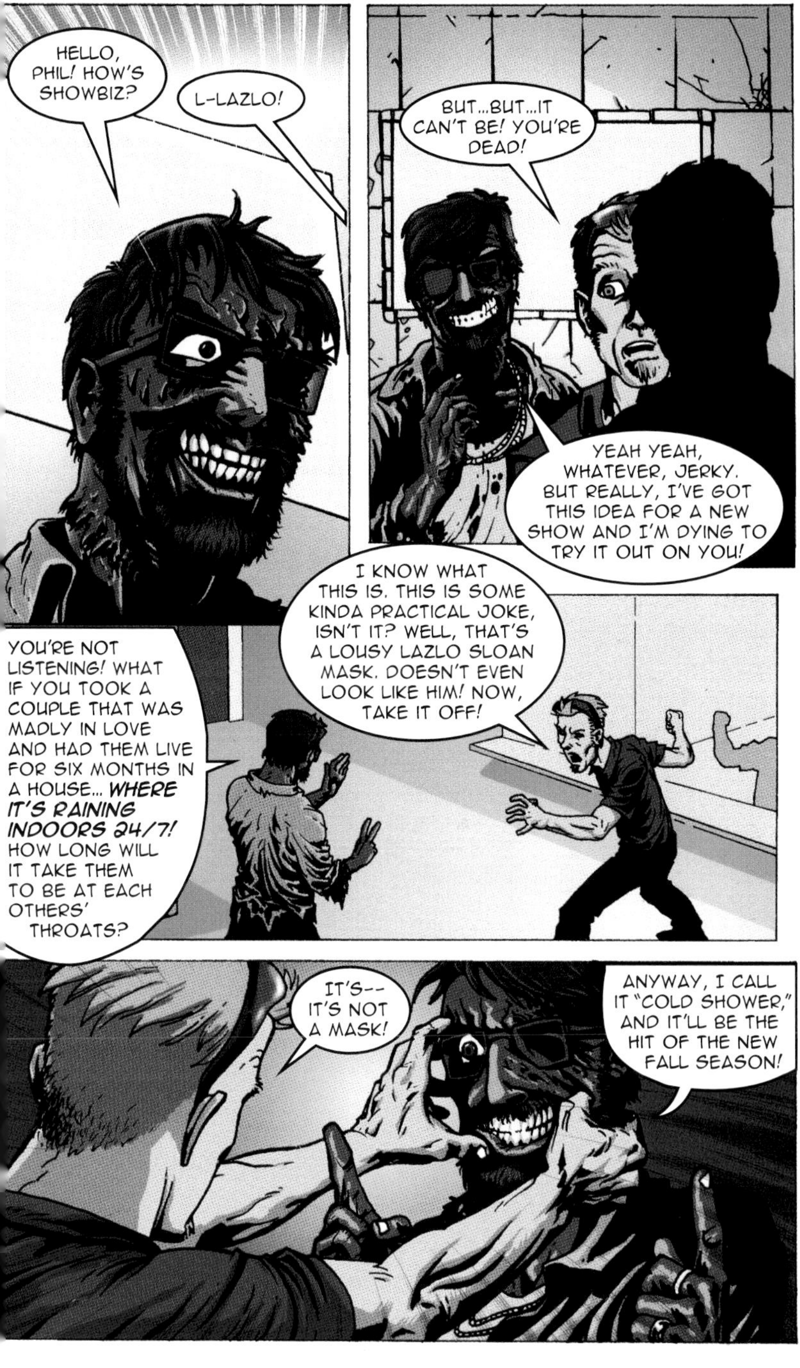
HELLO, PHIL! HOW'S SHOWBIZ?
L-LAZLO!
BUT...BUT...IT CAN'T BE! YOU'RE DEAD!
YEAH YEAH, WHATEVER, JERKY. BUT REALLY, I'VE GOT THIS IDEA FOR A NEW SHOW AND I'M DYING TO TRY IT OUT ON YOU!
I KNOW WHAT THIS IS. THIS IS SOME KINDA PRACTICAL JOKE, ISN'T IT? WELL, THAT'S A LOUSY LAZLO SLOAN MASK. DOESN'T EVEN LOOK LIKE HIM! NOW, TAKE IT OFF!
YOU'RE NOT LISTENING! WHAT IF YOU TOOK A COUPLE THAT WAS MADLY IN LOVE AND HAD THEM LIVE FOR SIX MONTHS IN A HOUSE... WHERE IT'S RAINING INDOORS 24/7! HOW LONG WILL IT TAKE THEM TO BE AT EACH OTHERS' THROATS?
IT'S-- IT'S NOT A MASK!
ANYWAY, I CALL IT "COLD SHOWER," AND IT'LL BE THE HIT OF THE NEW FALL SEASON!

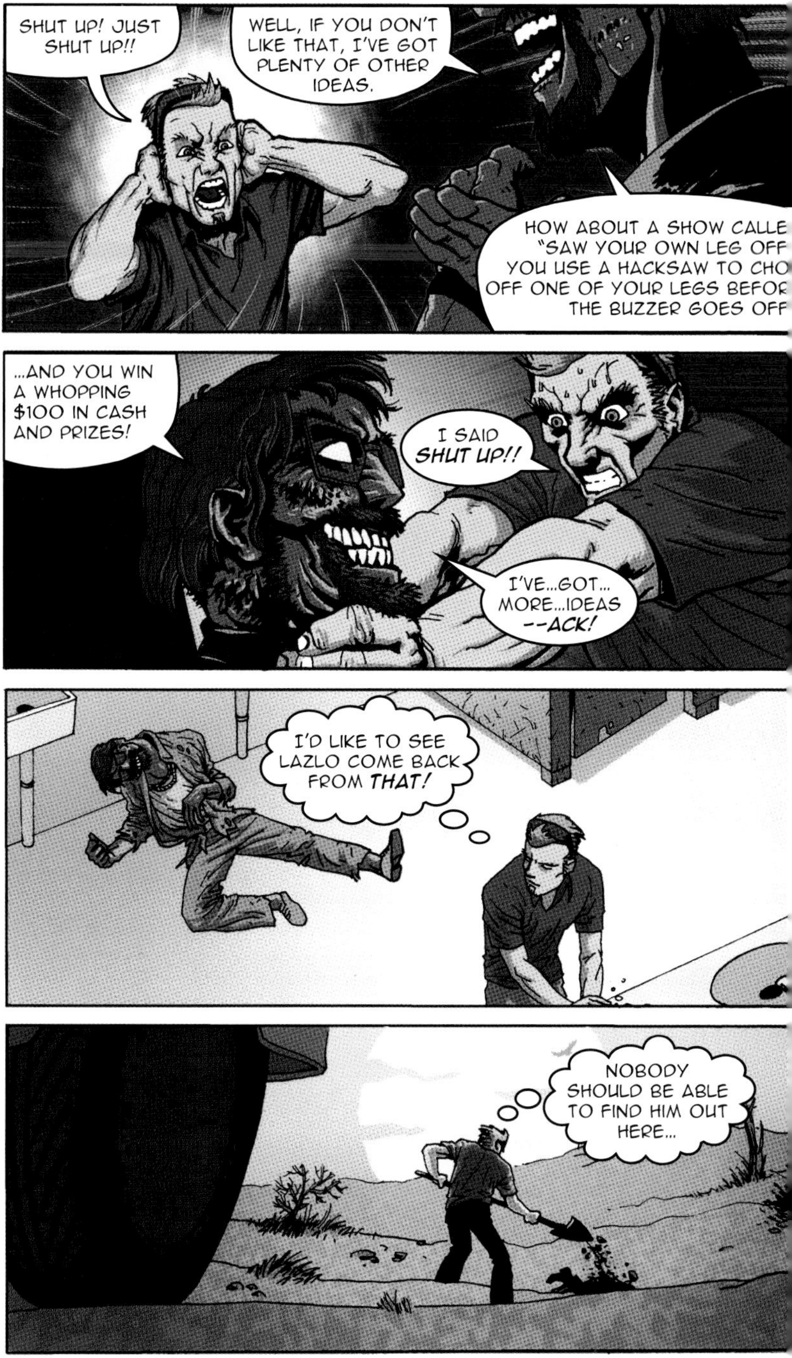
SHUT UP! JUST SHUT UP!!
WELL, IF YOU DON'T LIKE THAT, I'VE GOT PLENTY OF OTHER IDEAS.
HOW ABOUT A SHOW CALLE "SAW YOUR OWN LEG OFF YOU USE A HACKSAW TO CHO OFF ONE OF YOUR LEGS BEFOR THE BUZZER GOES OFF
...AND YOU WIN A WHOPPING $100 IN CASH AND PRIZES!
I SAID SHUT UP!!
I'VE...GOT... MORE...IDEAS --ACK!
I'D LIKE TO SEE LAZLO COME BACK FROM THAT!
NOBODY SHOULD BE ABLE TO FIND HIM OUT HERE...

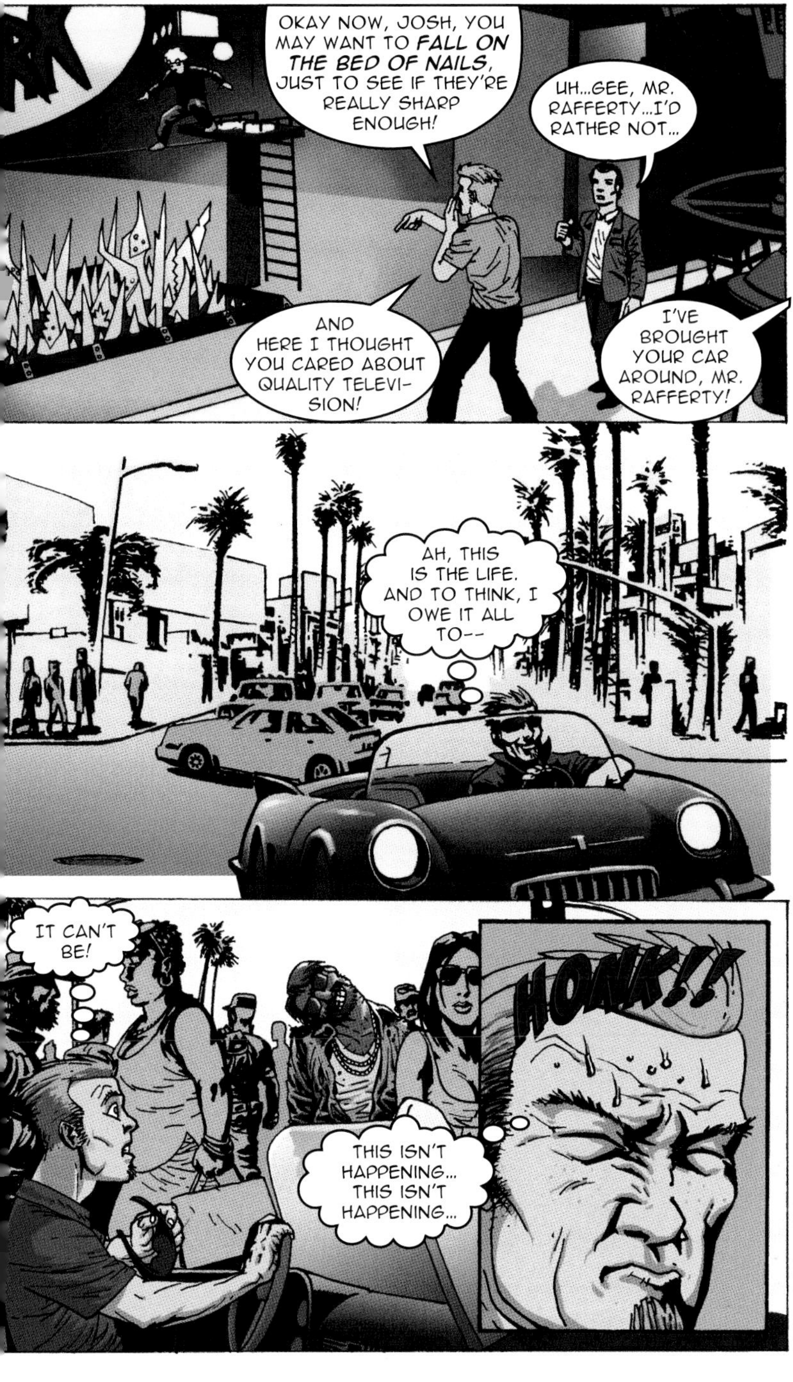
OKAY NOW, JOSH, YOU MAY WANT TO ***FALL ON THE BED OF NAILS***, JUST TO SEE IF THEY'RE REALLY SHARP ENOUGH!
UH...GEE, MR. RAFFERTY...I'D RATHER NOT...
AND HERE I THOUGHT YOU CARED ABOUT QUALITY TELEVI-SION!
I'VE BROUGHT YOUR CAR AROUND, MR. RAFFERTY!
AH, THIS IS THE LIFE. AND TO THINK, I OWE IT ALL TO--
IT CAN'T BE!
THIS ISN'T HAPPENING... THIS ISN'T HAPPENING...
HONK!!

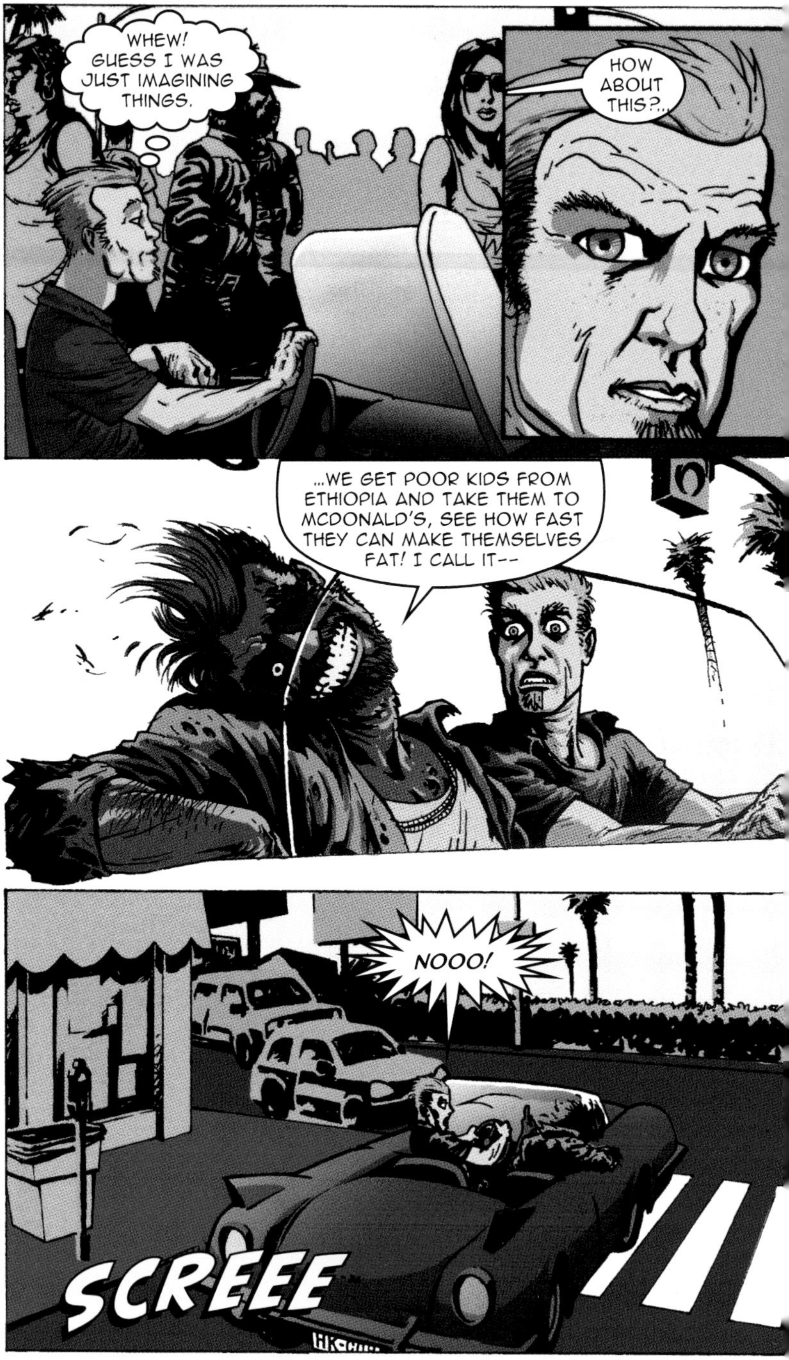
WHEW! GUESS I WAS JUST IMAGINING THINGS.
HOW ABOUT THIS?...
...WE GET POOR KIDS FROM ETHIOPIA AND TAKE THEM TO MCDONALD'S, SEE HOW FAST THEY CAN MAKE THEMSELVES FAT! I CALL IT--
NOOO!
SCREEE

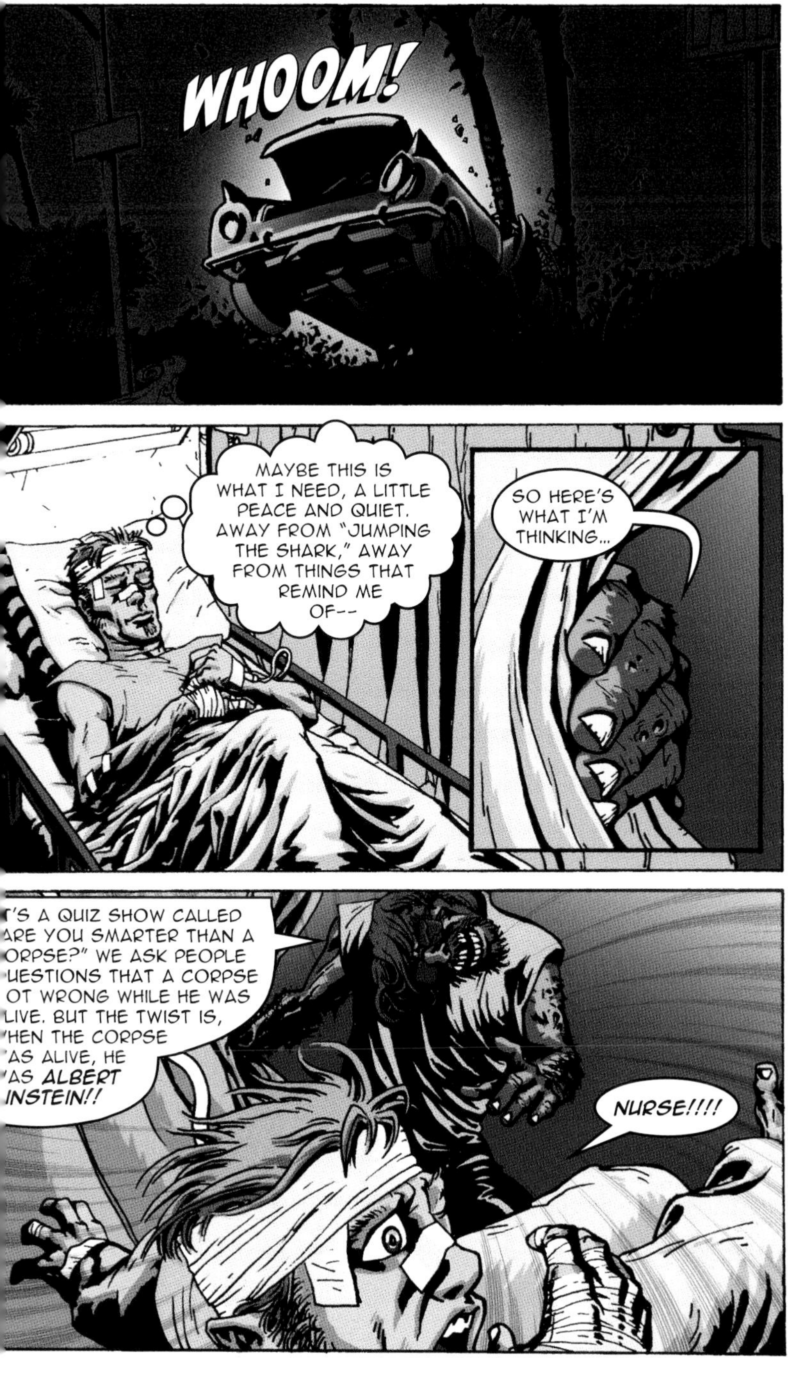
WHOOM!
MAYBE THIS IS WHAT I NEED, A LITTLE PEACE AND QUIET. AWAY FROM "JUMPING THE SHARK," AWAY FROM THINGS THAT REMIND ME OF--
SO HERE'S WHAT I'M THINKING...
'S A QUIZ SHOW CALLED ARE YOU SMARTER THAN A ORPSE?" WE ASK PEOPLE UESTIONS THAT A CORPSE OT WRONG WHILE HE WAS LIVE. BUT THE TWIST IS, HEN THE CORPSE AS ALIVE, HE AS ALBERT INSTEIN!!
NURSE!!!!

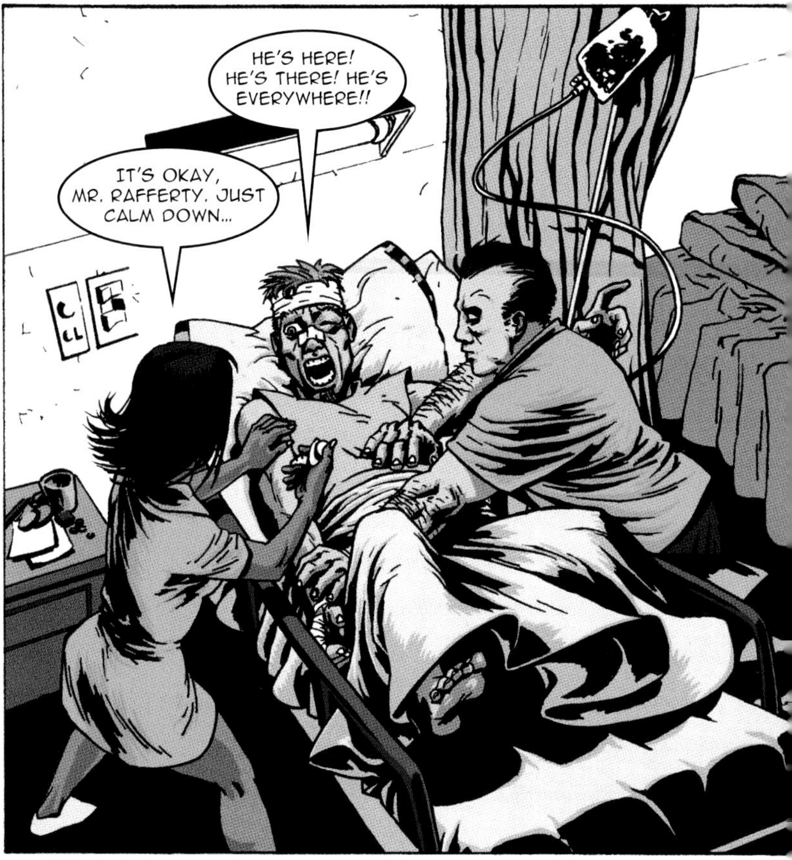
IT'S OKAY, MR. RAFFERTY. JUST CALM DOWN...
HE'S HERE! HE'S THERE! HE'S EVERYWHERE!!

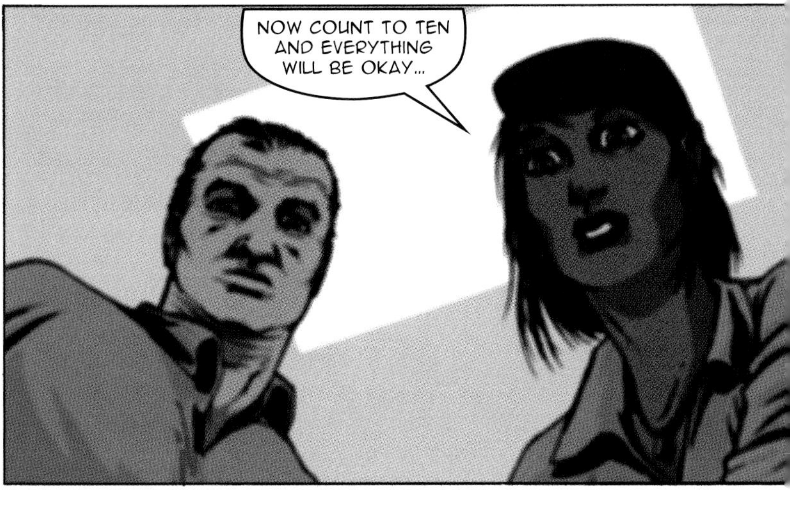
NOW COUNT TO TEN AND EVERYTHING WILL BE OKAY...

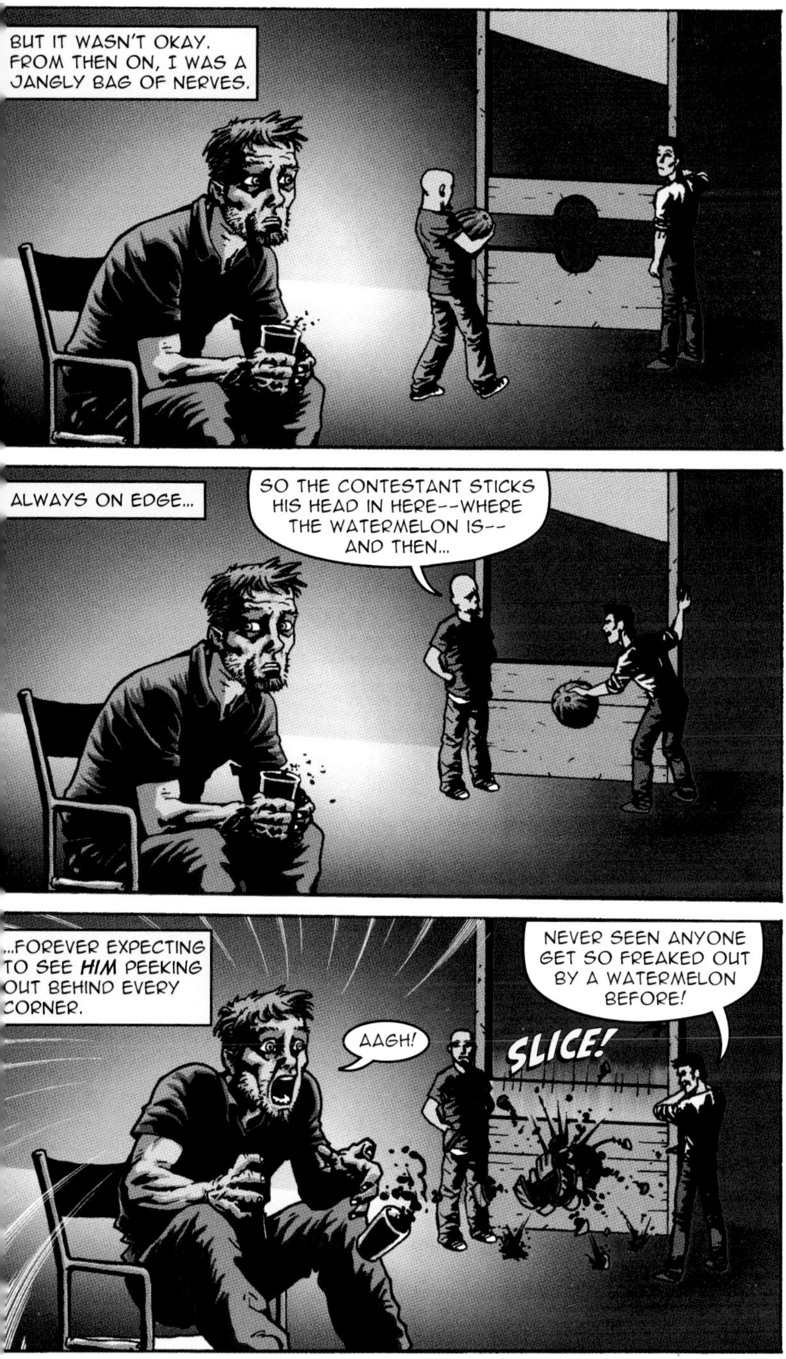
BUT IT WASN'T OKAY. FROM THEN ON, I WAS A JANGLY BAG OF NERVES.
ALWAYS ON EDGE...
SO THE CONTESTANT STICKS HIS HEAD IN HERE--WHERE THE WATERMELON IS--AND THEN...
...FOREVER EXPECTING TO SEE *HIM* PEEKING OUT BEHIND EVERY CORNER.
AAGH!
SLICE!
NEVER SEEN ANYONE GET SO FREAKED OUT BY A WATERMELON BEFORE!

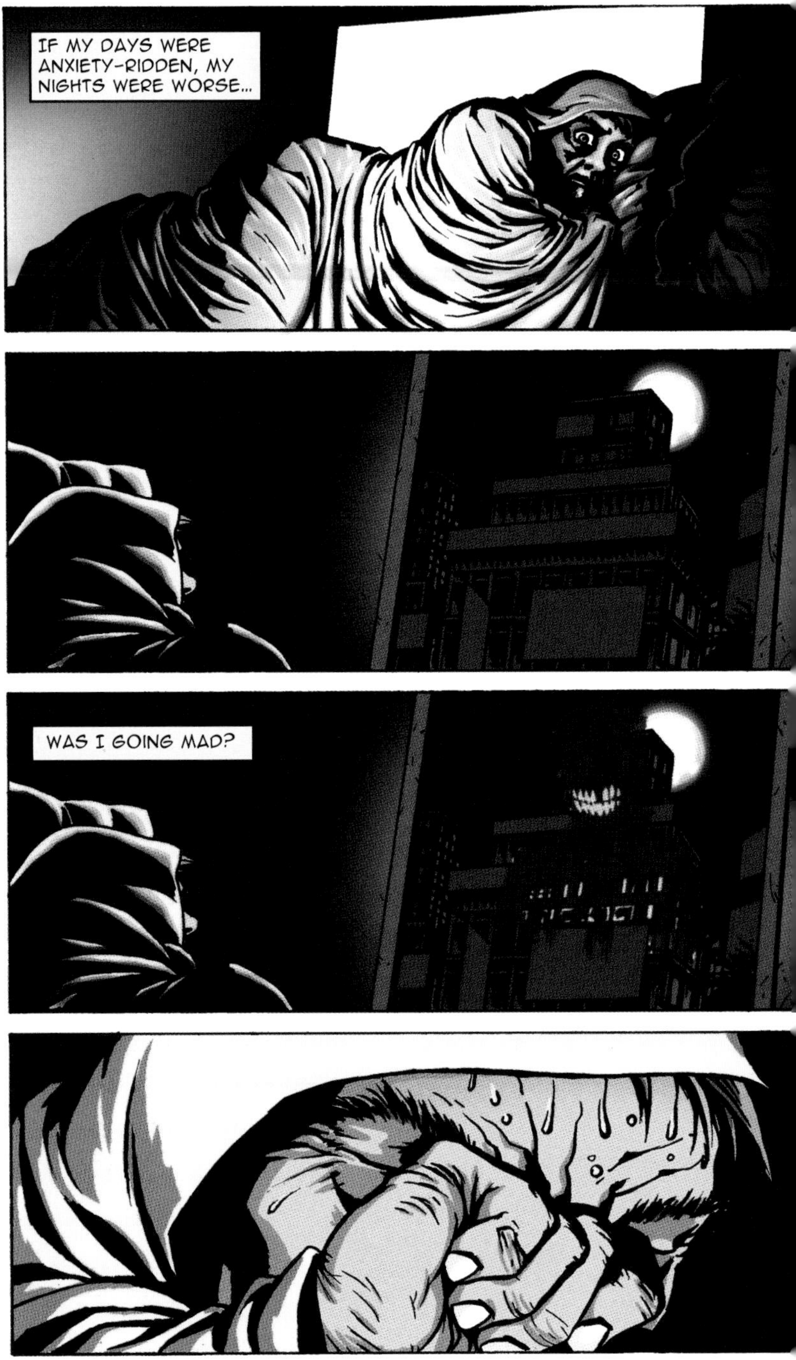
IF MY DAYS WERE ANXIETY-RIDDEN, MY NIGHTS WERE WORSE...
WAS I GOING MAD?

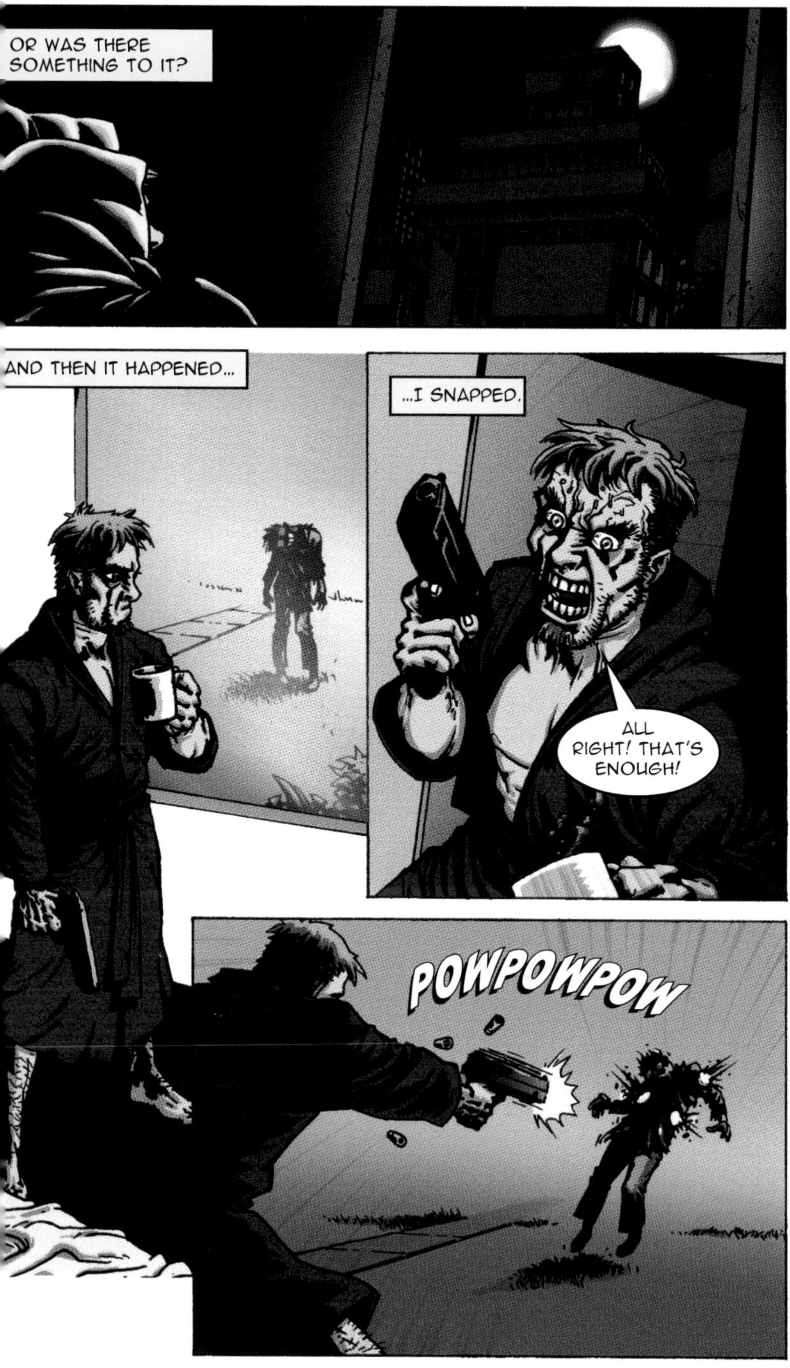
OR WAS THERE SOMETHING TO IT?
AND THEN IT HAPPENED...
...I SNAPPED.
ALL RIGHT! THAT'S ENOUGH!
POWPOWPOWPOW

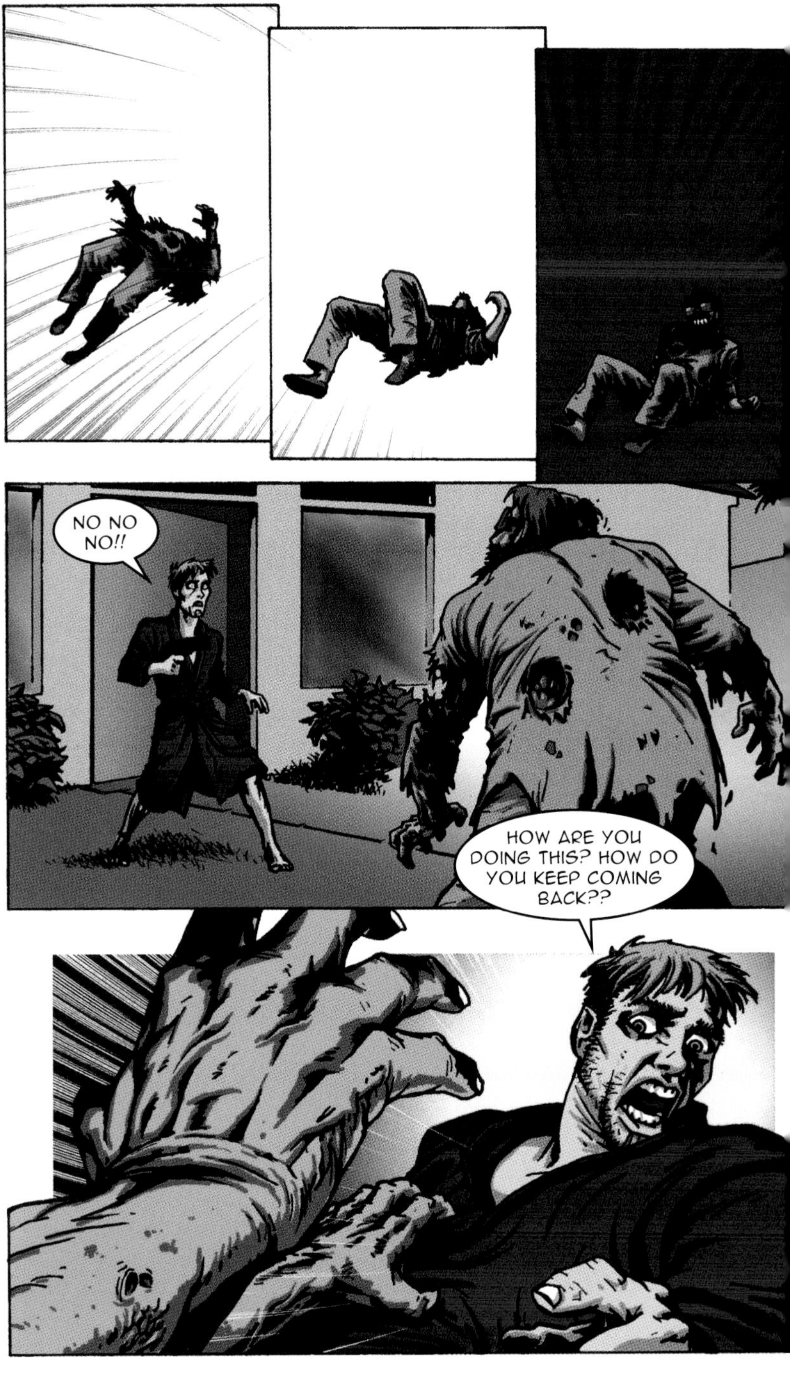
NO NO NO!!
HOW ARE YOU DOING THIS? HOW DO YOU KEEP COMING BACK??

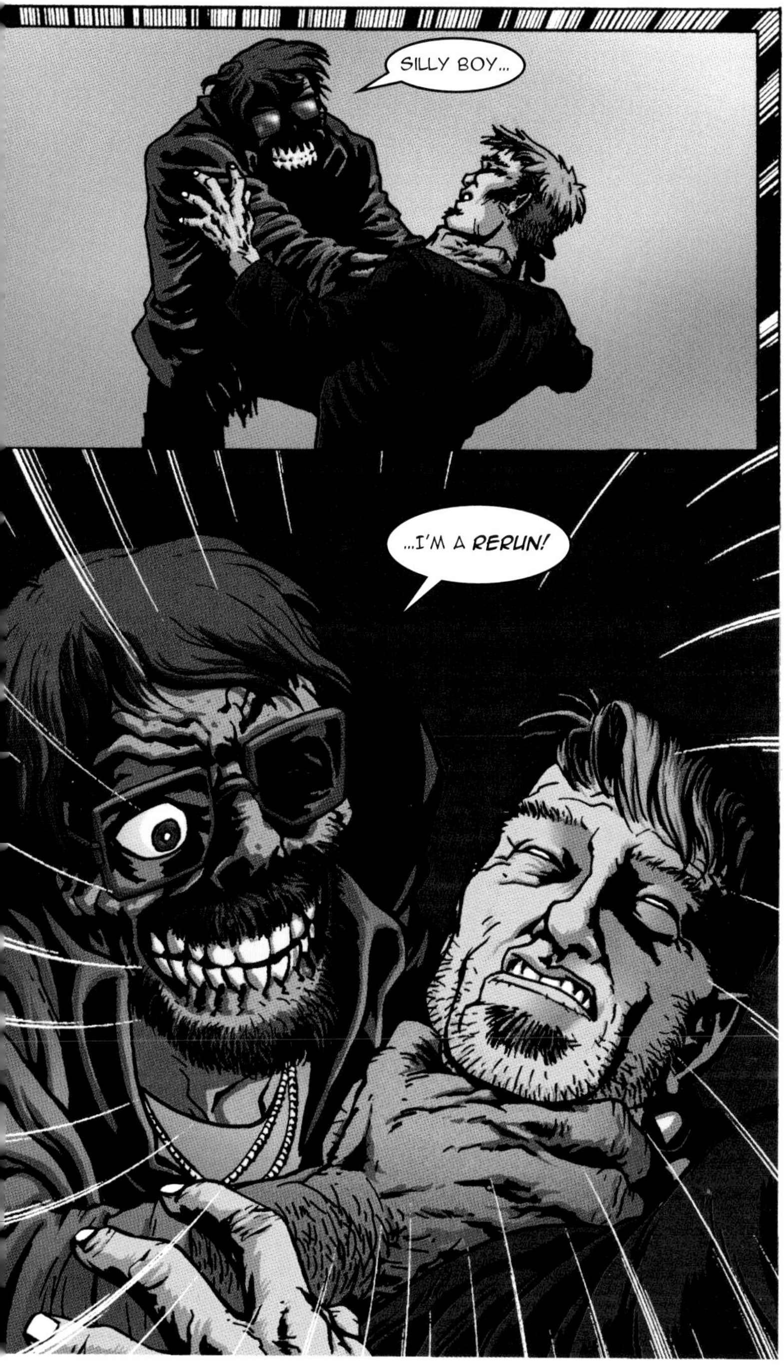
SILLY BOY...
...I'M A **RERUN!**

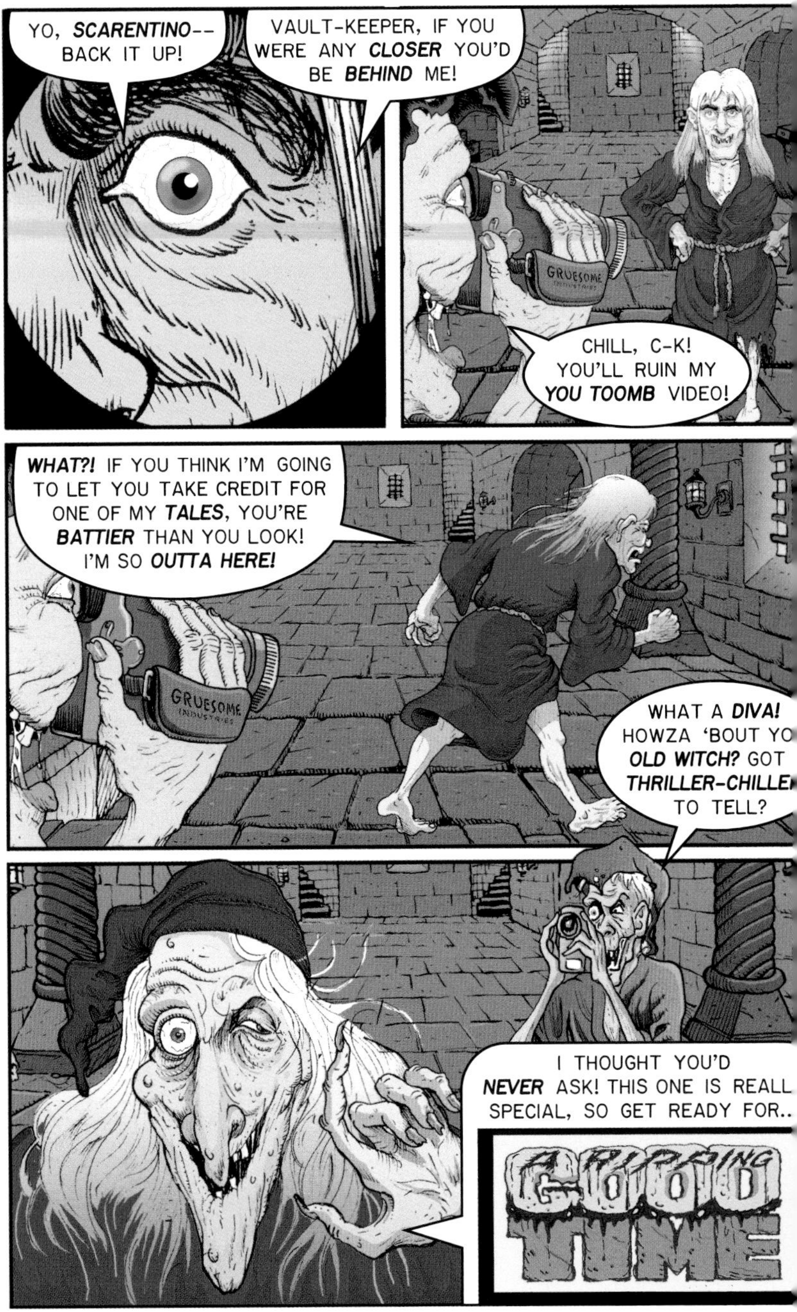
YO, SCARENTINO-- BACK IT UP!
VAULT-KEEPER, IF YOU WERE ANY CLOSER YOU'D BE BEHIND ME!
GRUESOME INDUSTRIES
CHILL, C-K! YOU'LL RUIN MY YOU TOOMB VIDEO!
WHAT?! IF YOU THINK I'M GOING TO LET YOU TAKE CREDIT FOR ONE OF MY TALES, YOU'RE BATTIER THAN YOU LOOK! I'M SO OUTTA HERE!
GRUESOME INDUSTRIES
WHAT A DIVA! HOWZA 'BOUT YO OLD WITCH? GOT THRILLER-CHILLE TO TELL?
I THOUGHT YOU'D NEVER ASK! THIS ONE IS REALL SPECIAL, SO GET READY FOR...
A RIPPING GOOD TIME

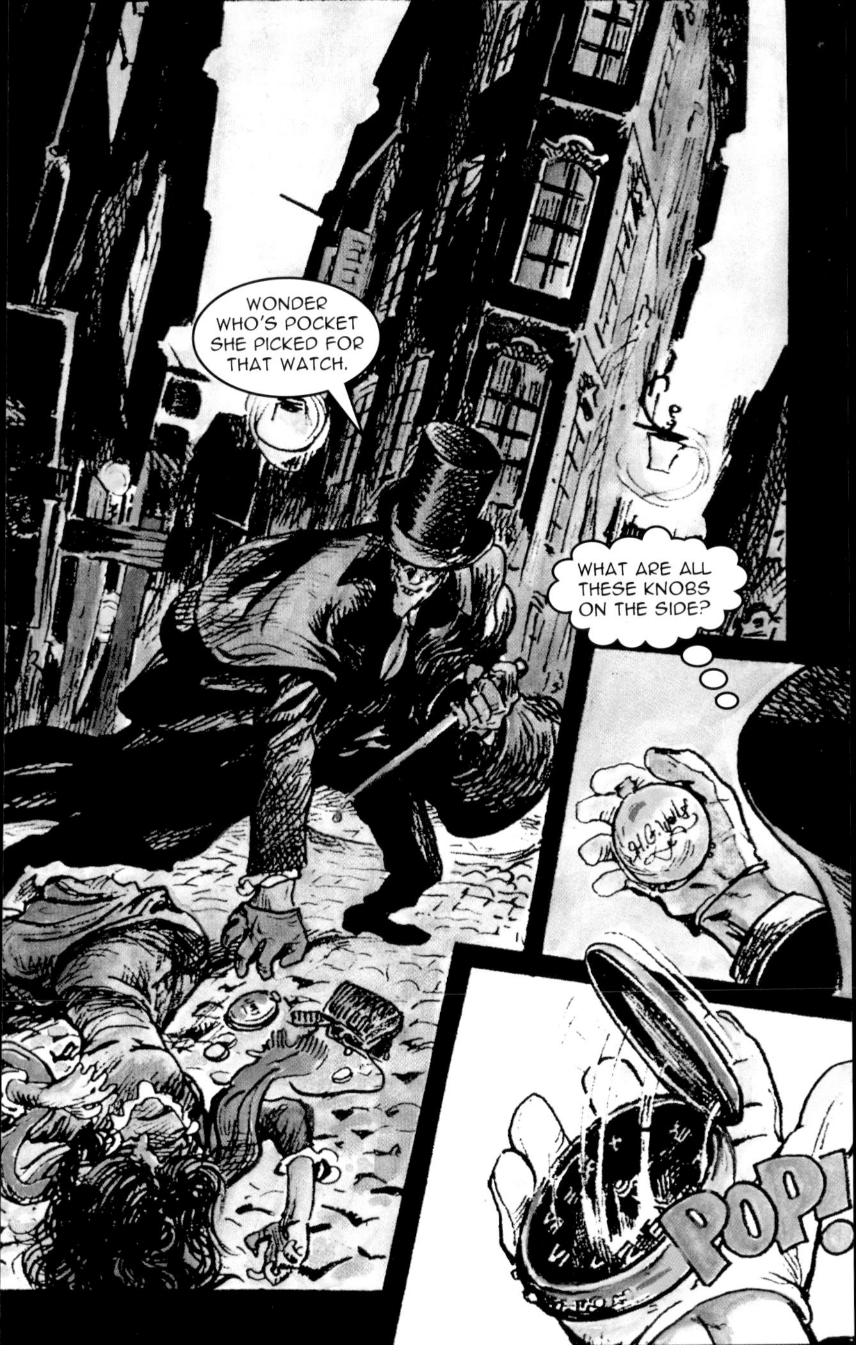
WONDER WHO'S POCKET SHE PICKED FOR THAT WATCH.
WHAT ARE ALL THESE KNOBS ON THE SIDE?
POP!

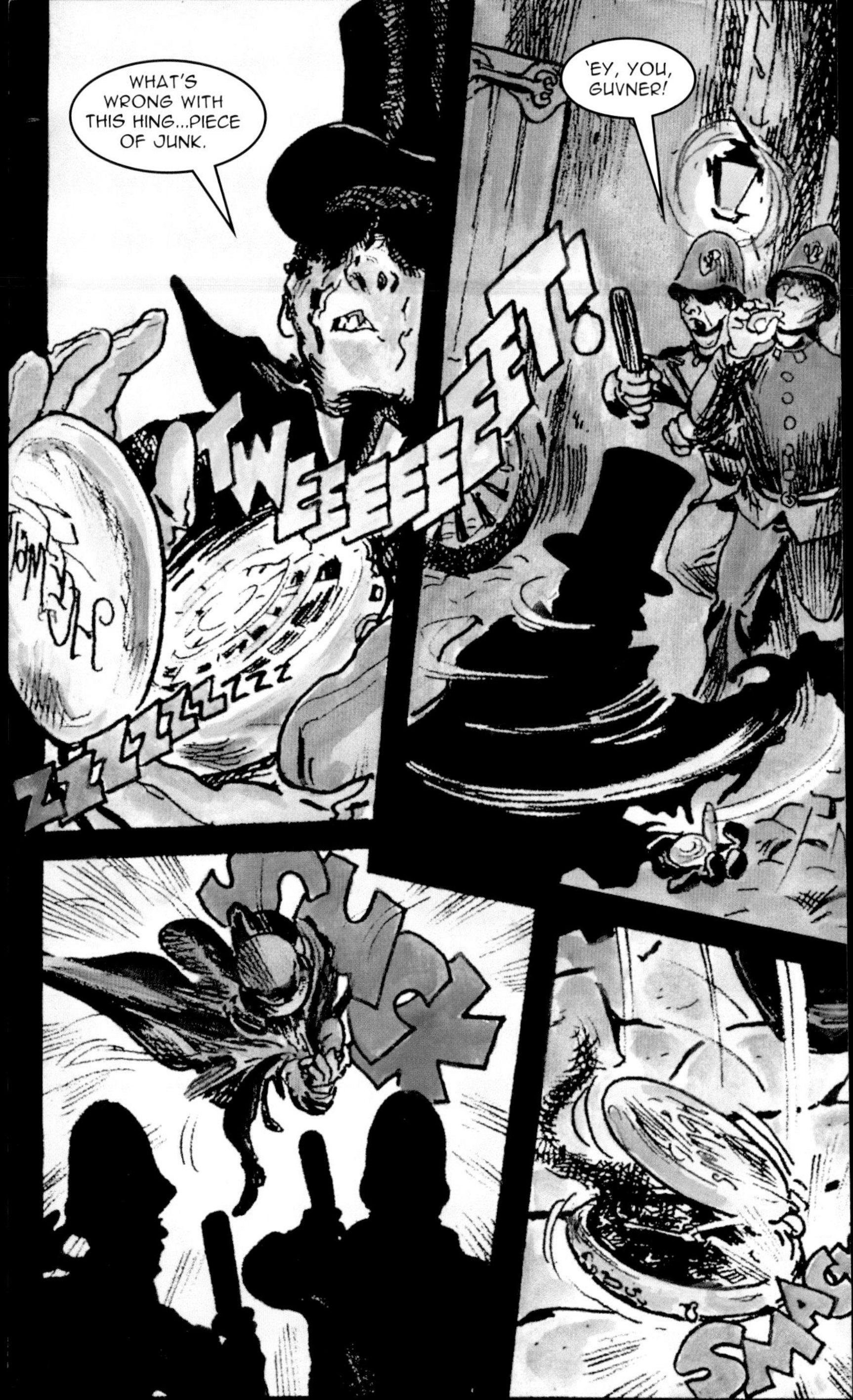
WHAT'S WRONG WITH THIS HING...PIECE OF JUNK.
'EY, YOU, GUVNER!

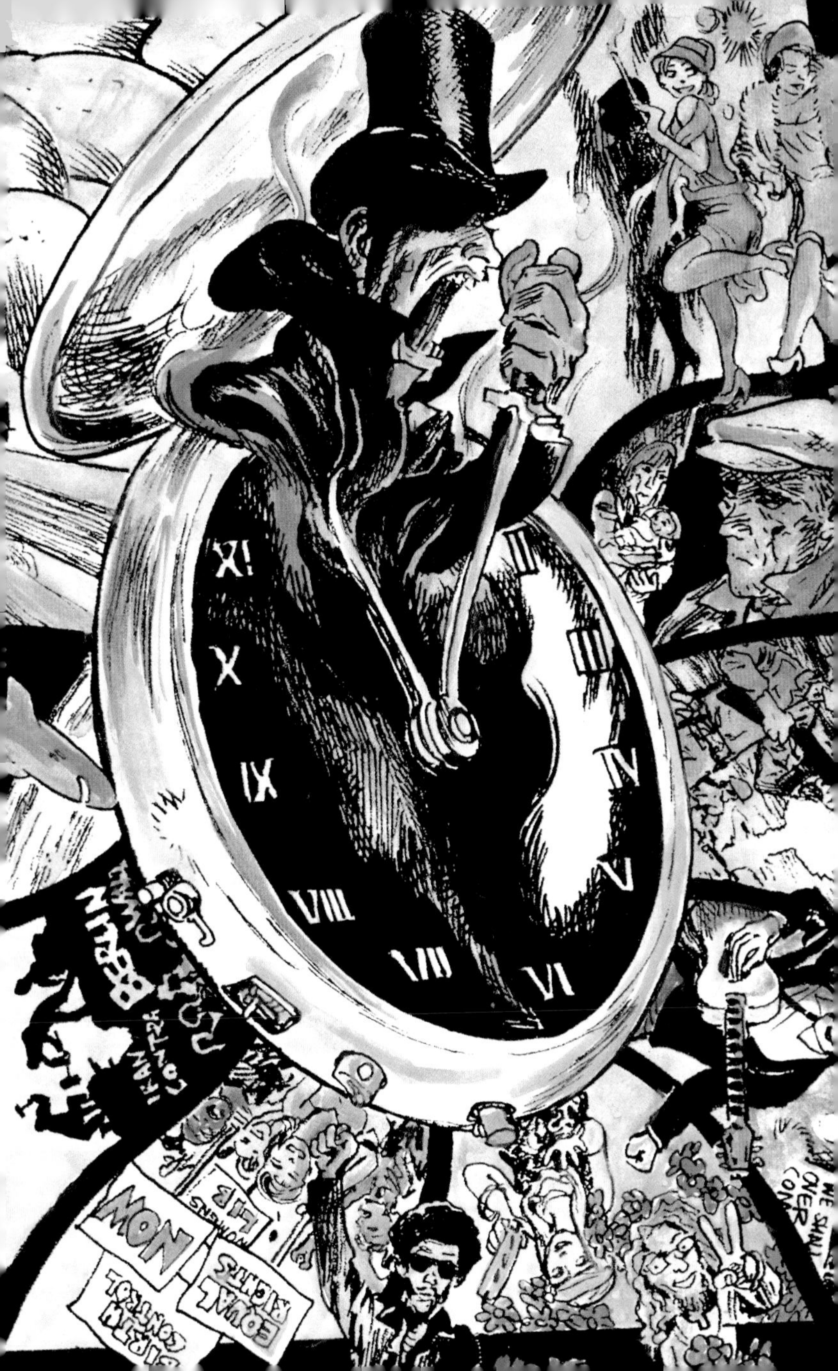

BIRTH CONTROL
NOW
EQUAL RIGHTS
WOMENS LIB
BERLIN

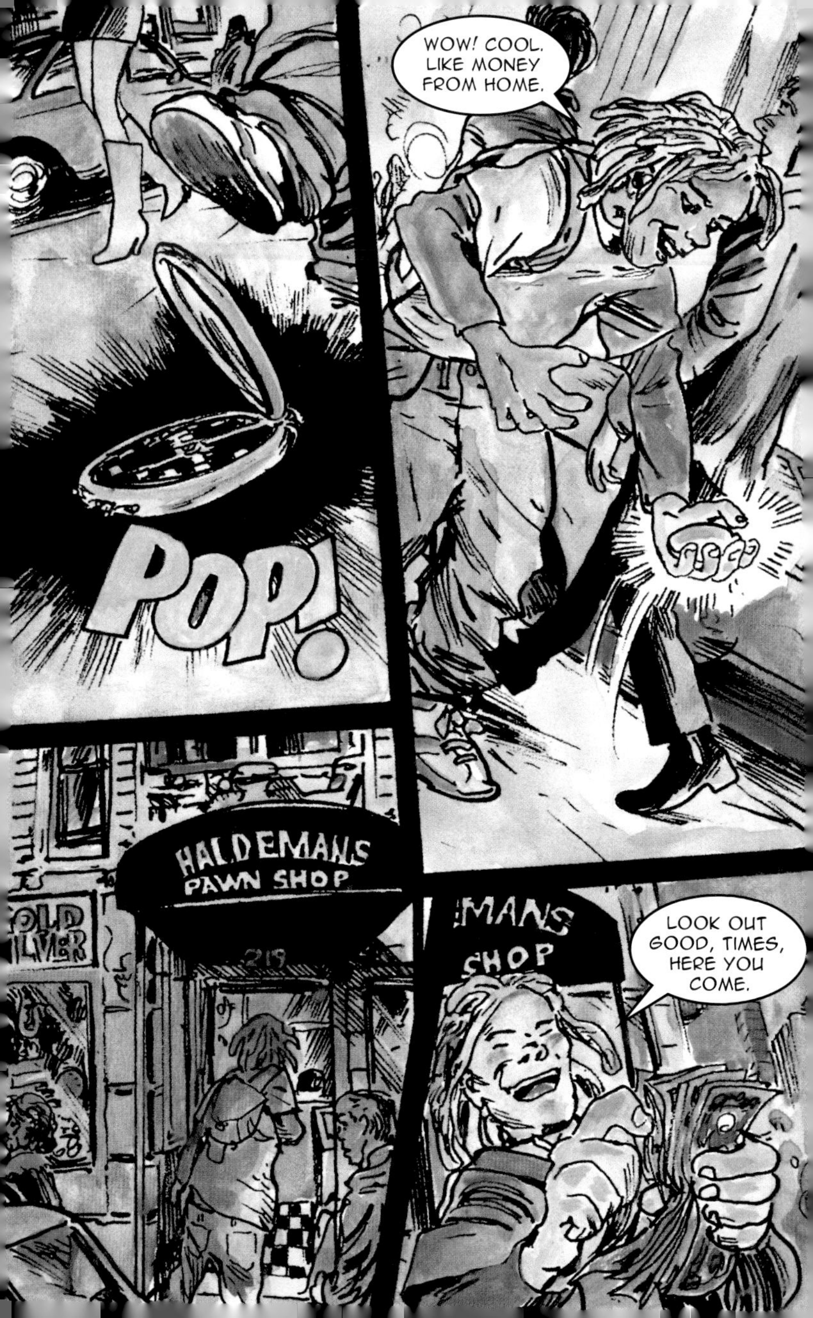
POP!
WOW! COOL. LIKE MONEY FROM HOME.
HALDEMANS PAWN SHOP
LOOK OUT GOOD, TIMES, HERE YOU COME.

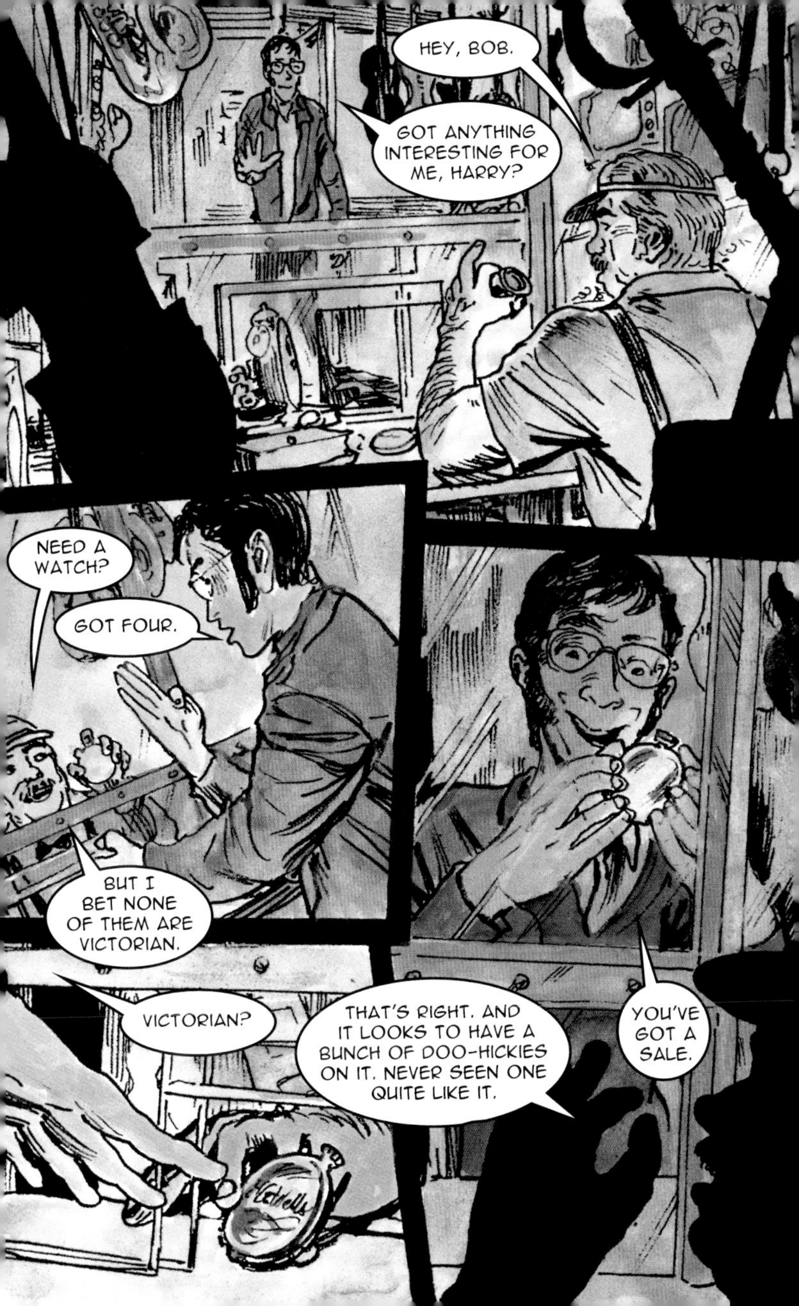
HEY, BOB.
GOT ANYTHING INTERESTING FOR ME, HARRY?
NEED A WATCH?
GOT FOUR.
BUT I BET NONE OF THEM ARE VICTORIAN.
VICTORIAN?
THAT'S RIGHT. AND IT LOOKS TO HAVE A BUNCH OF DOO-HICKIES ON IT. NEVER SEEN ONE QUITE LIKE IT.
YOU'VE GOT A SALE.

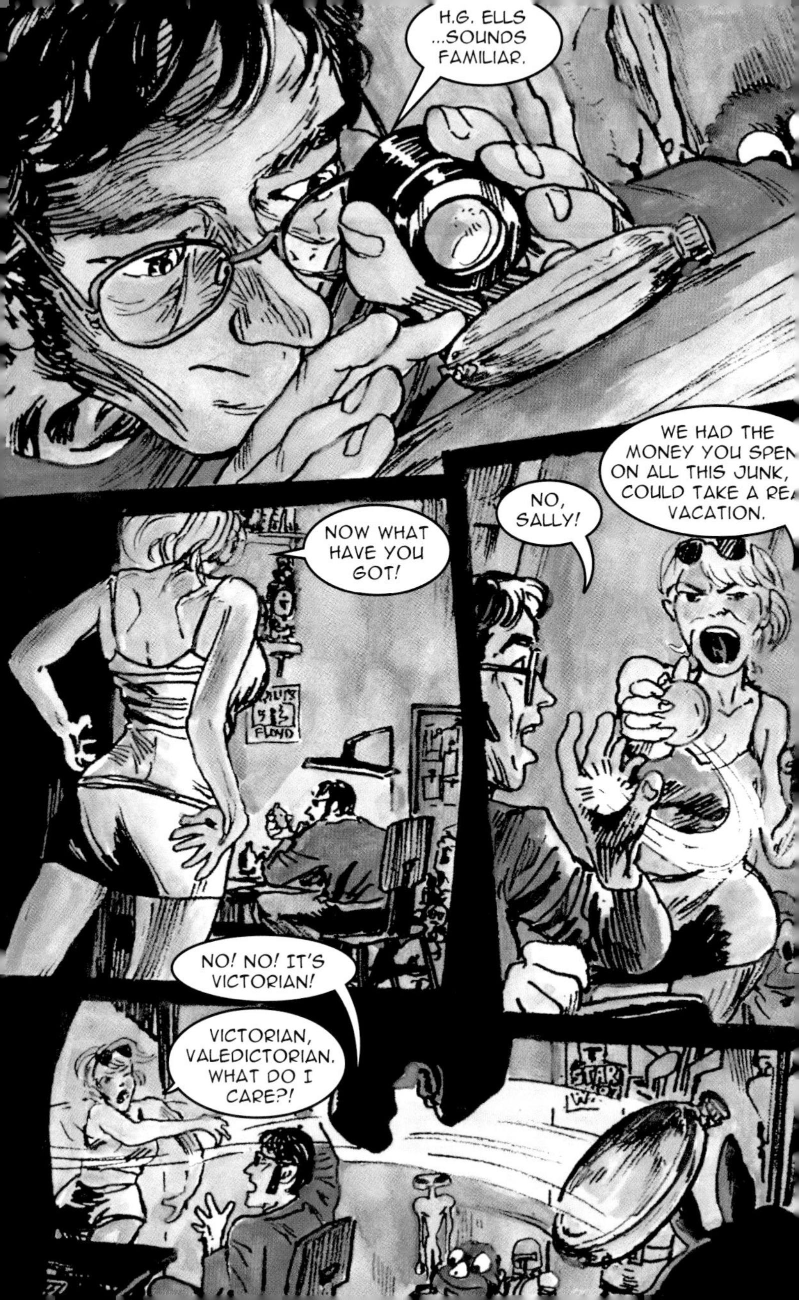
H.G. ELLS ...SOUNDS FAMILIAR.
NOW WHAT HAVE YOU GOT!
NO, SALLY!
WE HAD THE MONEY YOU SPEN
ON ALL THIS JUNK,
COULD TAKE A RE
VACATION.
NO! NO! IT'S VICTORIAN!
VICTORIAN, VALEDICTORIAN. WHAT DO I CARE?!

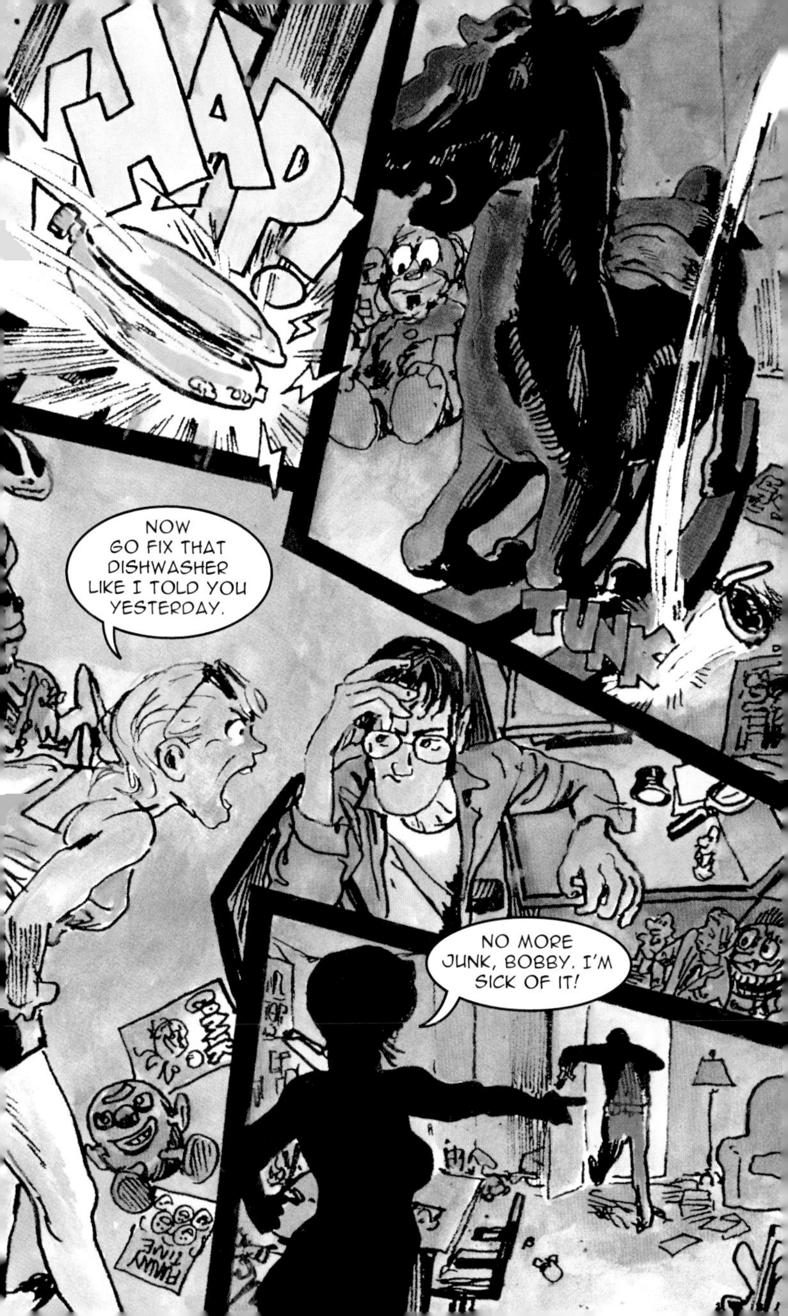
WHAP
TUNK
NOW GO FIX THAT DISHWASHER LIKE I TOLD YOU YESTERDAY.
NO MORE JUNK, BOBBY. I'M SICK OF IT!
COMICS
FUNNY TIME

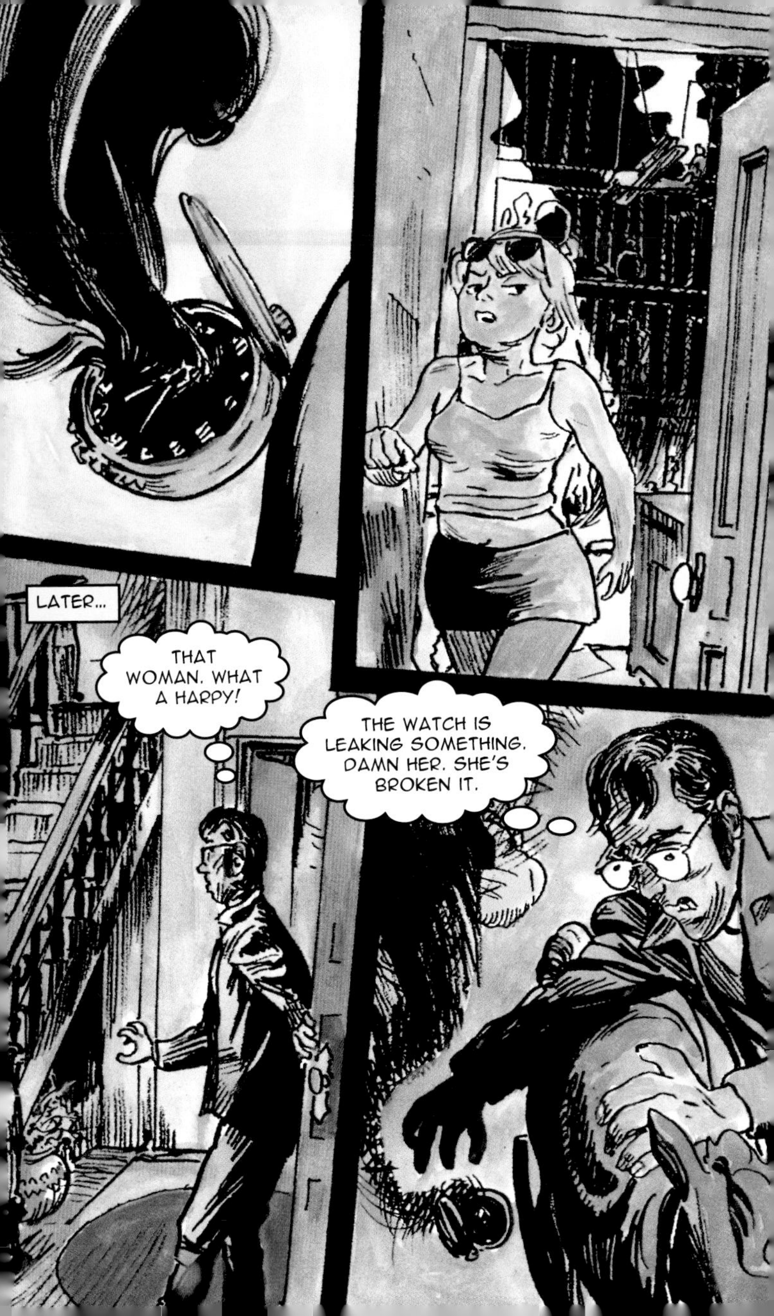
LATER...
THAT WOMAN. WHAT A HARPY!
THE WATCH IS LEAKING SOMETHING. DAMN HER. SHE'S BROKEN IT.